RUNNING THE GAUNTLET

Dragonsigns – Book One

Ken Hughes

Windward Road Press

LOS ANGELES, CA

Windward Road Press
11923 NE Sumner St Ste 879426
Portland, OR 97250-9601

Publisher's Note: This is a work of fiction. Names, characters, places, and incidents are a product of the author's imagination. Locales and public names are sometimes used for atmospheric purposes. Any resemblance to actual people, living or dead, or to businesses, companies, events, institutions, or locales is completely coincidental.

Book Layout © 2017 BookDesignTemplates.com
Cover © 2020 by Sleepy Fox Studio

ISBN paperback: 978-1-7350002-3-7
ISBN ebook: 978-1-7350002-4-4

Running the Gauntlet/ Ken Hughes -- 1st ed.

To Darklighter

— your town of Taylorville still has me in stitches

CONTENTS

CHAPTER ONE

THE FACELESS MAN

The intruder leaned around the corner, peering on up the stairway. Colin stood frozen—beyond those shoulders, the man *had no head*.

Then the moment passed, the figure stepped on around the corner, and Colin blinked and glimpsed a head in a ski mask after all as the burglar moved on upstairs. Still missing how Colin had walked in behind him.

And leaving the inspector slumped on the floor.

Blood spattered the victim's bald head. The footsteps faded up the stairs into the building's stillness, and Colin crept forward to the motionless man—Mike, why was he blanking on his last name?—to probe for a pulse. Weak but there.

He glanced up at the stairs. His fists clenched, and he *wished* he could hear the bastard descending from the library floor above. To have someone attacked, right here…

Mike's head lolled sideways. He croaked "someone… following me…" and the words slurred. A patch on the back of his skull looked sunken, the source of the blood.

Bashed from behind. Did that thief think someone he'd hit would just wake up unhurt in an hour, or did he not care? Just half an hour ago Colin had been showing Mike where to start the inspection here.

He grabbed for his phone. His finger slid so easily into 911.

"What is your emergency?" chirped the voice.

"I'm Colin da Costa, at the Vargas House. We have a burglar, and a man down—I don't want to move him."

"Understood. Can you get to a safe place?"

Sure. *But I'm Security here... my mother and I asked Mike to do his quake inspection after hours, that's why we're alone... No, don't start thinking it's my fault again...* And that missing head must have been a trick of the shadows.

Thunk.

The sound came from upstairs, a muted crunch like something slamming into wood. Colin was on his feet stuffing the phone away and heading for the stair, quiet as he could move and straining his ears for another blow, another footstep, filtering in through the street noises outside.

He crept up the stairs. The lights above were off, since Mike turned them off when each section was done. With each step up the wide boards wrapped the building tighter around him, all the turns and creakings he'd grown up with, and left a stranger's footsteps at night simply alien against it all. And this intruder was chopping into the place itself—

The footsteps above shifted. Colin froze. If the burglar heard him *now,* if he caught him on the stairway and had a gun... Too late, too many steps up or down to get clear. *And I'm still unarmed.*

But the feet above only moved around the library. Colin edged to the top and stepped into the dimness, pausing at the side of its doorway.

A good position. If the burglar came past him he could grab him right there, keep him from getting at Mike or using any weapon he had.

For one moment Colin wondered, *would I even be trying this if we hadn't asked Mike to come here at night, or if it wasn't an* earthquake *inspection that this attacked?*

Another *thunk* rang out. He peeked through the doorway.

By the moonlight through the tall windows, he saw the figure crouching at one end of the library. Right at the base of one of the columns, a stocky shape in dark clothes and that ski mask. Nothing strange about his head now.

A shape protruded from one of his gloved fingers, what looked like a pencil-thick blade. A useless thing that should snap itself or the single finger it attached to. But the intruder was drawing it back, sliding it out of the base of the column. Where he'd stabbed it into the wood.

The impossible *how* burned away from Colin's mind in a rage of *what* he saw: this man was slowly tearing, breaking, the House's *support columns, enough of that and this place could come down too like the quake buried my sister—*

A croak tore from his throat. A faint, helpless sound.

The masked man shifted in his crouch.

Colin ducked back behind the doorway. How loud had he been? If the intruder stepped too far out to check, he'd come within reach. Colin's heart hammered in his throat, his fists readied.

The burglar's footsteps walked deeper in.

"No skein here," he muttered.

Skayn, the word sounded like? What?

Colin peeked around again. The masked man stepped toward the wall, to the roped-off side, where he walked past the shelves of books and animal sculptures to stop at one of the paintings. The pale shape of Matt Vargas's painting of the library itself.

"There's the dragon."

The burglar's tone was a guttural sound, so low and thick with smugness it seemed like no voice Colin had ever heard. But he was walking deeper into the library, past one column after another in the row. The blade on his finger was gone.

Colin pulled back, listening. Whatever the masked man was up to, confronting him was still a risk, and the police would be on their way. The one who really needed him was Mike downstairs. But...

Is he sabotaging, searching? I don't even know how.

The pillars stretched in a row down the library, with the intruder walking toward the far end. Colin slipped into the room to crouch behind the nearest, with the whole line of supports to hide him. The old-paper smell of the room thickened around him.

Thunk.

From the far pillar—he was stabbing into that column too? Colin could just see him crouching by it, but his back and the row of pillars hid everything else.

Colin crouched down at his own pillar. In the moonlight, the hole in the wood might have been a gray stain, but the masked man had punched something right into it. Two joined holes.

He slid his finger in. The gap felt *wider* inside, and he wiggled around.

Instead of splinters, he touched a plastic smoothness. *A bomb*—but the shock was gone in an instant: even if the masked man had stuffed plastique in there, he couldn't have gotten a detonator in yet. Colin hooked his finger in the stuff, and drew it out.

With a softly sucking whisper, a dollop, a whole stream of some kind of putty slid out of the pillar. It looked colorless in the shadows, and it flowed like syrup—why would so much of it hold together and slide out? He caught it, and it pooled out and filled his cupped palm.

"Police! Anyone there?"

The sharp voice came from down by the House's front door, and the rapid footsteps showed they weren't wasting time before closing in. *We got you now!*

"*Damn* you—" The masked man's growl was pure viciousness, and he dashed down for the doorway.

Going after Mike. The thought crashed through Colin in one heartbeat, and in the next he was up and charging at the intruder's back as he passed. He had one instant to shuck the goo off his hand. Then he slammed into his target to shove him at the side of the doorway.

The stuff was still stuck to his hand, and his grip twisted. The thief wrenched away. Clothes shifted under his grasp as the thief wrenched free and shoved back.

Colin rocked back, ready. The thief stood just out of reach, bracing for one grand, telegraphed punch—

Something squirmed over that fist—

Colin blocked but the punch *slammed* against his deflecting arm, and burst against the wall with a savage crack. Colin stumbled away. The smell of sawdust bit at his nose.

The thief whirled and ran.

He bolted after him, the move bringing a surge of pain through his arm. The man was too fast—already down the steps? *Police still closing in in front, where can he go?* Colin ran for the steps. The putty was still stuck to his hand.

He reached the bottom of the stairs. Mike lay just the same as he'd left him, bringing a wash of relief to the part of Colin that wasn't staring around, looking one way and another for their enemy.

Two police burst into the room, staring around.

"Back exit!" he shouted. He spun, dashed through a door that had been closed, on into the kitchen, and raced through it with the two cops at his heels. The stove and the oversized fridge sprawled around him and gave him one moment to think the man might be lurking behind something to spring an ambush, but slowing down was unthinkable.

He hit the back door, and it wasn't even locked anymore. Instead it flew open, and he rushed into the back alley to find… nothing.

Only the back street, only the cars and birds of the summer night, not a glimpse or whisper of the thief. He stared up and down it, searching for cover, for anything. Nothing moved except the flicker of birds by the roof.

"Hands up! Don't you move!"

The two police closed in behind him. Both had their weapons ready—not trained on him, though. Yet.

He kept his body still, and his voice clear. "I'm Colin da Costa, Security and Assistant Director here. I'm the one who called you. The man in the mask ran this way."

The older cop raced down the back street. His younger, plumper partner eyed Colin, then trotted up to look in the other direction.

The stuff from the pillar still wobbled on his hand. Weird, weird... He shoved his hand in his pocket, and this time it scraped off and left his fingers clean.

The two cops marched back toward him.

"Nobody there, big surprise," the younger one said. "You should've run when you had the chance." A scowl began digging into his face.

His partner cut in "No, he *did* make the call. Anyway, first thing should be the injured man in there."

Mike... The three of them rushed back inside. Colin kept himself in the cops' view and just a few steps clear of them, forcing himself to simply let them work. The younger man glared at him and spat demands at his radio about the slow-running ambulance. The older one squeezed CPR compressions onto Mike's chest, and his motions grew more and more frantic in spite of the rigid rhythm.

Some endless minutes later, the cop came to a halt. "He's gone."

Colin slammed a fist against the wall. The impact made the cops jump, but it barely reached through the mire of guilt and regret. *If I'd heard the sounds one minute sooner...*

"Someone cracked his skull," the older cop said. "And you saw him?"

"That's right." Colin pushed out the clear, necessary words. "Ski mask and dark clothes, bulky, medium height. Vandalism or theft or something, I can show you."

"And your friend here?"

"Mike... Shane, I think. He was inspecting the place for signs of earthquake compliance."

At least he could leave it at that—they gave the same nods that anyone in Rayo Hill would, even years later. Not the same as what it meant to him, though, losing Terri.

Then the younger cop muttered "They always check that at night?"

"No. We asked him to, to miss all the community meetings we have here. I'm Security, so I let him in. Don't know what it means that this happened on the same night. He said he was being followed... I guess that's the *last* thing he said," he added.

"So he caught the thief in the act?"

The tight, suspicious looks hung on their faces, and they aimed them both at Colin and Mike—as if the dead man might have let the masked man in. At least they kept those thoughts to themselves now.

In the end, they took his statement and barely glanced at the holes in the pillars. Colin doubted they even wrote down what he mentioned about the stuff inside one, the putty that was still bulking his pocket. There had to be a better time to hand that in.

He knew better than to mention the moment the intruder had no head.

When the ambulance and the crime scene teams arrived, they showed him out. And he was free to call his mother and try to tell her the House wouldn't be opening tomorrow.

She didn't answer. She must think she had a busy night.

CHAPTER TWO

KNOCK ON WOOD

Pounding, pounding. Hammering, punching into wood, heaving to stir the dead man's ribs, pounding until the earth wobbled and swayed underneath. Someone he spoke to, saying the church was solid. Her running inside in the quake, and the arching shape thundering down to swallow her.

Terri's face. Mike's face.

Colin woke to feel his knuckles slap against the wall—the same fist he'd bruised when Mike slipped away. His other arm hurt worse, sore and stiff just from deflecting the masked man's punch, that *punch...*

He steadied his breathing; just a dream. *Why would my opinion on the building have anything to do with Terri going in? That's the dream speaking, when I wasn't even there.* His sister's death shouldn't be his fault, and neither was Mike's.

But his arm *ached*. He'd felt the power in that intruder shoving him back and cracking wood even after he turned the strike away. And cracking Mike's skull... the inspector was already dying before Colin found him.

I'm supposed to be Vargas House's security, and a thief got in.

Colin rolled over on the bed to sit up. He glanced over in the dark, at the shelf where his father's picture would be, in full dress uniform. At least that was one death he couldn't put on himself.

He muttered "My first real fight, not just clearing drunks out. And the only thing I won was not ending up beside Mike."

Faint shapes stood out in the room's dimness, just clear enough to remind him where the boxes stood in their rows. The night hid how many things had begun to spill out from them, thanks to all that work for the House and community, faster than he could pack them away. He was twenty-one now, he was *ready* to enlist and make a difference and find himself, but there was always more work here, and even more without Terri.

And now a man had been struck down at the site he was "watching," and he'd *missed* it. The ranks of boxes seemed to glare his failure back at him.

He tried to focus on the problem. How could the thief hit like that? More important, why had he been there?

For something to smash, or plant, or steal? And the inspector being there when it happened, was that just his brutally bad luck, or some connection... connected to Mike's inspection, or that the killer came to get Mike, or Mike let him in, or something... No, he said the killer had been following him...

Colin jumped to his feet. All he really knew was that the thief, the killer, might hit them again. The Vargas House would need new locks, better alarms, ways to keep everyone safe. After the police cleared the crime scene, so for now it would be planning and trying to keep the House going with what functions they could hold around the police search. So much regular work to adapt.

"Skein," the thief had said. To rhyme with "gain."

Maybe he *had* been a thief, looking for a skein of something. Threads, yarn, the word meant. Not this.

Colin clicked on the light and found the coffee flask he'd sealed the material up in. Carefully, he poured it out onto a cleaning cloth... the greenish-silver stuff felt syrupy-thick again.

He poked it with a corner of the cloth. Not sticky at all now.

He clicked on his phone and spent a few minutes on military sites, clearing away the last suspicion that it might still be some kind of plastic explosive. Sometimes it had stuck to his hand, sometimes it clung to itself so well that he'd dragged the whole handful out of the pillar.

Wrapping his finger in a corner of the cloth, he poked it again. His finger sunk into it, and this time it clung around that finger, sticking to the fabric. He cupped his left hand under the cloth to pull it off him. It slid free of the one finger, but the bulk of it sagged down around the edges of his hand underneath, and settled there.

It held there, thicker than it had been, sticking to the folds of the cloth and the rim of his hand. He tried working his hand free of the fabric, and shaking the whole mess free, but the stuff was stuck on.

He scraped it against the edge of the table. It *caught* there.

What? How fast did this stuff set, like some kind of fast-hardening clay? He rapped it against the edge.

The wood dented.

When the thief had wound up for his punch, something had flowed along his hand... *And now it's stuck on mine?*

He felt his heartbeat rising, as he shook his hand harder, scraped it on the table—

The stuff slid off as easily as a glove.

He let a breath sigh out. His finger reached gingerly for it again, but he pulled back. Instead he used the cloth to pour the stuff back into the flask, never touching it... and it peeled neatly off the cloth and settled back inside.

So, the thief had been looking for this "skein"? And he knew it was in the Vargas House?

The phone buzzed. The screen said simply *Zara*—the name everyone had for his mother.

Her voice was as warm and quick as ever. "I thought you'd be up. Sorry I didn't check my messages earlier. You're alright?"

"Sure, like I said." She knew he'd be awake? He grinned.

"Of course you are. And you gave the bastard a taste of what he deserved. The inspector's dead? Do you have any ideas why?"

"The police are looking into it. I guess," he had to add.

"We'll see if Mike had any family. And we'll see if we can move the Summer Breakfast outside while the police are in there—or away from the House if it isn't safe. Whatever we need to."

"Right. I've been thinking about some security ideas for when they let us back in."

"I bet you have. I'll see you soon."

Colin looked at the screen—still 4:30, but no chance he'd be able to sleep now. He opened a notes file and tapped out a few thoughts about where they could add alarms, if they could afford them.

When his first ideas were down, he dropped to the floor and began working on his pushups. The pain in his arm made him switch to sit-ups.

Again and again, he glanced over at the table with the... skein.

* * *

The Vargas House looked the same as ever—the round-edged manor near the top of the Hillside, the terrace in front setting it off from the smaller homes—except for the crime scene tape by the door, like the first grave marker Mike would ever have. A couple of police still moved in and out of that door.

The other sign of change was two regular House visitors, as well as several neighbors, all standing out on the terrace watching. At least the police hadn't left a coroner's truck in view.

The short distance here had made Colin leave his car behind. He had walked close enough to the door for the police to give him a warning glare, before the people closed around him.

"What happened? You all alright?" old Clarence began.

"Zara's fine, she wasn't even there." No need to mention the murder until they had a plan for talking about it. "We think it was some kind of burglar."

Sandy caught at her child that was trying to squirm away from her hand. "Do you know how long it'll be closed? Do you need any help? I can help out with the breakfast setup, if there is one."

Right. Their Foundation was offering the space for neighbors to bring in their cooking this morning, part charity and more community...

By ones and twos, more people began gathering out front. Each one added more volume, more momentum, to the forming crowd. Again and again, he told them they'd be ready when they were ready.

"So why police? After those kids robbed me last month?" Sandy said.

"It's not related, I'm sure," Colin had to say.

"I hope not. My place would still be in pieces if you hadn't run that cleanup-fest for us."

There was that worry starting to spread. He looked around at the faces stealing glances at the taped-off section—how many of them were still feeling the effects from the quake, years later? And now they had a death at the House too?

"What did they take? How is this going to change things for you?"

"It's too soon to say..." was the best he could answer.

"And why are the cops here *now?* When our place was hit it took them all day to show up!"

"Um..."

He scrambled to settle their questions for a moment, while the deeper problem kept pressing at the back of his mind: what had the "thief" really been doing there, and would he be back? The "skein" felt heavy on his belt, even sealed up in the flask.

A hand caught at his arm—Tom looked scruffier than usual today. "There's going to be a fundraiser after this, isn't there? You'll need me to play for it."

"Mmm. If there is, we may want the music for a larger group," Colin tried. *Where we won't notice you.*

Then a new voice swept in: "If there is one, the schedule isn't set yet. You can talk to me later. Sandy! Now that we've got the police's attention we have a chance to press them for better protection for the whole Hillside…" and Zara surged past them.

Colin followed a flash of the necklace his mother wore, the dark dress that stood out in the morning sun, as she slid through the growing crowd with himself falling in to follow her. She moved from one person to the next, with a few words for each and never losing momentum.

Tom trotted after them. "I'll take the idea to the Historical Society—"

"Of course. I was just re-elected as its president," she added.

Colin moved behind her, watching for anyone she might hand off to him. He saw her lean in for a few whispered words with Clarence, and the old man going pale; was he the first one she'd told about the death?

Finally the babble of voices was still, and Colin and Zara stood apart at a corner of the terrace.

Her hand settled on his shoulder. Drawing warmth and reassurance from his safety, instead of mentioning his brush with death again. What she said was "I'm afraid we have plans to make, and maybe a chance to scale up protection for all of us. I hope we don't need it—do you think this incident is over?"

Colin had to say "No. This wasn't some ordinary break-in. He was looking for something, and he was ready to kill for it." The cold words felt alien in the familiar daylight bustle of the crowd.

"Or an ordinary break-in surprised the inspector, and it turned tragic." Zara lowered her voice further. "Did you see a reason to think it was more?"

"Damn right I did. He was cutting into the pillars, looking for—"

Sandy scrambled toward them, still dragging her little daughter back. "It looks like the police are coming out."

"Thank you," Zara smiled. "We'll see what it means."

Two uniforms were standing by the crime scene tape. She headed toward them, but Colin moved with her and drew her to a slower walk. He whispered "You have to know, I've never seen anything like it."

"Anything like what?" She leaned closer.

"I'll show you later." He rushed the words out. "It was inside a library pillar. The thief almost found it—and I think he knew it was around there."

"In the pillar?" She stopped where she stood. "If it's so serious... Matt Vargas could have hidden it there himself. The library pillars haven't been redone since the House was built."

Of course she knew that. And... "The thief stopped to look at Vargas's painting of the room, and he said 'there's the dragon.' "

"Something to look up. And it sounds like we need Leo to look at the damage anyway. If it's his grandfather's secret, he might have an idea who could have learned about it, and who's coming after it."

"Leo? I guess it's worth a try," Colin sighed.

"Anything to help the police clear this threat up. And remind them they *can* protect us, all of us, if they listen to what we know."

"I'll handle Leo." They closed in on the uniforms at the door.

The older cop, the same one from last night, gave them a hard glare and a yawn. "Guess you've got some pull downtown. They tell me they're done with the crime scene, so you get to use that kitchen and anything else, just you keep away from the murder site itself."

Then it was Colin setting up warning signs on chairs around the hallway, and warning off the first curiosity-seekers that came nosing around the yellow-taped space. Traces of black fingerprint powder lay caked over the surfaces there. But the rest of the floor looked pretty much untouched... Colin's gratitude that they finished so quickly faded into a fear that they had barely looked. *We can't afford a full alarm system—at least let them have a decent crime lab.*

He pushed the worries down to focus on the moment. The people were milling and whispering at the disruption, even with Zara brushing reassurances around them. Still, the two of them soon had the kitchen organized to heat up the volunteers' dishes, and he hauled tables onto the terrace, enough for every needy volunteer and whoever had a donation to the House fund. One potluck breakfast, with a few nods to history and more to the Hillside community now.

Finally everything was settled and he had the right volunteers to keep half an eye on the crime scene, and he left the noise behind to head up to the library.

The air-conditioned floor was already cooler than the day had become outside. If the worried but familiar visitors had felt strange after last night's violence, the room's low-arching ceiling and the thinned sunlight through the tinted glass made it a halfway point between them. Still their own, but touched by something else now.

He eyed the paintings.

Matt Vargas had more than a dozen of different sizes gathered in this room, some of the buildings he'd designed and some of others simply around town. But there was no question the thief had gone to look at *Library at Sunset*.

Colin peered at the three feet of canvas. The space it showed looked barer, incomplete, showing the room from before it had been filled with memorials to the man. It was brighter too, full of shining golds compared to the muted light through the protective windows. The way the painted light reflected and caught swirls of dust…

Yes, that *could* be a winged dragon shape, curling in the shadow behind the farthest pillar, the one the thief had shifted to search. Colin studied the image of the first pillar—matching where the "skein" itself had been—but nothing his eyes did could pull the same kind of shape out of those painted lines.

He walked to the pillar it *had* marked and knelt down to look. In its base lay another hole, just big enough for his finger. He felt inside, found nothing but the rough edges at its rim.

There'd been no sound of a drill. The thief might have *stabbed* something into the wood... and then he'd cracked the wall with his punch.

His glove had worn a blade on one finger. For a moment, and the next moment it had been gone.

There was no way. But still, Colin pulled out the cloth from his pocket, and tipped the coffee flask to pour the skein onto it.

He'd felt it toughen up for a moment before, when it scraped his table. If the thief had been making skein do that himself... Keeping the wrapped, ball-like shape balanced over his palm and clear of his skin, Colin tapped it against the pillar's base.

Squoosh. The thing flexed like a water balloon.

Stubborn stuff. He rapped it again, shifted his grip. It was all guessing anyway, that the skein's changing substance could be how the thief had cracked the walls, but he'd felt it shift before. And... this had to be what the thief had come for, killed for.

He tapped it again, and as he swung it the wrappings rustled away from his fingertip. A prickle like static electricity brushed him.

Whack.

The skein struck the wood, and it felt solid as wood itself. Colin squinted at the base of the pillar and thought he saw a scratch on the dark grain. He swung again, harder.

A chip, a fragment of the wood, flew off. Colin froze, stared, looked at his own hand. And, his fingers hadn't even felt the impact.

Footsteps sounded outside. He stuffed the skein back in the flask.

A woman stepped into the library. She walked briskly, head turning slightly to take in each side of the room as she passed. Short blonde hair. Her clothes were downtown business casual, not part of the neighborhood. And the police had let her up here.

"You're the security guard who chased off the killer," she said. "Not much that scares you, is there?"

Was that a certain brightness in her eyes as she said it? Finally, a cop willing to listen.

He stood up beside the pillar. "Oh, I've still got a few fears."

"I hope so. We've got one dead and you could have joined him."
She held up her badge. "Bea Simms."

That shine in her face had crept away. *But she's not so many years
older than me...* He gave his best half-smile: "Colin. And I didn't say
it was dying that scared me."

She only crossed her arms—not that he'd expected any more response. "You let Inspector Michael Shane in last night. How well did
you know him?"

"We checked that the office sent him. And, you have to believe the
best in people, right?" *Wait, am I still flirting with her?*

"And this break-in happened on the same night." She raised an
eyebrow.

"Hold on, are you saying Mike was part of this?" He stared into
those eyes—no trace of that warmth now.

"I'm not saying anything. But you're assuming that?"

"No. I just don't like suspecting someone who's been taken from
us."

"And you have another explanation?"

"Several. From bad ones to what looks pretty good."

"Then let's hear them, 'detective,' " and she gave a small smile, a
challenge or a warning.

He tried a wider, calming smile in return. "Look, I know you're the
professionals, it's good to have you here. I'm just telling you what I
saw. Like the damage here." He motioned to the hole in the pillar. She
knelt smoothly down to it, and he added "This is where I saw him stab
it."

She rapped a knuckle on the wood. "Looks solid. That's a powerful
tool he brought."

"Powerful, yes. And then down here, he hit the wall too."

Colin strode back down the library, with her right behind him.
Good, good, the more he could point her at solid evidence the closer
she'd be to hearing the rest out.

The jagged crack stood waiting in the wall beside the doorway. "That was from him trying to hit me. Now I wonder, what could do that?"

She leaned toward it, squinting at it from one side, then another.

Then she turned and advanced on him, storms lowering over her face. "Some kind of hammer, that could have split your skull. And you saw what it did to your inspector—he was hit from behind, so he never had a chance, and yet you still went after the killer. You're only alive because you had more luck."

I know, already. Still, Colin faced her down and countered with "So what's your own explanation for why they were both here? You really think Mike was working with him, or was he the guy's target, or was it coincidence, or something else? We live up around here, we need to know what's going on."

She only shook her head. "It's my investigation. I ask questions, I don't need to share my answers yet."

"You sure about that? We've got more than a dozen people outside now, and they'll keep coming. If there's a reason this was connected to Mike, then it's over and they're safe. If we know it's not, we can shut the House down right now—and try to convince them the whole of Rayo Hill's original Hillside isn't slipping into crime." And the more he thought about the skein, the less simple it looked.

The detective shook her head again. "I don't have an easy answer. And again, it's not my job to share one with you."

Something in that cold, closed-off look... *We're talking about losing Mike and maybe the town, and she thinks I could have killed him, and staged all the rest?* But no, her gaze didn't seem harsh enough to believe that. Still, he felt a sour taste in his mouth at the idea of having to look at the world that way.

Heavy feet sounded behind them.

Colin knew Leo Tozer before he saw the blunt face, the bodybuilder's frame crammed into the expensive shirt that announced he was more than a contractor. Leo marched right past the two with a grunt that could have been *Hey* and began tromping down the library.

"Someone I should know?" the detective said softly.

"Leo's here about the damage. When the police cleared out, they said they got all the evidence they needed from this. Or we can work with your lab about leaving it intact for a while."

"They said they were done? Sloppy. You people keep rushing to have this place back to normal."

"Then give us a reason to slow down, or get on with it—"

He stopped. Leo was marching slowly down the library, looking at each of the pillars, and the tables too. Zara must have told him just where the damage was, so what was he up to?

Colin walked up to join him, steadying his thoughts as he did. Leo was one of the few people on the Hill bigger than him, and on some days that helped them understand each other.

"Hey, Leo."

"Hi." Leo folded his arms, and twitched one as he did, shifting the gold-toned watch on his wrist. From someone else it might be a hint that they were in a hurry. With Leo it would be simple restlessness.

"Did Zara say where the damage was?"

"I'm checking for any you missed. And I can get in some work on the other columns too."

"Some work?" He kept the words casual.

"Why just patch a couple bases when I can give them the full treatment, like how he put them in at the bank?" Leo thumped a foot on the floor by the nearest pillar.

And inflate the whole project's cost. "Not exactly a recreation then, is it? It's not how he kept his house."

Leo's brows lowered. "You want to tell me about *my grandfather?*" he rumbled.

No, I need you *to tell me about him*—not to rehash how much the old man had cut Leo and his parents out of the will, or how Zara had earned her place running the Foundation it formed. And Leo's temper was already simmering.

Still, if Leo knew some of Vargas's secrets... Colin found himself trying to look past Leo's glower and picture him in the intruder's mask. But no, the thief had never seemed that tall. *And Leo's no murderer.*

Light steps split the moment, as Detective Simms moved up behind them. "He did ask you a question: were you told where the damage was? Or can your eye pick it all out?"

Leo snarled "What are—"

She held up her badge.

Leo swallowed, and some of the lines of tension pushed themselves off his face. "Well. Sure, there were the marks in the first pillar, and the crack in the wall. She said there was one more." He crossed his arms again, and one finger brushed the watch. "What's it mean?"

"I'm not sure. But I could use an expert opinion," she added, and a bit of her smile peeked out now. "What could have done this kind of damage? Have you ever seen something like it?"

Other damage like it? Colin's eyes flickered to her. What if there *were* other attacks like this, from where the thief had gotten his "skein" already. What had she heard?

"Nothing like this," Leo said. "It's some kind of drill or chisel. Someone wanting to deface the place, I guess."

"Thank you. And please, check with us before you fix or replace anything. That is what you promised me, right?" she added to Colin.

Then she was handing cards to the both of them, and walking away. Her footsteps soon faded among the voices below.

Colin turned back to Leo, but the man was already stomping deeper into the library, this time with fewer glances at the pillars he passed. Better to let him cool off before they talked again—Colin said "Be back in a bit," and turned away.

Down below, the detective was already gone. Colin checked that the volunteers were still keeping visitors from wandering into where

Mike had been hit, then moved out to the back door. Since it had been open last night, he'd expected the lock to be broken, but it looked intact. Small scratches around the keyhole showed it might have been picked.

He walked around to the front. The Summer Breakfast was long over, but more visitors were lingering than usual at this hour.

He waved Zara over. "Listen, the more I look at this, the more I think the thief will be back."

She sighed. "Then we'll shut the House down until we know more. After today's speaker, that is. Don't look like that, it's our chance to plan how to appeal for better policing up here. And I can't believe a burglar would go near a crowd like this."

Colin opened his mouth—*was that her holding the neighborhood together or just holding court with her friends...* but she was probably right.

There were dishes to wash, tables to move inside, rounds to do again. When he was caught up and went back to the library, Leo was gone.

No chance to ask him about the House, then.

Did this all come down to the "skein" and the thief hunting for it? The detective's words stayed with him, the way she'd asked about other damage like this. There could have been other attacks, maybe at other Vargas buildings...

He glared at the "dragon" shape in the painting. Matt Vargas *could* have put the skein there, it might not be the strangest thing he'd done in his life. The House's archive was full of designs, speeches, rallies, and other efforts he'd made to keep the town going, all the way up to the different rumors about how he died.

If there were other attacks, other sites, would there be dragons hidden in paintings of them too? He'd never have seen one in the curled shape by the pillar if he hadn't known. He walked from one canvas to another searching their lines, but all he saw was his eyes blurring.

That left only the least enjoyable part of the House. Colin paced down the steps and around to the back room with the archives.

At least these would be clear print, instead of guesswork about paint shadings. He dug out the bound, preserved files—authentic copies of Vargas's work and the coverage of it. The speeches and news articles were grouped together, easy to bypass.

Instead Colin focused on the descriptions of his architecture, his art, and the notes behind it. One volume after another slid through his hands. He didn't even know what a clue would look like, or if it would make a difference...

Finally he stopped, glaring at a list of buildings Vargas had marked as earthquake-vulnerable. With St. Mary's Church at the top—*he was right that time, and this bit of paper could have saved Terri's life if we'd noticed...*

It took all Colin's control to close the binder gently, and put it back on the shelf. He should have left this search for Zara anyway.

There was nothing like standing in a historical preservation house when he needed to hit something. He stalked through the back ways of the House—

"I'm a teacher," Terri had said. "You want to save a community, there are places that need it more than the Hillside. With more people left to help." Except she took one moment trying to save a piece of this town, and the place killed her.

—He fished a defective wooden sign for a Puppet "Shuw" out of the trash. Then he made for the back corner behind the House, one pocket screened away from any curious eyes along the back street.

The skein poured from the flask like it was only a squishy cloth-wrapped lump—as if he'd only imagined the shifts it had made before. Still, what had it taken last time? He peeled back the cloth in one place.

Carefully he moved a fingertip to rest against the skein, bracing the cloth ready to pull himself free if he stuck. Then he rapped the skein against the sign on the ground.

Squoosh.

No. He struck it again—

Something sparked, a faint pins-and-needles sensation in his hand. The skein *thunked* on the sign like it had never been any weaker.

He felt a grin spreading. He pressed his hands against the cloth and kept pressing, and tapped his fingers on the substance under it, growing more confident every second. The skein softened like clay and let him mold it into a broad wedge-shape. When that solidified again, he slammed it against the sign.

Wood splintered. He heard it crack, but again his fingers felt like they hadn't struck it at all, he felt so little impact through them. He pulled back, but the wedge was caught in the wood.

And the pavement under it.

What might be a quarter-inch of the skein wedge had sunk into the asphalt. He tried wiggling it, then simply willed it to go slack and withdrew it—

The stuff is reacting to my thoughts.

Colin stared at the skein, still mostly covered in the cloth. He'd only been recreating what he'd already seen—the stuff had already shifted for him once, and he'd seen the thief stab some kind of blade into the pillar and then pull it around his fist for a killer punch.

But it really did respond to his thoughts.

What *did* that? Not simply some weapon or invention. And someone was killing for it, might even have killed for it somewhere else. Someone who'd been looking for a dragon clue, someone who would come back...

And he was controlling the stuff, the impossible skein that was driving it all, right in his hand. The stuff that could split pavement or melt away or...

Colin turned his eyes away from the splintered sign. Shoving the skein back in his pocket, he rushed back into the House. The warm, locked-in-time corridors squeezed back against his hurried footsteps.

Only, that agitation went beyond his own pace—he could hear hushed, angry sounds in the dining room ahead, rippling against Zara's calming words. Then he stepped into view.

Three, four regular visitors stood around, eyes fixed on Eric Rowe.

One growled "This'll be the last crime we have here, you'll see! Nobody asked you and your damn offers to come around…"

Eric looked back and forth between them, trapped. The suit and fine coat showed that Terri's old fiancé had been doing well for himself, but now they only made him a target for the others.

"Hey, Eric!" Colin waved him over, and the little man moved to his side and out of the room, still under the people's glares. *Some things never change—even now.*

"Thanks," Eric said when they left the sounds behind. Then he held up a finger and a rueful grin: "Though I should admit, I could only get away by telling my boss how any crime might make people here think about selling—and I know better than that. Really, I wanted to see you were all okay."

"We're fine." Then he had to add, "So that really is your job at Gardner? Buying up buildings for developers?"

"To improve them—" Eric stopped, looked at the floor. "Well, it's not what I expected when the shop closed."

"You always said you still had options." Terri and Eric. There'd been a time that nothing got those two down.

Eric looked up. "There's nothing like an earthquake to convince a guy something has to change."

The words hung between them, old wounds it did no good to hide.

A moment later Eric added "So, you had a burglar."

"Yeah. A moment of excitement, but now we're mostly busy dealing with the police. We'll get through it." It was reflex, waving away the House's problems even though they looked deeper the more he saw.

"Good to hear."

Except, this might be too big to face alone. "Listen…" He leaned closer, and lowered his voice to pull them in below the murmurs back in the room. "You say your work lets you hear about crimes and news here? Do you know if there are any weird patterns around town?"

"Weird? How?" Eric's eyes, always alert, narrowed further.

"Like… the kind of trouble that seemed random, no clear motivation. Maybe…" Other break-ins with nothing taken, except… No, it was all too strange to explain. "Never mind."

"Maybe…" Eric's eyes closed for a moment, then opened. "I'm part of a team, so it's not really me who watches for local information. But I could look. We owe each other that much."

"Thanks—hey!"

Sandy's fiend of a little boy was scurrying straight for the site of Mike's death and the crime-scene tape. Of course he would.

Colin dashed forward. In a few steps, he'd swept past the spot and cut the boy off, then crouched and spread his arms to block him.

"What are you doing?" Sandy stepped around the corner, and her sharp tone sounded more aimed at him than her boy—who took the moment to twist around and dodge past his grip.

Colin jumped back a pace to head the kid off. How irresistible could a few pieces of yellow tape be?

Behind him he heard "More vulture-watching us, Eric? Here to buy up anyone who blinks?" *Leo.*

"I didn't say that—" Eric began.

Sandy finally caught up to her wriggling child and scooped him up, and turned to march back where she'd been, without a glance back. Colin turned to get one glimpse of Leo rushing back toward the dining room, closing in on Eric's footsteps.

Colin raced after them. Two shouts clashed in the murmur ahead: a tangle of "—not finished with you—" and "—let me through—"

He slammed to a stop, just short of where Clarence's back blocked the room's entrance. Over his head he saw Leo herding Eric into a corner, with several other people watching in shock. Zara was no-where in sight.

Eric turned back to face Leo, but he was almost hidden by Leo's bulk. "If you're here at the House—does that mean they're listening to you here?"

Leo slowed, and his fists lowered a fraction. Colin slowed too—no need to set those two off again, and Zara had to hear the commotion soon.

"No," Leo rumbled. "They just call me every time the place needs something."

"I guess they would. You were, what, raised on Vargas designs?" Eric's words were steady enough, but his voice came out with a shrill edge. "You'd know—"

Leo twitched like he smelled that fear. "You... you're trying to *handle* me." He reached out, tapped a finger at Eric. "You think you can buy me for some goddamn takeover? Time I sent a message back to your bosses—you think you can just walk in here..."

Oh God. Leo's temper was going for full boil, even in front of eve-ryone. *Maybe I can take him, but we could trash the room and anyone within reach...*

His hand dropped down to his pocket, and the skein.

CHAPTER THREE

SPIKING THE PUNCH

It was a crazy thought, a trick out of an Eastwood movie. But Leo was howling "I build them up, you want to see me tear you down??" and still psyching himself up. For a few more seconds.

Colin stepped back, from the still-oblivious Clarence in the doorway. He pulled out the skein.

Move, flow with me!

He slid the stuff under his shirt, with his fiercest command for it to shift. It softened, molded under his fingers—no, it spread itself out in response and spilled across his chest.

"I'll show you!" Leo yelled over the murmurs.

No more time. Colin could only think *now, hold there!* and let his shirt drop as he pushed into the room.

Where the hell is Zara? came one last thought, as he called out "Leo, don't you think you've scared him enough?"

Leo halted, and motion flickered at the edge of Colin's sight that would be heads turning toward him.

Eric, little Eric shrieked "Stay out of—"

Colin cut in "There's a room full of people watching you, Leo. You know this doesn't end well."

Sandy gasped "Please, don't…" but let the words fade away in uncertainty.

"Why??" Leo glared right at Colin. "Why does your whole family keep sticking up for this *rat?*" He turned back to Eric, and there was no more waiting in his voice. "Little Terri isn't here to save you this time—"

"Or save *you,*" and Colin closed in.

Leo bellowed as he charged, with all his towering size. Colin's hands rose to guard, and a flash of instinct brought them up higher, too high even to fend off a taller opponent.

Those fists struck.

Leo's left caught against his arm, brushed aside. The right snaked in under that misplaced guard and slammed into his stomach—but instead of a crash of pain he felt only a massive shove.

Colin's hand caught at the higher, blocked fist, and that grip even held for a moment and helped break his momentum as he stumbled back. One step, something hit his unshielded back—

And his head, lights flashed—

Then they cleared, and he could see Leo screaming and clutching his hand. Those knuckles hung in a jumble on his hand.

Clarence shuffled in behind them. "Can you just—"

Leo howled "You... *you...*"

He turned and staggered away, heading for the front door. Not one person got in his way.

Colin turned back to Eric in the corner. "Are you alright—"

"Damn it!" Eric's face twisted, leaking tears of rage. He dashed past him, for a different doorway and toward the back. Colin moved after him, trying to screen his embarrassment from the others. At least he didn't look hurt, physically.

One chirp sounded behind them from Sandy's boy, that could have been *Do it again!*

Eric raced away from them all, out the kitchen and not slowing until he cleared the back door. Then he stopped, looked back at Colin, and his face was clear again.

"Sorry. Thank you, back there."

"Sure. Do you need—"

Eric was already spinning away. Colin watched him in case Leo showed up again, as Eric grabbed out his keys and ran to a silvery new car, and roared away.

Colin looked at his hands. Shaking, cold, and the coldness flooded through him and drained away as the adrenaline worked through him.

He tapped his stomach. The skein was still locked in place over it, but where the punch had landed he felt only a twitch of discomfort. *Body armor shouldn't do that, I should still feel the force of that hit.* Instead the blow had done nothing but fling him away, until he'd struck his head.

The others. He turned and headed back for the dining room.

He heard the shocked buzzing before he walked into the sound, before he saw Zara in the midst of the guests and already bringing order to their confusion. When their eyes swung toward him, he said "It's over. Everyone's fine."

"Are you—"

"What was—"

The questions swelled around him, everyone hungry for answers and promises that there was nothing here any bigger than Leo losing his temper... When he needed a way to *stop* the masked man from killing again, for this impossible "skein." He couldn't think.

He spun away from the room and marched deeper into the House.

His mother's footsteps were right behind him.

"Colin, what was that?"

He stopped, stepped into the next room. Vargas's craft room—he slumped against the desk, his hands shoving woodworking tools aside.

"I'm sorry I missed the trouble there," Zara added. "I got a call. What happened?"

"Leo went after Eric. And I had a way to stop him." He turned to face her. "Listen, we need to get the guests out of here. This thing, the skein, is bigger than I thought. So the next time they come after it... well, anyone here might get caught in the crossfire." Back through the corridor, those voices were still murmuring, not so different from any other day.

"But... Soon, then," Zara nodded. "We just got a speaker for today so we can close on a calm note. Everyone should be safe in a group—"

"Now!"

"You know I can't do that." Her voice, always a finely-tuned tool, thickened and softened with concern. "We'll be planning our appeal for more police protection all over the Hillside."

"The thief's going to be back. I think this is what he was after."

He reached under his shirt and pulled at the skein. It peeled away, still a thin curved plate in his hands.

He tapped a knuckle on it. "Instant armor. But any time I want..."

He pressed it between his hands. For a moment it stayed rigid, then he felt the static-like flicker and it softened and folded into a ball.

Zara looked at it, for long, breathless seconds. "If it can do all of that... was this what Leo punched? Then I *am* sorry I missed it." She gave a dark little laugh, before looking up at him. "But, you were saying this was inside the library pillar already? Inside it, not stashed near it?"

"The masked man muttered something about searching for it. And looking for a dragon in the painting." *And I can't just stand around telling people the danger's gone.* He stuffed the skein back in his pocket.

She blew out a breath. "Something that can do this, that goes that far back..."

Her eyes hardened.

"We can't let some murderer have it. And we can't let our friends be caught in it—I'll try to call the meeting off, but not everyone will get the message." Her phone was in her hand now, and she began pacing the room. "If Jessie comes, at least she might know more about the paintings. We need answers, and we need to get them to the police and *stop* him."

"Yes. Anything we can give them. And I met the detective—Bea Simms?"

"Her?" Zara smiled. "She seems like a capable young woman."

"I think so." *When she's not suspecting Mike and everyone else.* "We can hand the stuff over, soon. But I want to dig up enough that they'll listen."

"Of course we have to! Or else this could simply disappear into the police files. Even though it's part of Vargas history, if that painting's part of it."

"If it is…" There was no way around it, and he felt his shoulders slump. "His grandson might know. I have to talk to Leo."

First he humiliated him, now he had to ask him for favors. With *this* at stake, something someone had died for—

"Leo? Do you hear yourself?" Zara's eyes locked on his. "Yes, he might know something we don't. And that knowledge might make him part of this attack."

"He's not!" The idea brushed a shiver down his back. "Leo's got a temper, that's all. To *kill* someone, and from behind? I can't believe he'd do that."

"And if you walk into his hands and if you're wrong? In any case, you just made him look like a fool."

"I know. And I can't leave that hanging either."

* * *

The street outside was already hot under the afternoon sun.

Colin sent a quick call to Leo's business, but he hadn't been seen since early morning. Knowing Leo, he wouldn't be bringing his pain to the job or a bar where anyone could see it; he'd be home.

Colin set out on foot, even in the early summer heat. Just showing up there might remind Leo they used to be friends. Before Zara took control of the Foundation.

Trotting down the hill he passed a few of the residents on the street or in their yards, but too many homes that stood silent. Except, now someone was dead because of this thief and the skein, and there might be more deaths soon. And he had a chance to head it off.

By going to meet Leo alone. The idea still wrapped a coil of worry around him—but Leo simply wasn't a man who'd be part of that burglary. Or a friend to give up on.

A car turned down the street across his path, and Colin let it pass and glanced at the man at the wheel. He didn't look familiar, but he never glanced at Colin either. Was this how it felt to have a secret in his pocket, and know someone might be watching him?

And the thief would be back. He wouldn't give up on a weapon that someone could use—

That I just used, to humiliate a friend. Leo hadn't given him much choice, but... *I don't like the feel of me getting hold of power and finding I'm knocking people around.* Lines of summer sweat started down his back, a kind of penance.

While the masked man simply used his own skein to kill. That said far too much about what he wanted more of it for. And it had made armor, fists, blades...

Good thing the thief had missed this chunk of it.

He'd stabbed a probe into one pillar. Then pulled away, because the painted dragon said it was the wrong place.

Good thing he hadn't hooked the skein anyway. *And I got it all.*

Or did I?

A chill swept down him. If the masked man's probe had missed the skein... what if his own search hadn't gotten it all either? The stuff had been so eager to cling to itself, it had been easy to assume there was no more left in the pillar. There could be more—or much more.

His phone pulsed.

An update from Zara, even a report from Eric? He pulled it from his pocket.

What he had was a text: *not your fau*

"Fau"? He glared at the broken word. The sender's identity was blocked too, no answers there.

Another text popped up: *fault i*

He shifted the phone in his fingers. What was this supposed to mean? And, two fragmented texts in a row.

The screen's time display showed five seconds passing. Ten. Twenty.

Then: *went in church –terri*

The tiny little letters burned in his mind. He stared at them, saw the sun glare back off the screen, but they didn't change. Nothing changed.

Was that heaving sound his breath?

Whoever sent this might be following to watch him react—he spun around, swept a look along the streets, the houses and fences. Nobody there.

His fingertips slipped and beat at the screen, but he hammered out a response: *your prank's NOT funny*

Thirteen seconds later, a reply said simply: *please*

He stared, waiting, shaking the phone as if he could flush the bastard out of the line by brute force.

Except... when the quake happened, the rubble and the fires had damaged the remains under the church, so they only found DNA instead of his sister's body...

For all that that mattered. He'd always known she was gone—and if Terri had escaped she would never let them mourn for three years before contacting them. This thing was a vicious, poisonous prank.

Or worse. After all this time, it happened the day after he chased off the thief. *Is someone trying to rattle me now, and they came up with* this?

He dashed back up the sidewalk, staring down behind one fence, around the corner of another house. Still no sign of an enemy, only a few faces here and there that started to look at him now.

Colin turned and headed on again. His legs wanted to run the whole way, and he fought to bring his breathing back down. If someone wanted him distracted, then fighting back started with staying calm.

He glanced at the screen as he walked, but the messages had ended.

* * *

At the speed he marched at, he reached Leo's apartment in minutes.

A shape moved behind the shuttered window, good. Now that he was close enough, he could make him listen. Colin closed his eyes and tried to force away the idea that Leo could be an enemy, the outrage from the texts, and the awkward worry of following up a fight with asking for help.

First, get through the door. He stood outside it and punched in a call.

"What d'you want now?" Leo's voice grated through the phone.

"Leo… I'm sorry it came to this. We were never enemies, were we?"

"Why can't you just leave me alone?"

"I know you're better than this. You let Eric get to you, and you wish you could take it back."

"Because you made a fool out of me?" Leo snapped.

"I came to talk to you."

He knocked on the door, and he heard Leo muttering curses inside.

"I'm here because I need your help. I'm not going away, and there are some things you need to know. About your grandfather." And about their fight, but Colin's trick there was nothing to lead with.

Footsteps moved. The door opened.

"Alright, what?" Leo waved him in.

It had been years since Leo had thrown a party in his place, and it looked more crowded than ever. Knickknack shelves and paintings from his family dominated the walls, with Leo's own tools and souvenirs stacked up between them. And some of the Vargas possessions stood on the outer side of the stacks, as if he'd recently gathered them—or looted them from the House.

Colin tried to look past that, to what they had in common.

But Leo's hand was wrapped in bandages, where he'd tried to punch him. Colin had to start with "Are you alright?"

"Don't overrate yourself." Leo flexed his fingers, and Colin imagined he could hear the wrappings creak. "So talk already." He waved to a chair.

Colin sat, and Leo stayed on his feet, a few paces away.

Colin began "So you were told about the burglary, and the inspector getting caught in it. I think that thief will try again, and we want to head him off in whatever he's after. Before anyone else gets hurt."

"Always someone's protector, right?" Leo waved his battered hand.

"You want an apology? You're the one who went after Eric... " Colin let the words die away before the frustration could build. "You know you're better than that." He'd said that at the door, he was already repeating himself.

But Leo looked at the floor. "I know."

"Anyway, I think the thief was looking for something. And it might be your grandfather who hid it there."

"Hid what?"

Of course he went straight to that. Colin hesitated, and the silence stretched a moment, then another.

Leo took a heavy step toward him. "You're still doing it! You get your hands on something and then nobody touches it, right? Same as ever."

It's one house, one Foundation. Vargas set it up because your father was losing money—all things Colin couldn't say.

Instead he looked up at Leo and said "A lot of that's not my call. Besides, we're all doing alright these days."

Leo laughed bitterly. "Why are you even still around? It's your mother's place now. Let her wash her own windows." He leaned down and locked his gaze on Colin's. "Don't you tell me you aren't wishing you were long gone and in the army, wasn't that your plan?"

"She needs me—"

Colin halted again. This was what happened, arguing with friends. Leo knew him too well, the same as Colin knew how easy it was to strike back.

Instead he said "I try to be where I'm needed. My choice."

"I guess."

Leo looked away. Colin felt for a way to make him listen. From somewhere outside, the sound of children playing filtered in.

He said "Right now, I'm here because we need your help. And you were right, sometimes it does all come back to who grew up with Matt Vargas. And you can decide to sit back and let us flail around on our own, or you can be what we need right now."

"I hate when you're right." Leo leaned over against a wall, and the shelf creaked and rattled a moment. "What is it you need? Me standing up in a crowd and saying his heir's marching in step with the rest of you? You want Grandpa's lullabies? What?"

Colin grinned. "It's those pillars in the library, that the thief cut into. He was looking for something hidden inside them. And that means it was put there when the House was built, right? Nobody's redone those pillars since then."

"About right," Leo said. "The old man did stay hands-on when a building went up. And this was his home."

"And the thief let something slip. He was there following some of Vargas's art."

"Art? What art?"

Children laughing outside. Another moment where Colin could keep secrets, or—

"A sort of dragon shape, hidden in the painting of the library. But it's more complicated than that. From where the stuff really was, I don't know if the dragon marked it or if the key was something else."

"Could be. He had his secrets… a dragon sounds like something he'd use…"

Leo stopped, folded his arms.

"But, hidden treasure and codes, seriously? We have banks for that, or he could have told a friend. He could have told *Mom*, or me— and instead he's painting secret clues? That's crazy. No, you're saying *he* was crazy, and the old man was always sharp. What was he hiding that could be worth all that?"

"It's not… about worth," Colin sighed. "Not a stack of jewels or any of that. It's more dangerous than that."

"Dangerous…"

Leo's jaw dropped. He stumbled back a step.

"What did you do? That's what almost broke my hand, right? Something you found?"

"Yeah. I'm not proud of it."

Colin watched the emotions flicker over Leo's face. Was that more anger, greed, or something else? *And he's so touchy about his family's stuff, he could demand the skein was his just when we need to hand it off to the cops…*

Then Leo grunted a laugh. "I knew you couldn't beat me on your own. Look, I'll look up what I've got on the old man's secrets, and anything he did with dragons. Then tomorrow we talk, for real."

"Deal. And Zara and I do want to bury the hatchet, keep the doors open, all of that."

"Yeah, yeah. You have to—who else can keep the place from cracking and coming down around your ears?" His grin began to grow, as the tension slipped away.

*   *   *

The kids' voices and their games sounded just the same from outside as from within the apartment. As if nothing ever changed.

But I got Leo back with us. I guess reaching out and swallowing some pride really can work.

What *was* Vargas doing hiding the skein anyway? Leo was right, burying it in the pillars made no sense, and neither did painting the dragon over the pillar that didn't have it.

The thought came back to him again: what if there *was* skein in that other pillar, that the thief hadn't had time to find. Or maybe, more in the first pillar, that they'd both missed. The one piece in his pocket was powerful enough...

Colin quickened his steps. The afternoon heat was streaming over him now, making him wish he'd taken his car from the start. But the way back to the House wasn't far.

Just all uphill. Sometimes I get how people can resent Matt Vargas.

His phone pulsed. For an instant he thought of that damn prankster, and his fingers shook getting the cell out. Then he saw Zara's name on it.

"The speaker's going to be starting soon," she said. "Except, are you so certain that man could be back? You think we're at risk?"

What? "What's this about?"

"You might be getting your wish after all," she laughed ruefully. "I got a call from Detective Simms, and she wants to shut down the whole event right now and close the House up. I need you to show her we can keep our guests safe for one more hour. If you agree that we can, that is," she added.

She was asking him to support her now, when he'd begged her to shut it down in the first place. *Everyone's asking me to bend today.*

"What I think is..." He walked faster. "I left most of the doors locked, but that didn't stop him before. You're probably right, that he wouldn't risk going near a whole crowd. But if he does..." He swallowed, and added "Is having that crowd so important?"

"You know it is. It's our strategy for meeting the police halfway, and there are people here we can ask about that painting—Oh. Colin, did you really think I was just holding this for my own sake?"

He smiled. "I know you're not. I'll be back soon—" Then he remembered, and added "By the way, I got some kind of prank text. If you get one, ignore it."

He'd tried to keep his voice casual, no more than the cruel joke deserved. But Zara's voice tightened: "But you still mentioned it. Why is that?"

"Same as any prank, it's nothing. Or it's the thief trying to put us off-balance. I guess we should expect that from a killer who wants something from us—"

It was the motion that drew his eye. One of the few figures out across the street, the man looked up from his gardening and glanced over. Not at Colin, but back behind him.

Don't look, don't look—but Colin was already stealing a small glance back. He caught one glimpse of a broad figure and a hat worn too low even for shade, just ducking back behind one house and out of his sight.

The thief. It could be him.

"Gotta go," he said, and cut the call. His legs pushed harder and broke into a jog.

Chase him, trap him, or make for the House... pieces of ideas tumbled through his mind. But his eyes were scanning the neighborhood and already picking out the next turn ahead.

He followed it downhill, away from the House and adding speed to his jog with the steady slope. Bare yards and silent streets slid past him—the kind that could limit the thief's cover and slow his pursuit down. And it ran past more empty houses, Colin's best bet for keeping the thief away from bystanders. They'd be even safer if he could lose him.

There was a gap between Colin's footsteps, an instant where the slope pulled his weight along before the next step dug in.

Within those moments he heard feet closing in.

Too fast, like some animal, quick and tireless: *tap*, then *tap-tap* in the distance, then gone. Colin risked one glance back—saw a figure peeking around a house's corner, a glint of sunglasses and then out of sight—and wrenched his gaze forward to focus his balance on the slope.

Faster, faster, he'd just ride the hill down far enough ahead and duck out of sight...

Tap-tap, tap, between his steps, *tap,* and he ran faster, but it sounded at his heels, rushing in with a *tap-tap*—

He leaped aside. His shoes slammed into the street, scrabbling over asphalt to catch his weight. He spun to look.

Nothing. Only the empty street, the sidewalk, a single garbage can. But he *had* heard it.

He dashed to the far sidewalk and raced on. Nothing moved like that, so fast and then gone. Unless the thief was a ghost chasing him.

His steps pounded faster, pushing down the prickles at the back of his brain, sweeping him past house after house. Of course this was no ghost, just the thief trading his mask for a hat and sunglasses. He guessed Colin knew about the skein, and now...

Tap-tap. Not so far—he stole another glance back. Nothing, or maybe a blur of motion at the corner of a fence.

Light, childish laughter sounded ahead. He stared forward at a yard full of kids, a ball flying, figures scrambling in and out of the street—

Can't get through them, can't lead him into them—

No fence beside him here. Colin twisted away to ricochet off the side of a house, and spin up between it and its neighbor.

The turn let him grab one more look around. A modest gap between the walls, not the worst place to stop and fight, but those kids' voices were still too close. He dashed over the drying grass for the opposite end.

Tap scratch-scratch—

Something slammed into his back. He spun away, fell. Crashed down—his face landed in something soft, a pile of tossed-out *flowers.* He rolled up with his mouth spitting out petals.

Still nobody in sight. The gap between the houses looked empty.

He charged for the far exit, away from the kids. Something in the back of his mind traced the bruises and scrapes from his fall, knew he'd feel them later, but all that mattered was now. The open space beyond the houses swept up.

He slammed into thin air. Some arm that *wasn't there* clotheslined him, he caught one glimpse of the headless shoulders the limb was attached to. Waiting behind the house's corner, for him.

Then Colin's hands were clutching that arm, like any other kind of sparring, grabbing it and trying to drag his opponent down with him.

Feet scrabbled, grips shifted. Weight and leverage clashed—and then the thief flung him away with a surge of strength that that wiry arm should never have.

Colin rolled to his feet. His enemy stood back, watching him. The thief wore his ski mask again, instead of playing tricks with his sight. He looked less bulky in daylight, and Colin's moment of wrestling had confirmed he was deceptively light. *I knew it wasn't Leo.*

The thief raised a hand, and skein shimmered as it flowed over it, and settled into place.

Into a silvery glove, with two-inch long claws on his fingertips. Claws that could stab into a wooden pillar.

The thief took a slow step forward.

"Help!" burst from Colin's mouth. One single, traitorous sound echoing off the walls, with no thought for the kids nearby or what the thief had already done to Mike.

No.

No.

Colin thrust his hand into his pocket. His skein was a liquid lump, but when he pushed his fingers through it he felt it reacting, moving up his knuckles. He drew his hand out—and the thief actually stood back, watching, letting him shape it with his need. It formed a glove, a heavy-knuckled cestus ready to smash bone.

He curled his fingers into a fist, and the skein moved as he did. *This* was how it worked, the motion felt natural. Strong.

The thief still hung back. Then that clawed glove swung up higher, and the enemy's skein began to stretch down from his it, ready to cover his whole arm.

One chance— Colin lunged in, flowing into a jab at his enemy's face. The thief's arm swung up to block.

Colin twisted. His arm snaked around the thief's to immobilize it, and he pushed in to shove his lighter opponent back, his other fist readying.

The thief's arm bent. With that impossible strength, the skein's arm slid out of his grip and slammed an elbow in—

The house, that had to be the house's wall that he lay slumped against. His jaw felt like a lump of ice. Something moved in front of him.

The clawed hand dug into his wrist. He should move, knew he had to, but nothing worked. The claws pricked, dug so *gently* in under his glove, and pulled.

His glove slid up. Split apart, peeled away, into the thief's hand.

Then he brought his hands together. The skein flowed.

The thief held up two gloves, one arm-length and now one short.

Colin pushed himself off the wall with a growl.

The thief jabbed a quick punch, with the new glove. A short punch with no leverage behind it, that still crashed into his chest and flung him back to the wall.

The thief made a soft grunt of satisfaction.

Then he muttered "Now for the rest," and he spun away.

Colin looked around for him, not sure where the flashing lights in his eyes ended and what was simply the thief's speed.

As he pulled himself to his feet, voices swept in around him. Light, children's voices, and a man's with them. "You okay?"

The thief was gone.

CHAPTER FOUR

WE ALL FALL DOWN

"Now for the rest."

The enemy's words helped Colin drag himself up, and shake the muzziness from his head. The thief knew he'd found the skein, and he had known what place Colin had thought to look. Where the thief had almost found it himself. Where Zara and her guests were now.

He stepped around the kids, and his balance settled as he did.

—No, he was in no shape to run, and the thief was too strong to fight already. He grabbed at the arm of what seemed to be the children's father.

"Your car. I need a ride to the Vargas House, and forget the speed limits."

The plump little man stared. "What… you… I've seen you at…"

"I've got fifty dollars on me. There's a killer—"

"Come on!"

The man—shouldn't he know his name?—scrambled for the street, surprisingly fast for someone his weight. Or that could be Colin's own struggle to make his legs keep up.

The man's car was close by, a long, low beast of metal. The two piled in and roared out.

Colin fumbled for the seatbelt and braced himself against the first lurching turn. One street after another squealed by, and he felt hope racing too.

The thief could run all the way, but he couldn't match this engine. Even if the skein made him stronger and faster. *But he's got more skein now, he's got mine. And when he does get to the House he can tear through anyone who sees him.*

Unless I get more of it.

"You sure you're okay?" the driver said.

"I have to be."

His jaw was starting to ache, when he moved it. But his head was clear again—the lurches and screeches of the car left no doubt of that. The driver knew every turn up the hill.

Then they slammed to a stop. Right beside the line of cars in front of the House—too many cars, too many people.

"Thank you." He jumped out of the car, and pulled out his wallet.

"Keep it." The driver flashed him a smile, an ear-to-ear grin of someone sharing the rush of the chase. Colin grinned back and ran for the House.

A single, clear voice sounded from the meeting room, and he raced toward it. "Now, we must remember that recovering from the previous quake took years too—"

He burst into the room. A whole dozen people sat in their circle, with Zara in the back looking up in surprise. Detective Simms stood with her.

Colin throttled his voice back, down from the shout he was ready to give, to a simple firm announcement: "I'm sorry, but this meeting is over, as of this minute. The House is closing down for the day."

A woman called "But, I already paid my donation, I want to hear."

"Please!" He flung the word at them, then made for the door beyond them before anyone could block him off.

He heard Zara saying "I'll see what—"

"This is police business now," the detective told them all. "Let's start with those nearest the door."

Not bad, less charming than Zara but more forceful.

The craft room was only twelve quick steps away. No power drills in sight, so he grabbed up a hammer and a chisel. For an instant he wondered how Leo would react to what he had in mind, or if he'd just be grateful for the extra repair bill.

Sounds echoed from the meeting room—a clatter and ripple that might be someone tripping in the confusion. He glanced back ready to help, but no, the thief could be closing in any time now.

He charged for the stairs, right past Zara's shocked face. Then he was in the library and beside the pillar.

The pale wood opened out where it met the floor, smoothly as if its tree had grown this way too. The two fang-like holes the thief had sunk in it lay just above that "collar," and he set the chisel against one.

Zara shouted "Have you lost your mind?"

Behind him. Colin looked around at her, kept his hands in place. "The thief jumped me in the street. I think he's on his way here right now."

"You *think?* And your answer is to rip up—"

He swung the hammer. The blade of the chisel bit into wood, widening the hole he'd dug skein out of once. Not enough.

"Finding more of this is the only answer we've got. You didn't see him, he's *too strong*, he knows about this, and he could be here any second. You've got to get everyone out. Please!" He swung the hammer again.

"I... alright." The word slipped from Zara's mouth like she had to force it out.

He heard her footsteps moving away, and some man's voice at the doorway calling "What are you—" and her leading him back down.

No more hesitating. He pounded on the chisel, again and again, biting deeper into the pillar. *I could do this in seconds if I had my own skein.* His vision blurred a moment and forced him to clutch the hammer tighter.

Somewhere back where the stairs were, a man yelped in surprise and clattered on the stairs, then settled in to quiet cursing and Zara making calming sounds. Colin couldn't even look back.

There had to be more skein here, or else the thief would get to keep slashing through everyone in his path. *Or I'm missing something—I could be, he did hit my head.*

He drove the chisel deeper, then worked it side to side trying to widen the hole. *I did hit my head. I've got to be forgetting...*

Something smashed into his side. He toppled over, slammed down across the hard floor—the House's revenge for him stabbing it, came a random thought. He rolled to his feet.

The thief stood at the pillar. Skein gloves shimmered on both his hands and stretched up toward his shoulders.

He followed me. No, he let me hear he was going after the skein, and I lead him right to it, that's what I missed! But how, how could he get right through the House unseen, no matter how fast he was...

Colin gripped the hammer and chisel, still in his hands.

He stood facing the murderer—the *murderer!* He snapped "Why'd you kill Mike last night? Just for getting in your way, was that it?"

The masked man didn't move. Silence hung over the room, stirred only by babbling voices from the floor below, from where Colin tried tell himself was a whole safe world away.

The thief turned toward the pillar, still angling himself to keep his opponent in view. Ready for what would come next.

Colin charged. He held the chisel ready to follow up and hope for a lucky stab, and lashed out with the hammer.

The thief's gauntlets caught both.

Colin's charge swept on in to crash his weight against his lighter enemy. His shoulders and knees strained to push him past those hands' grip, anything to force his enemy off balance and take control. He shoved the thief stumbling back, back.

Then that momentum stopped cold. The thief braced and pushed out, and the strength in his arms sent Colin staggering away.

Colin lunged again, but skidded to a halt to keep clear of a warning swing of those claws. He'd dropped his hammer, and the thief's slash forced him back from where it lay.

The thief stepped away from the pillar, the thing he'd backed into that had saved his balance, and kicked the hammer aside. It clattered away far across the floor.

The thief took another step, just the smallest move this time. His masked face studied Colin.

He exhaled... a small, reluctant sigh, *like he knows me?* Then he took another step.

Thunder boomed through the air. The thief glanced over, as Colin placed the sound, a gunshot.

"Back away, now!"

The detective, Bea Simms, stood in the doorway. Gun leveled in both hands, feet braced, eyes locked straight on the thief.

"Get those hands up—"

The thief twisted away. The move might have used some of the skein's speed, or she might have lost an instant in surprise, but when the next shot boomed out the thief had still ducked behind the pillar.

She fired again and again, filling the room with echoing deafness and splintering holes through the wood.

The thief stepped back into view. His mask and dark clothes were gone, leaving only a much thinner figure completely sheathed in green-silver skein.

Completely sheathed. The thief must have been wearing more of the stuff all the time, under his clothes to bulk him up and disguise his skinny build. And now...

We're all dead, flashed Colin's thought, at the same instant she fired again and the bullet whined off the skein. The impact only drove the thief back one step.

Then he exploded toward her.

Colin rushed at his back, still clutching the chisel, but the thief was already beyond his reach. He got one glimpse of the green figure closing on the woman and the broad slash that sent her gun flying away, then the second strike. Of her diving away out of his reach, him letting her twist to her feet.

He's toying with her. But that might end at any moment.

Simple dark clothes still peeked through a wide section of his back: his skein couldn't armor all of him after all. So if both his enemies came at him from different sides—

But he was too *fast.*

Colin wrenched himself away from that elusive target and ran for the pillar. Shadows in the corner of his eye showed one figure driving the other back, tugging at his attention. But he forced himself to drop down beside the pillar and dig the chisel into the wood.

A crash made him look up. The thief's punch had cracked one of the tables, and in the moment he pulled his fist free the cop jabbed a finger at his eye, then ducked back, farther across the library. Leading him away.

Something glinted on her hand.

Colin wrenched the chisel in the wood. Faster, faster—

A clatter of feet pulled his gaze up again. The thief stood grappling with her, his skein against her strength… and somehow she twisted and held her balance. He shoved her away, and she skipped back on her feet ready for more.

The silver-green head turned. It looked over at Colin, then back as the detective lunged at him in that moment. He blocked her punch and sidestepped away.

The move put him beside the library's farthest pillar, the one marked in the painting.

The thief raised his hand, and his fingers *stretched.* No, the skein on his fingertips drew out into claws, blades, longer than his hand. The barer patch across his back spread, as if the blades' material had been drawn from there.

He stabbed them straight into the base of the pillar.

Colin felt the *crunch* clear across the room, too loud and fierce. The thief was digging for more skein there.

The cop rushed at him again, while his hand was trapped. He swung his other hand at her to drive her back, then tore his claws free.

Something bigger, more massive, than one handful of wood, gave a ponderous *creak*. The thief's claws had ripped part of the pillar right out.

Cold fear flooded through Colin.

The thief turned to the detective and pointed at the pillar. "This is the one over the meeting room."

No... That voice, hearing it aloud this time... how could that be Eric...

A section of wood on the pillar splintered half through. The detective rushed toward the remaining support, and the thief—the small, green-covered figure—turned and advanced on Colin.

He strode down the library, spreading his taloned fingers. Halfway across, he looked over and with slow deliberation smashed his claws into another pillar. He lingered there a moment, straining those blades through the wood, then wrenching them and a piece of the pillar free.

Timber groaned. Something like sawdust hung in the air.

And the thief drew closer, inescapable. That small, implacable figure was Eric, *how?*

"Get out of here!" Detective Simms shouted. "Run! I can't hold it!"

Hold it? He looked past Eric, to her.

She knelt beside the crippled pillar, arms around it. Those arms glimmered in green skein.

He'd already seen it on her. A glint of green as she fought, and the way she held her own against skein, but how, how did she get...

And I'm still staring instead of digging out my own weapon. "Damn!" He wrenched the chisel at the pillar, dug his fingers into the gap.

A foot thumped down, and he *had* to look up to see the thief standing right behind the pillar. Drawing back his clawed hand ready to strike it.

He moved slowly now. Openly giving Colin time to get clear.

Colin stared at Eric's silver-green form. The groans of pillars behind him. The resolute stance of someone with no hesitation about skewering his target. Or any "friend" crouching behind it.

Colin flung himself clear as the blow slammed in. The crash ripped through the air, through the wood, through everything, and it spread cracks all along the damaged pillar and the creaking above.

He got one glimpse of Eric scooping out a great handful of skein—*there had been more in there, there always had been*—and drawing it around to cover the last bare section on his back.

Then the crack raced across the ceiling. A chunk of wood sagged loose over their heads.

Eric bolted for the doorway, without taking one glance back.

As he stepped through it, the skein around him shimmered, greenish changing to silver, and he faded from sight.

Disappeared. He *vanished.*

Colin stared after him. But the room, the whole room, was crumbling...

This is what the quake did, to everywhere unsafe. To Terri—

He shoved the thought in a cold box in his head and buried it deep.

But the doorway Eric had taken, that led away from the pillars, clear of the shattered, collapsing parts of the world. The way out was right there.

And Bea Simms couldn't leave.

He dashed back up the library toward her, as the thought shook loose that he had no way to help. He could only run, as the ceiling came down.

His skin crawled and went cold—for one moment he knew what an ant might feel knowing some huge boot was descending down somewhere, and he had only blind faith that it would fall somewhere behind him.

He reached the detective. Her pillar was still holding.

The ceiling cascaded down with a thunder that smashed ears as if they'd never hear again, and the sound beat against flesh to shatter all the senses.

But the rending, spreading damage was all real. The wave of impact only tore open more clatters, more shakings, as the crashing ceiling ripped the floor open in some great devouring sinkhole.

All on the room's *other* side—it *had* to be. Her holding the pillar kept the collapsing away from them, away from anyone left in the meeting room below them. The world shook and dust swallowed his sight, but he had to hope the destruction stayed back...

Silence.

The clamor was gone, only shock and a ringing sound in his ears.

No, he *could* hear again. He heard smaller, lighter pieces of rubble still shifting, and one voice moaning in fear.

Until more voices spread out below. A prayer, another shout for help and someone else crying out for his family—answered moments later, mercifully, but the voices kept stirring here and there and rattling in the shocked, unsteady stillness.

Colin and the detective stood still at the edge of the hole, watching for signs that more of the floor or ceiling would give way. Finally someone from far behind them called out for them to make their way to the back stairs.

Carefully, Bea Simms unwrapped her skein-coated arms from the pillar. The wood grumbled, but it held.

Then she gave a slow look around, at the remains of the library, at the rubble below. As she did, she lifted a bit of her skein up to cling to her face, hanging over one eye like some oversized monocle.

She turned away before Colin could speak. The skein *slid* out of sight under her coat, and she said "Walk slowly now," and led the way out of the shattered room.

The floor held. With every step the walls around them and the remaining floor seemed to remember some of their strength, and she moved faster. Colin pushed to keep moving behind her, but his mouth couldn't work, couldn't break the bubble of stillness with his questions about the skein and Eric.

Then they stepped down the back stairs, coughing as the dust thickened. Out of those clouds Zara rushed up and grabbed his arm and steered him away.

People stood around the edges of the ruined House—staring, crying, asking if anyone was inside—and Zara led him around urging the people back and passing out calming words everywhere.

"Not a quake, it's not a quake," someone said. The thought Colin had sealed away earlier *unlocked,* the day of the quake and the sight of the weakest buildings falling...

But it only coiled in his gut and tugged at his thoughts, it never slowed his steps or the calming words he had to say. He spotted the glassy eyes of the people who'd been closest to the fall, and the hardened gazes of those who'd been outside, who'd seen the difference from a real earthquake at once.

And losing Terri... *I got a text in her name, and now I find out her fiancé's a killer*—don't *try putting those two together.*

He saw Detective Simms managing crowd control at another side of the site. His own work with Zara kept him away from her, as he mouthed promises and eyed which windows or walls were most cracked now. Zara waved him back and forth to different parts of the crowd, always keeping him in her sight, always grabbing hard onto his arm again whenever he came back within reach.

More and more police gathered around the site, still too few of them, all trying to push the crowds further and further back.

Two uniforms closed in on Colin. At first glance they seemed the same two that had shown up last night—*was it really just last night?*—but his dazed eyes cleared as one said "You saw it start? You were up there with Simms?"

"I saw... something," Colin hedged. "The detective wants to take my statement herself, I bet. You know where she is?"

"Somewhere around," was all the cop had.

The struggle wore on, calming watchers and pushing through his own crippling sense of how much of their world had just crumbled away. He glimpsed the detective again, but Zara kept him in motion.

Until they faded away. Until the murmurings grew lower and the eddying demands of the people left him and his mother sliding away, enough steps away to let the two of them speak for themselves.

He gripped the hand that was still clutching his arm. "I'm alright. Really."

"Of course you are."

She took a slow breath, and drew her hand away.

Then she smiled. "If I'm ever like that again, give me a good shake. Yes, even if there *is* another moment like this. What... what happened, anyway?"

"Not what, who. Eric."

He felt the rage thickening to fill his throat.

"I know it's him, his voice clinched it. It's Eric, he's been... I don't know, he's lost his mind or broke it something, but Eric's been attacking us to get the skein, and he just *brought all that down* just to cover his escape. And she, Detective Simms, has her own skein to fight him off."

"Eric." Zara said it slowly, eyes closed. *"Eric.* But even for him... And Ms. Simms, she saved you?"

"Yes. Me and some of the House."

"The House..." Her eyes squeezed tighter. "How could we just *lose* so much? What's the Hillside going to do if we can't pull them together now? We have to show them, that it's not all..."

She looked up, and motioned around. The scattered, irregular heaps of rubble where one ceiling had crashed down through another. The crumbled walls. The dust, the noise and the people still so close.

Her gaze jolted back to Colin. "But there's more, isn't there? More behind this? We always pulled together before, the whole community. But this is something bigger, that was always part of the House and the history? Something this powerful, that has Eric killing and destroying for it... We have to get away!"

"What?"

"We have to hide. If this is part of the history, we have to grab every record we have, and go somewhere safe before Eric comes after us. We can reassure the town from anywhere. But we need to find out what's going on. And we stay out of sight until we know."

"Hide?" The word wanted to roar out, to smash back at her. "There's a cop on Eric's trail now. And Eric did this, he can kill again... God, I was just at Leo's, what if he saw me there and goes after him next?"

"Listen to me." Zara locked her eyes on his. "We need time, to get to the truth about this. We need to do that in a safe place—"

"So hide. I have to stop him."

He pulled Zara into a hug. When he pulled back, she caught at him, but he twisted away.

The back door was right there. He walked straight to it—there were still too few police to watch everywhere. The House archive was close by.

The room looked exactly the same... except invaded by the smells of destruction, and eerily exposed to the noise outside instead of the shelter it should have had.

Two whole shelves of records tried to capture what Matt Vargas had been. Colin brushed his fingers over them, and grabbed out the few volumes that focused on Vargas's architecture—at least he could look for patterns about *where* the skein might be. For what the stuff was, he had no idea where anyone would start.

That left so many books, too many to carry. The police would probably want those as evidence, but Zara should get them sooner or later. He marched out again.

With all the layers of crowd and police, he thought Detective Simms might be impossible to find. Instead he spotted her looking over the rubble and making notes on a pad. She waved him in past the uniforms to her side.

He greeted her with "Looking for any skein that we missed?"

"What? Skein?" She kept her eyes on the damage.

"The thief called it that, the stuff you both use as armor. And you're hunting for him. You think he'll be back here, or heading somewhere else?"

"Look. I don't know what you think you saw. But..."

She gestured slowly around the damage. Just like Zara had.

She added "What should be obvious is just how dangerous this is. You need to accept that there's no way you can get involved."

"No way? You think I can just stop? I saw what he did, I saw him when he first snuck in here—"

"Detective?" One of the uniforms started toward them, and Colin realized his voice had been rising enough to hear over the chaos.

"Under control," she said, and the cop stepped back.

She turned back to Colin. Before her mouth could move, he whispered "They want to take a statement from me. And someone needs to know about the dragon painting, the skein, what I've seen him do with it. So who do I tell who'll believe it? Just you?"

She looked at him a moment. A hint of a smile lightened her face. "At least you're not trying to blackmail me about it. Of course the police at large wouldn't listen about this. So you tell me whatever you know—"

"I know who the thief is."

He flung the words at her, and her eyes sharpened in alertness. An instant later they went cold, suspicious.

"I'm not making it up. I *know* his voice. And I'd never put strings on sharing something that important. His name's Eric Rowe.

"I thought he was my friend, but I haven't seen him much since my sister passed... I never guessed he'd turn out like this. And he's *smart,*

I hear he's a rising star down at the Gardner corporation. Plus, he's way too good with his skein, I found some myself but he chased me down the street, right in the afternoon, and he beat me and took it. Then he followed me here to get the rest."

She nodded slowly. "Then you should see that you've done everything you can, and it's time to—"

"I see that I *have* to stop him. I couldn't save the inspector, or Terri, or the House. You think I can walk away now?"

"You're certainly determined. Determined to get yourself killed. I have an *investigation* here. I already found some—"

She only hesitated a moment, looking for the word, but Colin jumped right in. "Skein, it's called, like it was some kind of yarn. I'm sure you've got a plan, I saw you fight him. But you said none of the police will believe any of this. So can you really turn down someone who's already seen it all, and fought Eric already? And how's he finding it? From the dragon in the painting?"

"What? What painting?"

"The one Eric looked at—"

He glanced toward the House, and his throat caught. It was *gone*, devastated, maybe beyond saving one scrap of it...

He rushed on, spitting the words out before he lost his momentum. "He was following something in the Vargas paintings, and it almost worked. The pictures are buried in that pile now, but they're all digitized, plus I've got these records to start with." He tapped the books in his hands.

"Those books are evidence." She reached toward them, then halted and drew her hand back. "So you can identify him, just from his voice? Anything else? Think."

"Mostly that, sorry. Can you grab him for that or not?"

She shook her head. "I'd rather have more on him. Both to make the case stick and to bring more manpower when we do. Which is also why you can't think of going after him on your own."

"I'm not chasing him, I'm trying to find *how* to stop him. Like more skein, or more answers. Like Vargas's grandson—I asked Leo to look for other clues. *And* we need to get to him *now* before Eric gets to him first. The way Leo bullied him today, Eric would love an excuse to pay him back. And if he saw me asking him for help before…"

Colin stopped. His rush of thoughts, and words, had worked their way to the end and he had nothing left to argue with. In their place was the crushing fear that Leo *had* to be next and he had no excuse for losing another second.

All he could do was take a step away, and look back and add "Coming?"

She shut her eyes. "That's a decent plan. Except you could get killed doing it alone."

CHAPTER FIVE

UP THE SLEEVE

The detective's car stood right outside. A practical, nimble Ford of almost the latest year, with a subtle dent in the black paint in front of one tire and the inside spotlessly clean. Colin could just picture Bea Simms buying it from some police impound lot and making it her own.

Someone whose respect he wanted to keep. So once she eased the car out of the fringe of onlookers, he turned his gaze away from the rubble in the mirror. "I've... got a theory about Mike Shane, the earthquake inspector. Say, Eric was meaning to search the House for hidden skein, but he wanted to see if Mike spotted anything in his own search. Except Mike saw *him,* and... Eric killed him." Colin shifted the books on his lap. "Those were his last words, that someone had been following him."

"Possible. If Shane found a trace of something, Rowe could use that. And if he missed it, nobody'd see Rowe follow it up." Her gaze edged from the road over to him for a moment.

"Better than thinking Mike was part of it."

"Except it's my job to consider how anyone could be part of a crime. You could be here just so I can keep an eye on you."

"You don't believe that." *Anymore.* His voice came out oddly light, hollow.

"Not as much, the more I find out about him. And you."

"Or if you did suspect either of us, you'd deny it?" he grinned.

"I might." She actually smiled back.

And I just went to flirting with her again, like there was any point to it. He looked away, tried to feel how much his nerves were still jagged and twisted up with pain after what they'd been through. Better not to sweep that under the rug, he had to face his reaction to all the danger he'd seen—

And then *not* seen. They already had Leo's block in sight, he had to tell her what they could be walking into.

"I saw Eric *vanish!* Just disappear in thin air when he left us. He did some of the same trick on the street too. I don't mean just being fast or smart but..."

She pulled the car to the side, and gave him a silent, measuring look.

He added "I'm not delirious, I know what I saw." Like the time Eric had made his *head* disappear. "He vanished!"

She reached a hand into her coat's sleeve. With one motion she pulled out her silver-green skein and it slid out and flowed over her hand.

The skein, the hand, shimmered and faded from sight.

He blinked, stared harder. Some dim shape was still there, like a hand made of the finest mist. She turned her arm over, making the outline move above the dashboard. Not impossible to see, but...

"It really does that? So Eric did make his head disappear to look around corners... but why just his head—"

Her mouth was opening, and he rushed on:

"Wait, I get it. In the fight, I saw it, he didn't have enough skein to cover his whole body. Even when he chased me, he could still have been using speed and cover, and just hiding parts of himself. Except that now he's got so much that all of him can vanish."

"I think you're right," she said.

"And now? Now he can just be completely *invisible?*"

He glanced up and down the streets—it all looked so ordinary. Could Eric be standing there, anywhere, *any time?* Her hand still showed as a blur, but that kind of trace was a thing he could look right past, right until Eric stabbed them through... His gaze couldn't stop searching, looking at every shadow...

What kind of armor, weapon, something is *this stuff?*

"Mr. da Costa? Colin? Do you want to leave this to me, now that you see the kind of threats I have to be ready for?"

"You know I don't work like that." He looked back to her. "Say, after Eric left, was that why you pulled some skein over your eyes? To help you look for him?"

"Good," she nodded. "That does make it, call it, a little easier to see this trick."

"Then can you give me a bit of skein?" The words rushed out, with the reasoning forming right behind them. "Think about it. I don't mean I need so much that you can't fight without it—I saw how you took on Eric and held the pillar and all. But, would it take that much of the stuff to cover an eye, so I can at least keep watch for him?"

She looked at him, and he saw her eyes narrow, evaluating.

Only for a moment. "Sorry. I can't risk it, Colin."

"I can deal with it. Bea," he added.

She winced at him using her first name, but then that smile flickered again.

Then she turned forward and started the car up again.

Colin worked his fingers against the books on his lap, trying to settle his thoughts—Leo's apartment was just ahead. He'd faced Eric without skein of his own before, and now he had to stay focused on what help he could give.

The apartment building rolled up. Rows of windows, bushes here and there under them, a man exiting a car while children's voices sounded somewhere nearby...

The detective, Bea, held up a hand as if to shade her face—or hide it—and set a bit of skein over her eyes. She took a long look around the street for hidden enemies before tucking the skein back into her sleeve.

She walked up and rapped on Leo's door.

No answer. Colin pulled out his phone, and got nothing but Leo's voice mail.

"This is where you left him? Where Rowe could have seen you with him?" she said.

"Right. I asked him to look into his grandfather's secrets... he could be out looking for them now."

"Or not." She pointed over along the wall, at the nearest window. One speck of the glass glinted back.

"A crack?" But that would leave a paler patch in the glass, with a spider web of more cracks around it.

"A cut. Just enough to let someone outside listen, or more."

She led the way over to the window. As Colin walked he cocked an ear to the sounds of the kids around the block: they'd been almost this clear while he'd been inside with Leo. *Like how the crowd's noises had reached into the House's archive, after some of the walls were gone... Oh God, the* House *is gone...*

Bea stood in front of the window, hidden waist-down in the bushes. Colin saw faces here and there on the street turning to look at her. She tapped a finger on the half-inch gap, and a tiny tendril of her skein slid on inside.

She frowned in concentration, and the probe moved slowly, clumsily within. Colin watched it, letting the idea sink in again: this was a substance someone could *control with a thought.* On top of all its strength and stealth uses.

When the tendril touched the window's latch, she drew it back and sighed "So Eric Rowe could have opened this. With practice."

"Opened it?" He forced his voice down. "You mean—is Leo alright or not?"

She looked at him, and he could almost feel her slowing down to push her thoughts out in words. "There's no sound inside, so no reason to think either of them is here now. I don't want to argue probable cause that he had a break-in, and have to explain how I know what that little slit could be."

Instead she led him around in search of the super. Colin remembered the skinny old man from when they'd all helped Leo move in, and he was opening his mouth to remind him he was a friend. Bea held up her badge first.

Half a minute later, the super was opening Leo's door. Bea gave them both a warning wave back, and stepped inside.

Colin swept his gaze around the sidewalk, trying to catch any faint shimmer or footsteps of an invisible enemy lurking in plain sight. He listened to her footsteps, moving slowly through the apartment, waiting for the moment something attacked her...

I came here so nobody else would die, and I let her go in alone? He stepped through the doorway.

Leo's place looked the same as when he'd left, the same piling up of too many generations of possessions in too small a place. Too full of shadows that could hide some deadly blur, if Eric was still here.

Bea stepped back into view from the bathroom. "Empty," she said.

"So it's a false alarm?" the super said.

"I still need to find him. Mind if we look around?"

"Sure." And the old man simply walked away without questioning. As if her badge settled all of that.

Colin shut the door behind him.

The detective gave him a cold look. "I wanted you to stay back first." She cast a slow glance around the crowded rooms. "This is really your big expert on all this?"

"Matt Vargas's grandson. There's nothing like growing up around some of the answers. And don't worry, I know not to touch anything now."

"Good. Now look here."

She motioned to one open door. In the bedroom beyond, an old dresser had one drawer hanging open, and clothes strewn around the floor.

"So your friend packed and left in a hurry," Bea said. "Or someone could want us to think that. But, no signs of a struggle... I think. Hard to tell with a place like this."

"Not that hard," and Colin grinned. "Because, I was here just hours ago. Maybe I can see if anything was knocked over, that wasn't that way before. Or what else anyone's been digging through."

Or I can try—I had to open my mouth here. He moved slowly out to the front room, and closed his eyes to shut out the shape of the stacks now. *I've spent years making sure a place kept every chair and flowerpot in line, so that should be good for something.* He tried to fill in the lines, the details, the *intent* of how Leo had piled things up or left them spilled.

Those books looked about right, all stacked up cleanly but with boxes heaped in front of them. Good, the more the room matched his memory the more likely Leo had escaped. Those old lamps, had they been shoved that far into the corner before?

One slender lamp had fallen over, right at the edge of the group. He looked at it, tried to picture someone walking by and brushing it... but it was too far out of the path of traffic. Someone must have *wanted* to go to those lamps.

Or to the space behind them. A distinct crack ran through the wall there.

Colin pulled out his pocketknife and was just starting to kneel down when he caught himself. "Right. No touching anything, I said."

He backed away, and the detective leaned in. She must have slipped on plastic gloves at some point, and she probed the crack with a finger. Then she slid one glove off, and slowly stretched a bit of skein from her finger into the space.

When she slid it out, a bulb of skein the size of a finger bone clung to the end of her probe. Just the way it quivered as it slid free showed it was separate from the stuff she controlled… until it flowed and merged into her own skein and it all slid away beneath her shirt cuff.

But I found that hiding place. I could have used just that bit of skein to practice using it.

He pushed down that resentment to focus on what they'd found. "So Leo had some of it too? He knew about the stuff all along, and when he ran he hid this here? Or checked on it, or grabbed a chunk of it and missed some. Just when I'd asked him to help me find answers…"

Oh. He slumped where he stood, feeling stupid.

He finished "I told him this was dangerous. Then he heard the House collapsed, and of course he ran."

"Sounds reasonable." Bea took a long, slow glance around the apartment, that ended with her eyes locked on his. "So the rest of this looks undisturbed, suggesting that your friend got out without being interrupted?"

"Yes. Or, I think so, from what I can remember." He had to hedge that, much as he wanted a firm conclusion to show her, one that would mean Leo got out safe.

She nodded. "We can try tracking Leo down. And Eric Rowe—but you still only identified him from his voice."

"Right. And his size, and how he passed up a chance to kill me after he got the skein."

Softly, calmly, she said "After you led him to it."

"I *know*. I know I led him to it and I let him get away. I know he destroyed the Vargas House, and he could be chasing Leo right now."

The crowded room seemed to press in on him, and he took a quick step—his foot brushed a stack of books, and he felt them sway before he leaned in to steady them. It looked like a stack of classic poetry, more magpie collections from the Vargas family that looked nothing like a clue. For a moment his leg tensed ready to kick it over, to do anything.

Instead of lashing out, he told her "I have to stay on this. Maybe I can figure out where Leo would go. Or, I know Eric... I *thought* I knew him. Look, I just need to stop him."

"You need to?" She didn't move, but something in her eyes shifted, closed off. "You take a lesson from your mother, and get out of sight; the two of you can probably dig up more about where this started than Leo ever could. I think I can clear the rest of those books from the site for you to hang onto—"

"No." He met that gaze, tried to settle on some kind of answer for her, but his hands wouldn't stop shaking. "I'm telling you I need to get out there and *do* something about it. You, you said nobody else knew about the skein, so you need someone who does to watch your back..."

Her voice went softer, sadder. "I didn't say nobody knew."

Somehow, those words bled the last of Colin's reasons out of him and left him slumping where he stood. He'd fought Eric, given Bea their enemy's name, and now he'd retraced Leo's steps and found more skein, and she simply shut him down? With no chance, none, to do any better?

Long seconds later, his phone pulsed.

Bea said "That could be your mother now. Ready for you two to get started."

The screen showed a text. From the same meaningless set of digits that had claimed to be Terri:

get the skein

have to get it all away

-T

The screen shook, the letters blurred in his sight as the rage slashed through him. He'd actually pushed the other messages from his mind, with everything else that had gutted him, but now *this*—

"How bad is it?" Bea's voice was soft now, trying to reach through all the pain.

"Just a goddamn prank. No, it must be Eric, trying to rattle me," he said through gritted teeth.

"Then it looks like it's working."

He angled the phone toward her, then flipped back to show her the other set of texts. And he slumped, sagged down to sit on the floor.

"It says it's from my sister. She's *dead*—they found her DNA under St. Mary's ruins. And Eric was engaged to her. Maybe losing her was what broke him... he told me this morning that the quake changed him. Or he was *laughing* at me then, and he still is. Or she was too trusting all along..." He knew he was rambling. "The texts started just today, and now they know about skein—it has to be Eric trying to break me..."

He looked up.

For a moment he got his head, his voice, clear enough to ask "You think you can trace that?"

"We can try."

"You have to. Eric has already destroyed... and now he pulls *this?*" His voice still came out too calm, too quiet.

She crouched to bring her head down to his level. "Colin. What is it you really want now?"

"I *want* Eric to never hurt anyone else." That was the truth, but saying that much dug his thoughts deeper like fingers into a tainted garden. "I want, well, answers, but if the only way is to rip Eric open with my bare hands I don't think I'll have any regrets. I *hate* feeling like that."

"I... know."

Her voice was softer than he'd ever heard her.

"Look. I could lock you up as a protected witness, to try to keep you from running into danger again. Or, there's someone you can meet. You can tell both of us all about this."

"What? Who's that?"

"I did say I wasn't the only one who knew."

* * *

Bea drove without a word. She steered them down from the Hillside, clear out of the original Rayo Hill neighborhood, and Colin felt more out of place as the buildings around grew more modern, more filled with glass and steel.

She hadn't spoken since they'd set out. He couldn't guess what thoughts were running behind those silent features, or what he could say, only that he'd hate to try chasing Eric with her against him too.

And Bea Simms herself... she was so sure, so together, that just being around her kept him feeling out of his league in this hunt. But then there'd be moments when he pulled a smile out of her, or thought how unlikely it was that she'd taken him along this far. The most he could think now was to keep silent and not risk whatever chance he had.

She pulled up at a two-story house that looked almost taller than it was wide, standing alone in a small unfenced yard. Colin spotted discolorations along some of the siding trim, a sign it had taken damage back in the quake and long since been repaired.

Bea turned off the engine, but instead of rising from the seat she said "One thing first."

He couldn't read her voice. "Yes?"

"When you had your own 'skein,' did you ever just pull it off you and set it aside?"

"Sure. Wait, are you saying you can't?" He stared at her.

"No, no. Or, that is what I've been saying," and she chuckled bitterly. "I lied to my partner that I can't remove mine."

"Your police partner? That's who we're meeting?" *And you lied to him?*

He left the last unsaid, but she might have heard it in his voice— she closed her eyes for a moment. "It was the only way to stop him from reporting the whole story to the department, skein and all: I had to say that he couldn't turn this stuff over to some lab without them cutting me up too. I'm still trying to guess what a weapon like this would do for the world, or to it."

"Like the army Special Forces—I mean, *invisibility?*"

"Exactly. Or it's already one of their projects, but I can't see how it does all this... Anyway, ever since, I've been trying to think how to tell him it's not stuck to me after all."

"How to tell your partner. You hid that from him. But now you're trusting me to keep a secret like that. I'm flattered." *And concerned—* he felt prickles of unease moving through him. The skein really was a huge can of worms to open, and yet her first response was to lie to a partner, to someone she trusted her life with? *I really don't know this woman.*

They walked to the door, buzzed, and it clicked right open.

The inside could have been a gift shop, from the balloons tied up that bumped against the ceiling. Or the layered smell of maybe a dozen different vases of flowers, all standing on tables with cards beside them, and air freshener trying to tame the scents that had gone sour. A sound rolled over the floorboards and into view.

The man in the wheelchair had to be in his fifties, a figure of lean, corded muscle propelling the chair out to meet them. His blond, military haircut matched with the piercing gaze he darted between both of them.

Partner, Bea had called him? A cop this old had to be more like a mentor to a young detective, but how did that wheelchair change it...

The veteran cop's words broke into those thoughts. "All right. Who's this?"

Bea nodded to her partner. "Meet Detective Sergeant Ed Jordan, the one who came closest—too close—to catching Eric Rowe."

Jordan's eyes widened at the name. And Bea meant that Eric had put him in that chair?

She went on "And, Colin da Costa. He knows something about where this—" she raised a hand and brought a flicker of skein peeping out— "is hidden, and he was chasing Rowe too."

"And you're bringing a witness around here?" Jordan said. "You think that's safe?"

"The stuff is called skein," Colin said, and he took a step toward Jordan. *It worked to get Bea's attention.* "The man who attacked us is Eric Rowe. He used to be my friend, but now he's attacking and killing to get—"

"Why?"

Jordan's single, sharp word knocked Colin's sentence off its tracks and left him grabbing for breath. "What d'you mean?"

"You know so much?" Jordan's eyes searched his face, the way he stood, like they missed nothing. "We'll get back to how you found out. Right now, cut to the chase: what does he want this *skein* for?"

Colin glanced at Bea. She didn't even seem to notice, with her eyes on her mentor.

"Well, going by the power it has?" he began. "You use it right and it makes you bulletproof, fast, strong..."

His hand crept over to rub the arm he'd bruised, fending off Eric's first punch last night. Jordan's gaze shifted a fraction as he did, and Colin's hand slid back. A few bruises were nothing to be wincing over, not in front of this man.

Colin went on "He's unstoppable. He brought down most of the Vargas House with a few slashes."

"So he's out to destroy? A terrorist?" There was no emotion in Jordan's voice.

"No. Or... Look, we've been out of touch, but I always remember Eric as the smartest in the neighborhood. And also, the smallest."

Jordan's face didn't change, didn't consider it.

Of course not, not if I'm reaching all the way back to us as kids to explain it. Colin tried "Just today, he was getting shoved around right in front of a roomful of the House's guests, like nothing had ever changed. And, I bet he let that happen because there were witnesses. If he does catch Leo alone, I don't want to think what he'd do to him."

"So he's got a mean streak. Or did Bea tell you to say that?"

"Tell me? No." He glanced at the younger detective.

Bea gave a tight-lipped smile. "I keep saying, any arrest we made, we'd have to choose the right location. Where he couldn't cut loose on bystanders."

"Could be." Colin tried to picture Eric turning those claws on a crowd, going from killer to worse. "He did tear through the House, and he killed the inspector for convenience, I think. He gets more dangerous the more skein he gets. The stuff just makes it too easy to turn assassin."

"That's a motive there," Jordan said. "Easiest way to cash in on this thing."

"No! That's not him."

"You're the one that used the word." Jordan's lip tugged in a grin.

" 'Assassin'? It's just a word! I think…" He closed his eyes a moment, then glared back. "I think if I ever knew Eric at all, I know he'd have some kind of reason behind what he did, something that suited him more than money. My sister thought he was more than just greedy, and I can't believe we were all *that* wrong."

He pointed a finger at Jordan, and his voice gathered force.

"Don't you see, that makes him *more* dangerous. I've seen what he can do too—"

"Relax."

Jordan raised a hand, and his word brought Colin to a stop again.

"We can stop putting you on the spot. You sit down and tell us from the beginning."

*   *   *

Just up the hallway, Jordan had a table out with chairs ready. All set for letting guests sit and be more comfortable with their injured host.

Colin worked his way through the tale. All about knowing Eric and Leo, the intruder in the House, going after Leo and being stalked by Eric—and being followed to the House. Himself and Bea finding Leo gone.

He realized he'd left out some of the details about his skein, when Bea said "There, you see, Rowe *tore* the skein off him with his own. So there's one way we can disarm this threat after all."

That's Bea's lie again, that her own skein is stuck to her. He glanced at her, at her mentor. Why would she put that kind of poison between them?

"If we get that far," Jordan told her. "Confirm it's Rowe, and get everything there is to know about him."

"And more skein." She and Jordan could have been alone in the room now. "We can try tracking Leo Tozer down too, and see if he has some of his own. The stuff's better protection than Kevlar. I can't take Rowe without more of it."

"Oh, I think seeing a sniper rifle pointed at his center mass would take the wind out of him. You really want to take on more 'skein'?"

"To bring him down? Of course. And it keeps it away from him, if we find it first."

Colin added a short nod to her words.

Just that faint motion brought Jordan's gaze to him again. "Then why's your sister saying to just get the skein *away?*"

"That's not Terri. I told you—"

"I heard you," Jordan cut in. "All your reasons it's a prank. Now I'm asking you, is it possible it's her?"

Just like that, he threw the question at him? Colin forced his teeth to unclench, and answered "It's *possible.* But don't you assume it's real just because it gives you an extra clue. You don't want to count on it turning out the easy way, right?"

He smiled at that. One point for him, against the uncompromising detective.

Jordan smiled back. "Or count on the simplest, least painful way. Right?"

Damn, he got me there. Colin forced himself not to look away from that knowing grin. "Right. Whichever it is."

"We'll see if we can trace the texts." Jordan's grin softened, warmed a fraction.

Then he turned to Bea.

"So you really want this person tagging along?"

Colin felt his eyes widen. Bea hadn't called Jordan since he'd joined her, and Jordan's surprise at seeing him felt real. So the detective had simply read Bea's intention off of her bringing him here?

She wanted him along?

Bea looked right back at Jordan. "He doesn't panic. He's got eyes, sometimes, when there's something to see. He does the work."

"Leg work."

Jordan could have been making an ordinary joke; if there was any bitterness in his voice it buried deep.

Then Jordan's eyes narrowed. "Don't think of it as my permission, more that I'm not reporting you for this. If he gets hurt, it's on you."

Colin snapped "It'll be on *me*. I asked for this, and after that it's up to me to move fast and listen to her."

Jordan waved that aside. "The audition's over. Save the promises and try living them."

Colin opened his mouth, stopped, and gave him a slow nod.

"Then we'll get going on this Mr. Rowe. And, one more thing." Jordan's gaze had shifted to Bea, but now it swung back to Colin.

"What?"

"Stop flirting with my partner. Letting that into the job gets people killed."

Colin winced, swallowed an *I'm not!* He'd kept his eyes off Bea for almost the whole time here, what had Jordan seen? And the cop just tossed the warning out in the open so the whole idea would die of embarrassment.

Bea's face didn't even twitch.

When they walked outside, the sun was lowering in the sky.

He looked at Bea beside him. "What next?" he said, hoping she'd keep silent about Jordan's last warning.

All she said was "You heard him, we start investigating your friend Eric. And at this hour I can get more of that on my own."

"Huh. So you're being a cop and I'm just digging through Vargas history? Sounds a lot like when you were sending me away." The words came out more complaining than he wanted.

But she didn't even glance over. "I'll have more on him in the morning. Then I can catch you up. Show you where it started for us."

They climbed into her car.

As Colin strapped in, he asked "Is Jordan going to be out of that chair someday? Or did Eric…"

"We don't know."

Bea said it softly, no feeling in her voice except the hush itself. She set the key in the ignition.

Then she paused. "Thank you. For keeping quiet about how the skein works."

"I… are you sure you're fooling him at all? Anyway, a lie like that is a nasty place to put us in. All of us."

She glanced at the mirrors. "I thought it was the only way." She started the car. "Someone has to keep this under control. And that means some hard choices."

CHAPTER SIX

ONE WRONG STEP

His apartment had never seemed less like home.

After Leo's several crowded rooms and Jordan's house, Colin's "temporary" one-bedroom spot felt smaller than ever. But it still had windows to check, and corners of open boxes to stare at trying to remember how much of that not-quite-invisibility could be seen, if Eric was here.

Then he had every corner searched, and the rest came flooding in.

Terri could be alive. The Vargas House is gone, and Eric *brought it down. I'm hunting Eric—I'm betting my life that he won't bother hunting me down as long as he thinks I'll give up, and he should know me better than that already.*

When a pipe creaked in the walls, he jumped. Sounds down the hall frayed at his nerves, cover that footsteps could creep up under...

He set out the Vargas records he'd gathered, and called Zara.

She answered with a simple "Hi."

She sounded cheerful, unshaken—or she would have if he hadn't spent the afternoon learning how two detectives could keep their own emotions masked.

"Hi," he answered. "So you did it? You're all tucked away at some hotel?" She'd been so sure Eric would come after her next.

But she only said "I'm at the Wyngard, and I'm doing fine. I've been looking for answers about what this 'skein' could be."

"You sure that's where you want to be? Not making the rounds promising you'll bring the House back?"

"You think I can't do both? There've been supporters to call, insurance forms to check, promises to make... so many promises. After a few rounds of that, it's easier to search for why it happened than stand around pretending everything will be the way it was." Something dark thickened in her voice.

A pause gathered, lengthened. A sound moved just at his window—no, that was out by the street.

Finally he said "I know the feeling. So... what have you got?"

"No signs about Matt Vargas and any secret bulletproofing study. But seriously, what should I be looking for? For instance, you showed me what looked like a plate of armor, and then you made it change form. How did that work?"

He took a slow breath. "Yeah, that's the weirdest part. One of the weirdest," he had to add. "I *thought* it, and the skein responded."

"You thought it." She went quiet a moment. "Are you calling it some kind of magic?"

"I don't know *what* it is, or how Vargas got involved with it. Just when you think you know someone," he added, but the joke came out sour. *Because of Eric again.*

"Anyway, here's some progress," and her voice lightened. "I started looking through his paintings, and I mean scrolling over them inch by inch. I think I found one more dragon, so far."

A file popped into the phone. Colin clicked it open to stare at the shape. One curl that could be wings and tail, a pattern in sunset shadows... He could barely make it out even with the circle she'd drawn around it. But she'd *found* one.

At the base of a Greek-style pillar at the front of... Rayo Hill City Bank?

"You're the best!"

"Or Vargas could have used other clues as well as this." Her words came faster, lifted by the excitement of the riddle. "Or dragon marks on a site itself, where we'd never know to look. Anywhere he had access to could be part of this—whatever "it" is. But I'll keep looking."

"I bet you find even more of them. And I'll get this to Bea right away."

He was on his feet now, pushing the books away and feeling a grin cut across his face. *If this really is where the skein is, we might get there ahead of Eric, we can beat him!*

That Terri-fake had said to get the skein away…

He added "They're already investigating Eric. Bea and her police mentor, I mean. They're working on how to prove what Eric's done and trap him." If there was a way that kept the skein itself quiet. He added "They'll get him."

They, I said?

Zara said "I'm sure you will."

Colin swallowed.

And, Jordan had been right about something else he had to face. He forced out the words "You remember those texts I said came from Eric?"

"The ones you got cut off from explaining? Of course."

"They said…" He let himself take one more breath. "Said they were from Terri."

Silence. The phone could have been a dead piece of plastic in his hand. The room was a pocket of stillness in the night.

He rushed on with "There's not one reason to think it's anything besides Eric using another weapon on us. But… nothing's changed, about her, except that now we know how far Eric can go." Maybe because he lost Terri. Or he was always that twisted, down deep, and she had been all that kept him in line.

"Oh. God, how could he… Thank you for telling me."

He heard her voice break for a moment. Eric had crippled two of Zara's treasures in one day, torn one building down and dug the other memory up.

She breathed "Just, don't let him get you. All of this is too crazy, and it only keeps getting deeper. You have to put a stop to him."

"I will, I swear."

He hung up, and shot a text to Bea: *Just found another dragon!* and attached the image.

He'd just broken out his first aid kit before her answer came back: *Already got that one. Just keep looking, till tomorrow.*

He frowned at the screen. Just like that, their chance at more skein was gone...

Wait. "Got" meant there *had* been skein right where Zara's clue said it was, and she was still searching for more. Or Leo could be out there somewhere with skein of his own, and more answers.

He took the first aid kit and worked over his cuts and bruises—from Leo's punch and *two* new scraps with Eric—to clean them and bandage one gash. Then he boiled up a quick mac and cheese and tried to sit still.

Too many small sounds around the apartment had him staring at corners again. He laid out the bound records from the House's archive and tried to search them, but his hand kept going back to the phone.

Soon. They *were* reading this trail right, he knew it. The next time they faced Eric, he might have a real weapon in his hand again.

Unless Bea insisted she take it all, to "save" him from the stuff she was pretending they couldn't put down.

Maybe it is magic, and it gets in our heads. Or it could be that's just how Bea is.

I can't figure her out. But he'd never seen anyone so at home with hunting down an enemy, or fighting like she did. So focused... but then, she had to be.

And a couple of times, he *had* made her smile.

* * *

The summer air was still holding on to its early morning chill, when too few people were out to notice it yet. Colin stood out front for a few of the longer minutes of his life, until Bea's car pulled into view. Her face was unreadable, and she brought up some skein to her eyes for a long look around the sidewalk for any hidden enemy.

Once she drove them away, he let the excitement bubble up. "Zara found *another two* dragon clues last night. There might still be skein out there."

"If Eric Rowe didn't get it already." She didn't look over.

"I know, but think how easy these shapes are to miss. I think we're on to something here."

"There's something I want you to see first. Let's see if you're right."

They drove along the winding road, up the Rayo Hill hillside itself and away from the houses. The stillness and the underbrush grew around them with each turn.

We're heading for the two statues at the top. Zara was right, came the growing thought.

They pulled over at the hill's crest. There were no tourists up here at this hour, and the simple stone statue of Peace in her robes stood alone there.

Bea climbed out, and glanced along the crest and the scraggly trees. The other statue, Hope, was just about visible through the vegetation. Bea stood where she could take in both of them. The hillside was silent, only some bird stirring in the distance.

Then she turned back, and Colin saw a line of pain on her face.

"That City Bank clue was also where Jordan and I started on the case. Two of the guards were injured, but nothing was stolen. Except that we found this."

She held up her phone. The image showed the stone pillar in front of the stately bank—with a familiar puncture sunk into the base of it.

Right at the first dragon marking Zara found.

"Yeah. Looks like the way Eric dug for skein in the library. The first time there anyway, when he wasn't rushed or trying to bring the place down," he added with a growl. "If that was the only damage to the bank, he must have found the skein right off."

She led him onto the gravel trail, that wound between the trees toward the other statue.

"We didn't know that at the time. Only that Matt Vargas had designed the bank, and days later we got a call about some trouble up here, another Vargas site. Jordan and I went up here from opposite sides to catch him between us. And then—"

She thumped a foot down on the path, and the gravel crunched.

She looked back at the statue behind them. "Then he ran *this* way. Jordan was closing in here by the Peace statue, and he got his legs cut out from under him, and the man in the mask... got away in the dark."

It was one small hitch in her voice, before she went on.

"I was on the other side. I saw he had cut into this statue, so I came back with a ground-penetrating radar set to see why, and I checked both of them. And the statue *I* was near, that's where I found my skein, and he missed it. Just one choice, that could have gone the other way."

She added in a whisper:

"Just like *anything* could."

Colin met her gaze, tried to find words to say to someone who'd seen that much, and come so close to being the one struck down instead.

All he could say was "Your partner got hurt, and you got a way to fight. So you fight." *Because now you have to.*

He didn't say the last out loud. But her eyes twitched wider, and for an instant he wondered if he had.

Then she looked away. "Worst trade-off there is. But... maybe you get it."

"I'm trying to," he said.

"Then you know how fast *you* can die," and she stomped her foot on the gravel again, "if you waste *one second* any time I tell you to duck. Or how anyone could die, from making the wrong call or the right one, it might not matter. And you still want to be a target?"

Her voice had gone calm, controlled again.

He could only nod.

Then he dug out his phone. "Here are those dragon paintings we found. You're right, there's one on the painting for the statues, see? So Eric's on the same trail, and that makes three times out of three that the clue works—"

He stopped, and held up the screen to compare them—the painted cliffside view of the two figures, aligned with the real statue on the actual cliff. "This is the one. The dragon's on this statue, Peace, and he cut into it there." He could see the hole, another precise little mark sunk into the base of the statue.

"And Jordan found him here," Bea said. "But the skein was in the *other* statue."

"So it's like the House library, the dragon's only on a place near-by? But—" He flipped to the bank painting again. "Here it's right on the only pillar he needed to hit. Or did you go check the others here?"

"Of course I did, nothing. Hmm, a pillar there, a pillar at the House. Two out of three were in pillars?"

"Three..." Colin jumped to the last image. "Zara found four drag-ons. There's the House, the bank, and here. That leaves just one. We have to get to the docks—"

He was just spinning for the car when her hand closed on his arm.

She held up her own phone. The image was of a wall of concrete, that aligned with Vargas's painting of the little Rayo Hill harbor and its pier at sunset. With a small hole reaching into the pier's concrete, right where the hidden dragon had been painted.

"From a vandalism report," she said softly. "After what happened up here. We know that mark, don't we?"

His head sank, staring at the stones under him. "So we were too late. He's already got all the skein we know about. Or else the dragon clue isn't enough and there's stuff we may never be able to find."

"Although he won't either, if he's been following the same clue."

"Yeah." He forced a grin. "And I saw you fight him before, with the skein you have now."

"Just holding him off. *Before* he got his last batch—he can armor his whole body now, did you see that?" She shook her head. "It keeps coming back to that. Nothing really stops him, unless I get more skein."

The bitter, hungry growl of her words hung in the air. Colin nodded, and the image of Eric slashing through those pillars filled his mind again.

And something about Bea's voice. One thing about it, and her, felt off now.

He forced the thought out: "You say you lied to Detective Jordan. That you couldn't remove your skein."

She glanced away. "Yeah. I'm not proud of that."

"The way you talk about needing more now… Is the truth that you can remove it, or that you really can't?"

Her gaze swung back, and he saw the tiniest widening in her eyes. Surprise, or even hurt.

He rushed on "I mean, that text did say to 'get it away from there,' like it was dangerous. And, you lying to me instead of to your partner makes more sense."

And she *smiled*. A small, gentle curve of her lips.

"You're learning. But, see?"

She swung her hand downward, and a rush of silver-green slid down from her sleeve and splashed at her feet.

She moved away from the pool, two long steps. "I'm not stuck to this thing, or stuck on the idea of it either. I told you, I said that to *keep* control, to make Jordan think before he tells the brass about this and the genie's out of the bottle. So I have time to think what happens if the world at large finds out."

He looked down again. "Sorry for doubting you. I'm still trying to wrap my head around this many secrets."

"Well, you're doing fine. And I'll say it again: you're dealing with a killer now. It just takes one choice to change everything, and sometimes all your planning won't show you which one it is."

I get it. Colin nodded, tried to think of some kind of answer.

Bea's phone chimed. A simple, brisk ring.

She brought it to her ear. "Jordan?"

That was all she said, and all Colin could hear. Instead he watched her face harden and her body grow still, for what had to be the better part of a minute.

Finally, "Set it up, thanks," and she hung up.

He held his mouth closed. Right now, speaking just to prompt her felt unprofessional.

She said "Now we can start on our elusive Mr. Rowe. Jordan just confirmed a point about his job."

"At Gardner Development," he nodded. "Eric's one of the ones buying up properties from us, because he came from the Hillside himself."

"You know how he got promoted to that spot? Someone on his team died."

She reached down and scooped up her skein, pulling and summoning it into her hand before she led the way to her car.

* * *

Getting into the Gardner lobby was easy. Bea simply gave her name to the receptionist, with no explanation about Colin behind her, and said it was all set up.

Then they waited there, and Colin got a good long view of the wide space and cubicles beyond that desk. Again and again he spotted a chart or a full model of some bulky business or apartment complex—many of them on blocks he knew still belonged to their proper local owners. The models and much of the office trim were always colored green.

What felt odd was the sound in the air. Instead of hungry corporate sharks, he heard laughter and a sense of people at ease with each other, the kind of sound he knew.

The elevator opened and Eric's supervisor walked toward them, a skinny Asian man named Dennis Fields—*the perfect name for working in this green-covered place,* Colin thought.

He walked straight to Bea, quick with nervous energy. "Detective Simms, isn't it? I'm glad to help with the investigation. But weren't there other detectives looking into this?"

"We're trying a new angle. The sergeant told you?" Fields nodded, and she went on "Since Mr. Andrews had his fall while you were setting up your community fair, I'd like to know which of his team was on the site with him."

"His... well, we can—" Fields turned to start toward the receptionist.

"Without involving anyone else," Bea cut in softly. "Yes, I'm saying there is a chance someone on your team might be responsible. If that should turn out to be true and then they find out they're a suspect, that makes you the only one who could have leaked it. You see the problem if that happens," and her voice sharpened.

Or if word gets to Eric, and he finds out we've traced the attacks back to him, before we're ready to take him. Bea was risking plenty on being able to keep this man quiet.

"I... I see. But, you're wrong. All the signs say it was an accident. You're talking about one of us being a..." Fields couldn't finish the sentence.

And Bea nodded. "We certainly could be, and then all of this blows over. But if we're not, it might all come down to keeping this under control."

"Alright then. But you do have it wrong."

"So where can we talk?"

Fields led them in, past a few tables of those demo models, to grab the first door they reached and bring them into a conference room.

Bea's warning look softened then, as the door shut behind them. "Thank you for cooperating with us. First thing: this happened early while the fair was setting up. So which of your team was there?"

"All of them, I think. From me in the lead to a junior like Eric. I *asked* them to be there, that doesn't make them killers."

"And where are they right now?"

"Today, out seeing people. Community relations is the root of what we do, you know."

At least until you've bought a place away from that community. And then there's the killer you hired. Colin kept his mouth shut and tried to let Bea work without distractions.

"And which of them was here yesterday?"

His eyebrows went up. "I'm sorry, yesterday? What are you implying now?"

"Just answer the question, please." Bea's voice was still calm, almost friendly, even with that implacable hint peeping out now.

"We had Lisa, John—the senior members only. I can give you those two's schedules if it clears them."

"All of their schedules, if you don't mind."

Colin held down a smile. Bea had to be edging up to checking Eric's alibi for his rampage yesterday, and Fields might never guess.

"Yes, yes. Really, it's hard to believe any of this. We like to think of ourselves as family here."

"And you know the statistics for families?" Bea said. "They're where the bulk of murders happen—but, the bulk of the accidents too," and she smiled. "Now, the video? What the cameras caught while they were testing?"

Video? *It can't be that easy.*

"Didn't the other detectives get that copy? Come on—"

He bounced out of his chair and out the door, swept up by that same nervousness. Colin thought of calling him back, but Bea fell in place behind Fields and he followed her. Making a fuss now would probably draw more attention, more chance it might get back to Eric. And they'd said Eric himself was away.

The elevator ride up was silent. It was only when they reached the upper floor and started across the rows of cubicles that Fields began muttering "Andy Anderson was the best, nobody was better with a neighborhood than him. It was just a *fall...* "

Bea drew closer behind him and whispered a warning. His muttering faded.

Then Fields stopped in his tracks. He nodded to the far end of the floor, where six, no, seven people clustered together in what looked like an improvised party, from the brightly-wrapped boxes around them.

Fields spoke from the corner of his mouth. "Right next to my desk. They should break up in a minute, Jade's getting her real party later."

"We can wait," Bea said.

Colin leaned back against the wall, trying to blend in.

As he leaned back his gaze fell right on a diagram on the opposite wall. A drawing of the Hillside... with a sprawling green Gardner shape lying across where the Vargas House was.

Had been.

He blinked, stared, gritted his teeth. It could have been any of the other designs he'd glimpsed—it looked older than many, half-covered with note cards and sticky notes. Just another plan for property they *wanted.* While they called themselves family and pushed actual families out of their homes. And now Eric had cleared the House itself away.

Colin's fists clenched. None of this was working, this walking around asking questions, when they knew the name of their enemy—

Eric walked across the floor.

He was just a figure strolling for the elevator behind them, a small shape half-hidden by two larger men. He looked comfortable, focused on his destination, never glancing toward Colin or Bea. Innocent, even.

Colin wrenched his head away before the gaze itself made Eric notice them. *I don't care how he acts, I know that voice! Keep still, don't stand out...* He noted the number of suit jackets on the people around him, and wondered why he'd ever thought he could blend in.

"Mr. da Costa?"

A woman's voice, right at his elbow. He started, looked at the aging black woman beside him.

At least her voice was low, and Eric was out of sight now.

"I thought that was you," she went on. "I can't tell you how sorry we are to hear about a landmark like the Vargas House. Have you considered some kind of monument—"

Like a small one, while you get most of the land? Colin held still, pressure boiling inside him so he couldn't trust himself to move one muscle.

Fields and Bea walked away. From the corner of his eye he saw the crowd had finally broken up, and Fields headed to his computer.

Colin forced his clenched throat to shape something like a calm "Sorry, not now" and he turned on wobbling knees to move after the others.

His phone buzzed.

A gasp tore through him. His hand yanked the phone out by reflex.

A text waited there:

dont trust cop

–T

The screen shook, his eyes blurred. The babble of voices around was suddenly gone. It was another lie, another trick of Eric's, it was always that...

Up ahead came Bea's voice, insisting "You don't have to play the video now," and Fields saying "It's right here—"

Colin stumbled the last steps to the cubicle and locked his gaze on the image that Fields was clicking through. *Please, let there be some simple, clear sign on this, let someone have missed something that lets us take Eric down.*

What filled the frame was an empty stage, not an event. An outdoor stage in front of a clear space, sprinkled with people going through the work of readying the mics and banners and all the rest it would need. Camera testing, Bea had said.

"Here. There's Andy at the left edge, see?"

And Fields froze the image. Off at the side of the picture, a bearded man in a Gardner-green T-shirt had just begun to topple over. Right next to what had to be a lane of busy traffic.

Colin's chest went tight, his eyes blurred. The last moments of a man's life, and they were at the periphery of cameras aimed at a damn festival. Like the world refused to more than glance at his death.

"You see?" Fields said. "There's nobody near him. All he did was trip."

Space around that frozen figure was clear, empty. The nearest person was ten feet away from his back, and that man faced the other way.

Eric.

Colin blinked, stared harder at the shrunken images on the screen. What could be just morning light and shadow could also be the dim blur of hidden skein. Stretching out from Eric's hand to reach his teammate's back.

One shove. From a shapeshifting, near-invisible weapon, in plain sight—of course, Eric picked *this moment so there'd be a camera to show it was "impossible" for this to be… murder.*

His stomach lurched. He clenched a hand over his mouth and spun away from the mocking, damning sight.

Eric stood behind him.

A whole row of cubicles separated them, with people moving here and there between them. But in that moment his face seemed as clear as if he'd been only a step away. Eric looked back at his old friend, and the detective and the video with him, and there was no pain or fear on the killer's face. No hint of a smirk.

He showed… nothing.

Colin's eyes stayed locked on Eric, as he leaned over blindly to nudge at Bea. He heard more than saw her shift to follow his gaze.

Eric turned and walked away. He simply walked off, in among the cubicles and gone.

A harsh breath rasped near Colin's ear—Bea sounded as angry as him, he realized. She must know it better than he did: they still couldn't touch the murderer.

A chill washed through him. *We just lost our advantage. Eric knows we're onto him.*

Dennis Fields's nervous laugh rattled from a couple of paces away. "Is there something I'm missing—"

"Just send the video to here." Bea's voice was a model of control now, as she passed him a card. "I'll be in touch. Thank you for your cooperation."

They made their way out. Colin could see the watchful glances Bea gave in every direction, watching for Eric, and he tried to stay just as alert. At the elevator they waited, until a group of three people stepped in together before riding down with them, and even in that cramped space he couldn't keep from eyeing every inch of space for an invisible danger.

Eric had killed, stalked, even sent that mockery of a text... unless somehow that was the real Terri alive and warning him against Bea...

Finally they reached Bea's car, remembered to check its back seat, and roared away.

Bea gritted her teeth. "I *had* to get greedy."

"Huh?" Her words rattled in his head, made no sense.

"A suspect's boss could be a perfect source of information. I figured I could intimidate Fields in private, where our target would never know we were onto him. Fields dashes away to get us that video, I figure it's safe to follow because he says Eric Rowe isn't around to notice. Look how that worked out."

Colin crossed his arms and shivered—the car felt too cold even for summer AC. "So now he's coming after us?" And this was Eric, *Eric,* maybe hunting them now?

"You saw what he did in that video. Keep your guard up."

"I know," he sighed. "So, all we really did there was warn him that we knew?"

"Almost. I never thought we'd get much evidence on him anyway." Her gaze was locked on the road now, and she swung them smoothly through morning traffic as if she never meant to slow down.

"No evidence? What's that mean?"

"Oh, we can still work through that video. We might get a picture good enough to show that blur to the victim was something—but we can't admit what the murder weapon is."

"So what good is it? What good is any of it?"

"If we're lucky? There'll be other pieces. There could still be a fingerprint from the Vargas House. Or some conspirators with him in the company, if he brought the House down so Gardner can buy it up."

"He didn't! Or..." Colin shook his head. "If Eric were part of something that twisted, would he even let them in on it? I mean, you saw him there, he killed that man and he made the cameras cover for him. If he can do that, he *could* kill again any time, or he could just sit back and be untouchable. And you think we can wait around for him to make a mistake?"

"No, I don't." Now, finally, her face twisted in a scowl.

"So we let him get away with it?"

His rising voice echoed in the car, and the sound made him cut off. What had Eric, "Terri," said in that text, not to trust Bea?

She said "I think he'll keep killing. It's too easy for him now. He won't stop until we get enough skein to contain him without him cutting up everyone around him. Or else we have to..."

"What?" The word caught in Colin's throat.

"If it comes to that, we work out how the course of his day goes. He can't keep that armor over his head every second."

Her words were a low whisper, just louder than the air conditioner.

To catch Eric at some place where he'd have to come quietly?

No. Bea wasn't talking about a surrender.

Then she shook her head. "I need to drop you off somewhere. I'm due down at the station to keep pretending this is a normal case."

CHAPTER SEVEN

ALLEYS

Bea didn't mention it again. She only drove on with him, and let him sit beside her with the idea hanging in the air—that the more she worked out the options about Eric, the fewer she found except simply ambushing him. As if there could never have been another choice.

And she steered them toward the police station, ready to make those excuses that she was working under Jordan's approval on a normal case.

Instead of her bringing me along, and thinking of executions.

Colin had a moment's thought of going back to Gardner, trying to watch Eric and lay the ground for... some plan besides that. A useless, dangerous waste.

And the site of St. Mary's Church was near the station. He had Bea let him out there.

In the several years since the earthquake, the building stood partly rebuilt. Its just-finished wooden walls stood just back from the street like a hollow shell. Or a skeleton.

Colin stood staring at that shape and tried to take it as a sign that the House could be brought back too. But all he could think was how Terri had gone inside what this place had been, and never came out, and he hadn't come near it since.

The front had no doors yet, but plastic sheeting draped over the doorway, and a sawhorse stood in front of the threshold. He kept his distance from it and watched what passed for sidewalk traffic here. Any glint or twist of light there could be Eric closing in on him.

He brushed back sweat from the morning sun. A man he'd known for half his life was killing in cold blood... he glared at the building. Was that where it started, did losing Terri in there break Eric even more than it did him?

Unless the texts *were* from her—*please, let the cops get some trace on where they came from.* But no, of course Eric must have seen him in the office and fired off that new text to shake him again. It always seemed to lead back to whatever had changed Eric. Or changed Terri.

Colin stood at the edge of the church.

He barely remembered walking up to it. A shiver twitched and built within him, even in the heat.

One sliver of a gap lay between the doorway hangings, enough to peek inside. The basic shape of a church, the pathway into the main cross-shaped nave, were formed out of bare wood. He heard scattered sounds, like some fraction of a work crew somewhere within.

What am I thinking, that I'll find Terri inside? She was *gone,* leaving him with just Eric and these killings, and a detective who thought of putting Eric down like a dog.

Or Terri was out there somewhere, warning him against Bea. He stepped around the sawhorse and inside, rubbing his arms as he shivered.

The walls looked heavier from inside. They also looked rougher, not quite put together right... he knew that was just his nerves, but he still forced his gaze away from those, down and inward beyond the narthex, the outer chamber.

In the nave they'd even recreated the church's central pillar, where it would be just to the side of a broad aisle and ready to hang with art and notices without blocking the view of the altar. The sight sent a new frisson of worry through him—but of course the original pillar was long gone, and no skein-hunter would have an interest in this newly-built shape.

He ambled into that chamber, hugging his arms now. They'd set out one actual pew in the back corner, a rough thing that was little more than a bench, maybe some way for them to estimate sizes. Portable lights glinted off more plastic that they'd hung to curtain off sections along the sides. A scraping sound from one here, a hammering there... sounds that should be familiar to him, but now he could only stare at the gray screens and think something *else* might be behind them.

No, no, Terri's not in here, Eric's secrets won't be lying around somewhere... The shivering bit deeper into his flesh. If the walls cracked, if just one echo of Terri appeared—

A curtain pushed back. A scowling workman in overalls said "Hey! No wandering in, didn't you see the sign?"

"Sorry. Leaving."

The grim fascination felt scoured away, his head suddenly clear again, but the shaking settled into his knees and made him wobble as he staggered out. Of course there were no clues here, the quake simply *took* Terri and now Eric was taking everything else.

He stepped out from the cold workmans' lights to the daylight again.

His phone buzzed.

For one moment his hands couldn't move. *Please, let it be anything but another Terri prank, not* now.

He gripped the phone. Bea.

Her usual brisk, steadying sound filled his ear. "I'm on my way."

"That was quick." Or else the whole police station didn't care about Eric or any of it. His fingers tightened on the phone.

"Sometimes it is. But, are you alright?"

"After all of this? Sure, I'm as okay as I'll ever be."

"No, I mean... you sound like you had one of those moments, where it all catches up to us. We all have them, you know. Anyway, I'll be there soon."

Just one weak moment, yes. He looked away from the church and said "No need to rush—"

His gaze fell on a name, a shape, parked in the driveway of a house far down the street. The brown van marked *Tozer Restorations.*

"Or maybe you should. I think I spotted Leo."

"On my way."

Colin trotted across the street toward it. He could be wrong, Leo could still be on the run and this was simply one of his assistants taking the van out. But it could be him, it could be the only one who had the knowledge or the skein to let them face Eric.

The house could have been any in the Hillside: wide, low, bright colors and bits of patching along the wood. A low wall ran around the yard. The driveway was a spiderweb of darker asphalt lines filling in cracks. All the signs of a building that hadn't quite escaped the church's fate.

A voice came from the side of the house, and Colin angled around behind the van to listen.

"I told you, I just want it cleaned up." The voice could have been an old man, raised in anger.

"You think those timbers will hold forever?" Leo's was louder. "Rain, insects, all of it, they'll just keep working their way in. Sooner or later, boom."

"So what happened to last week's quote? You think you can just raise your fee now?"

"No!"

Leo's shout was so fierce, Colin risked peeking around the van to head off trouble. Leo loomed over the aging homeowner, but his hands were clutching above himself as if he meant to shake something out of the air—not out of the old man.

"Look, I'm trying to help you! Just look at the rates again. We can prop you up for a couple of years, give you time to think about the future. You know how it goes, every year here lets the offers you can get go up. Just, don't wait too long. *Please,"* Leo added.

"Are you… are you telling me to sell the place?"

"I said I'm trying to help you. Just look at my rates, and think it over. Right now I've got other visits to make."

"Uh. Well, thank you," the old man managed, confusion still rippling through his voice.

Leo's heavy footsteps trudged toward the van. Colin edged for its rear, trying to keep the van between him and Leo as he climbed in—

No. I'm not his enemy, I need him to talk to me.

He stepped back to the driver's side, as Leo swung open the door.

"I thought you were on the run," he told him. "Or even dead."

Leo stared at him, eyes wide. Then he pulled his face together and said "Why'd you think that?" He stepped back from the van and slammed the door shut, hard enough to make the metal ring.

Colin held himself in place, trying not to think how he had no skein now and the huge man might have grabbed some of his own before he ran.

At the edge of his vision, he saw a black shape rolling up the road. Bea.

He said "Running must have sounded good, when you heard the House was destroyed. And, we saw the hole someone cut in your window. We know you're a target too."

"You saw…" Leo swallowed, and he slumped a fraction.

Then his head jerked around, to Bea's car closing in. He grabbed for his door again and dove into the van.

The engine behind them roared first. Bea's car surged across the last stretch of distance and screeched to a stop to block the driveway.

The yard's wall had no other gaps through it, but Leo still started his motor. It revved once, a single sharp threat.

Then the engine faded away. Colin looked at the confusion on Leo's face, and waved for him to come out. Bea stepped from her car and walked to meet them.

Leo's door burst open—Colin jumped back clear of it, and Leo stomped past him, past the van, advancing on Bea.

She raised her hand. A gauntlet of skein flowed up around it.

Leo froze in his tracks. Colin moved up behind him, taking in how his face twisted. That shock had to go deeper than surprise, deeper than fear. If there was ever any doubt Leo knew about the stuff hidden in his apartment, the dread on his face now put an end to that.

A *moan* slid from Leo's lips, and the huge man twisted away and bolted across the lawn.

Colin lost a moment staring. He heard Bea's shout of "Police!" as she dashed after him, felt his own feet come to life and join the chase, as Leo's long legs hurdled the waist-high fence and swept up him the street.

The man was too *big*. His stride and his frantic pace pushed his figure ahead, growing smaller every second. Colin forced his breathing under control and his legs to drive for every inch forward. He heard, saw, the shorter Bea falling back behind them. Voices and figures stirred at the edge of his awareness, none of them in his path.

Four houses ahead, Leo twisted off the street to dodge between two houses. Colin pounded after him, trying not to think of how well Leo's work on the buildings might let him find a place to hide.

Colin twisted between the houses, to see a wooden wall of what must be seven feet height between them—none of that mattered, his headlong pace flung him at it and up to the top before he could pause.

Out by the corner of the house, he saw Leo, standing slumped over beside a tangle of trash bags. Leo reached into his pocket and flung something in among the bags, a liquid shape that vanished among them. He straightened up, gasping, and ran on.

Colin twisted over the fence to the ground. It couldn't be, Leo wouldn't have...

He scrabbled in among the bags. Khaki plastic slid against his fingers, the smell of coffee grounds filled his nose.

Then came the smoothness, the texture his fingers knew. He dug his hands in and half scooped, half *called* the skein to gather into his grasp. When he shoved it into his pocket, it felt heavier than the clump he'd found at the House.

Leo was out of sight. Colin charged to the sidewalk, glanced around, and saw him struggling up the sidewalk leftward. Three, four, people around the street stared.

Colin closed in. He picked out the clumsiness pulling at Leo's steps, and as he drew closer he heard that breath wheezing—tall or not, Leo was too heavy to run like a panicked sprinter and not pay the price.

Colin edged nearer. His own lungs ached too, but he forced out a shout of "Just let us help you!"

Leo glanced back, then pushed on. Just breaking his rhythm cost him; his steps looked even slower now. Colin dropped to a jog to keep closing the gap.

A familiar motor's roar swept up the street. Bea's car rushed into view, and the sound eased back with an almost smug tone as she pulled up beside the street ahead of their quarry.

Leo halted. He looked at her, then back at Colin at his rear. His face was pale, stricken, broken. He slumped in place with a whoosh of breath.

Colin tried to find words, but Bea was already moving up, hands lifted in reassurance. "You're not under arrest, Mr. Tozer. We only want to talk to you."

Leo didn't look up.

More softly, she added "I know you know about…" She gestured with her skein hand, and that motion did make Leo glance over. "Is that why you tried to leave town?"

Leo didn't answer.

Colin tried "Leo, we saw where you were packing up. But now here you are—"

Leo grunted "Can we just… get off the street? Before someone sees?"

More and more faces were watching every second, Colin knew that without glancing away. But Bea said gently "Of course we can."

She opened her car, and Leo climbed in with a squeak of springs and lay down flat along the back seat. Bea and Colin settled in front, and they drove away.

Leo squirmed and tried to press himself low, as if his half-folded knees weren't sticking up in full view of one window. He said "I'm doing what he told me. He caught me on the road, I'm just doing what he said."

"He? Who was that?" Bea asked.

"I never saw. Just a ski mask, he could be anybody."

"So what did you see? Size, scars, any marks you could recognize?"

"He was *different*. Kind of thin the first time I saw him, but when he ran me down he looked bigger. You can do that too, right, spread the thing around under your clothes to bulk up?"

"Right," Colin said. Like Eric had looked too big on the first night.

Oh. Colin twisted around the seat to look at where Leo cowered. *Does he think it was* Bea *in that mask, and all this is his tormentor come back for him...*

Bea only went on "Or was it the same person? Can you be sure, when you say you don't know?"

"Yes I do, I know! The way he looked at me—it was all him!"

The frightened edge pulled tighter in Leo's voice, but Colin felt some of his own muscles unclench. At least Leo knew his masked enemy wasn't one of them.

"And his voice?" Bea added.

"He never used it, not once. All he showed me was a note with what he wanted."

"What was that?" She spoke more gently now.

"To go to the places I worked at, start telling people they're unsafe. Any way I wanted. And maybe I'm doing them a favor, you know?" His voice was firmer now.

Colin said "Not sure I do. What kind of favor?"

"Well... get them thinking about going somewhere with no quakes. Or even..." His voice died away.

"Even what, Leo?" Colin let the words drift out, easy and reassuring.

"He already... He tore down the House. He could bring down anything, right? And I'm just getting folks out?"

"What?" Colin leaned around, stared down at Leo's face. "Did he say that?"

Leo only looked away, cowered lower.

"Leo... Please. Did he say that, was there any sign that's what he's planning?"

"No. But if it is, it means I'm saving them, right?"

Leo still didn't look up, only twisted where he lay. His shirt had come loose, and a network of vicious red lines peeped out along his back. Small, sharp lines, so many.

It was Eric Rowe that did that to you—are you going to let that little man break you? But no, saying that might rip Leo up even more.

The car's engine eased back, and Bea edged it toward the side of the street. She said "He tore down the Vargas House, and you know what he used to do it."

"You've got it too," Leo whimpered. "Please, I never did any of that. I don't have it, I'm no threat."

The car rolled to a stop. Bea leaned around to study their battered prisoner. "Leo, you *are* a threat to him, because this man has already been in contact with you. He's already killed two people we know of. He's going to come back for you, and deal with you the same way as them. Unless you help us trap him."

Leo looked up—to lock his eyes right on Colin. "Keep her away from me! Grandpa said the skein was death." His eyes stared at him, past him, out of focus.

"She won't hurt you, Leo. What did your grandpa say?"

"Keep her away. Away!" Leo shrieked.

Bea drew back. "It's alright. It's that danger I'm trying to stop."

"Danger, death..." Leo rolled behind the seats, and his shirt slid higher to show more scratches. *"Night and day, gratshay kodo, far away, gratshay kodo va... "* The sound was a child's singsong tone.

"Mister Tozer," Bea snapped. "The killer will be coming for you again. Will you let us help you or not?"

Leo burbled something that might have been *Night and day, night and day.*

Softly as he could, Colin said "It's the only way. Please."

This time Leo managed a weak answer: "No, no more..."

* * *

It hardly seemed real. Leo, the giant, the bully, the rumbling rebel who fought for his rights as a Vargas, lay curled up helpless in the back seat. And *Eric* was a man who could reduce Leo to *this.*

Colin kept still as they drove, mouthing reassurances and trying to draw Leo out of his shell of fear. In the end, Bea brought him a clinic to have his cuts looked after, with two uniformed cops to keep an eye on him.

As Leo stepped from the car, he shot a look at Bea and pleaded "I won't tell them, I swear!"

But he went with the officers quietly enough, glad to be away from the two that had run him down. Bea and Colin left him there, only to drive up the block and pull over.

"You think it's safe?" Colin asked. His hand gripped his bruised arm, from his first scrap with Eric. "Leo's shaken up enough to do anything."

"They're police officers. They can handle anything. Except believing in invisible men," she added.

"Eric did that to Leo, just to make him say the buildings were unsafe?" Colin shut his eyes, tried to fit it together. "That means, what, Eric's doing all this so people will sell to Gardner Development and get him promoted again? That just seems too *petty* for him, even now. Unless, you think Gardner itself is up to something bigger?" he added.

Bea considered a moment, and her eyebrows drew together. "It's possible. Everything I've heard about Gardner Development has them harmless enough. But it could be this goes much deeper, and your friend Eric was only sucked in to that. Is that what you'd rather believe?"

"Sure."

But Bea was looking at him, alert eyes wanting the whole truth.

He rubbed his arm again. "I wish it was that, but... I saw him in that video. I heard his voice when he attacked the House." And Eric had broken Leo—maybe *not* so hard to believe, after Eric had had to let Leo bully him before.

"And what do you think he'll do next?" Bea asked.

Her voice, and her face, had softened. She wasn't pushing him for the truth, she wanted to help him bear it.

And I still haven't told her about Leo's skein. His hand shifted from his arm toward his pocket.

"I don't know," he said. "I hope it's not more killing. And I really hope it's not demolishing homes just to buy the property. If it's someone else he wants dead... I can't let that happen."

"It could have already happened. Or any minute now. That's what using the skein invisibly lets him do." Her voice was cold now. "There simply aren't many ways left to stop that."

Colin looked away. She was back to that again, not *saying* she'd execute Eric, but hinting.

"We'll... see if there are others," he said, and it came out like a concession.

Other ways like having more skein. But, he moved his hand from his pocket. Bea didn't need to know about that skein, if she'd only want to use it for her own kind of ruthless strategy.

There had to be another way. Didn't there?

CHAPTER EIGHT

ALLIES

Only a block from the clinic was a fast-food place, where they stopped for lunch. Colin's chase had left him ready to wolf down hamburgers, and Bea ate just as fast—but they devoured them in her car, and she ate with her usual precision to keep any crumbs from spilling.

Then she stepped out of the car and walked a few steps away to make some calls. He watched her standing at the restaurant's corner, and wondered how much she'd keep from the police about Leo. Or what she was keeping from him.

He pulled out his own phone and called Zara.

When she answered, he began with "Hi there. Everything okay?"

"Of course." He heard a thump like her hand against a cushion, then a knuckle knocking on wood. "The police are keeping an eye on me when they can. The hotel's not one of their 'safe houses,' but it's safe enough. You're probably better off than I am with the actual detective watching you."

He shut his eyes. Of course going out after Eric *wasn't* safer, and his mother was talking around that. Any thoughts of mentioning Eric's daylight murder shriveled away.

Instead he said "We found Leo. Eric caught up with him, and he really worked him over. And he ordered him to tell people their houses are unsafe." He looked out at Bea, still engrossed in her own call. "I guess that fits with his work at Gardner, but I just don't get it."

"Eric can turn the tables on Leo now? The skein is that strong?"

That was twice she talked about dangers or protections, about his own danger. He pushed confidence into his voice: "Well, Leo thinks so. I'm thinking that means we need more of it ourselves." He could feel the skein's weight in his pocket, but that wouldn't be enough either. "But, for those four dragon designs you found? Eric's been to all of them. And Leo wasn't up to telling us anything more."

"Then I suppose I'll keep looking."

He heard her take a heavy breath.

Then: "Do you think it's Terri out there?" Her words came like a punch, unflinching. "Is it possible?"

The hamburgers twisted in his stomach. "It's... possible." He swallowed, shifted his grip on the phone. "Listen, I tried going to St. Mary's today. And now, what I think is, it's still likely she did die there, and it's part of what twisted Eric up. But that doesn't change what we can hope for," he added.

"Of course it doesn't. But..." Her voice went softer. "I keep thinking about how one of the ties between Terri and Eric was that they both kept looking outside the community. And yet when the quake hit, people saw her run into the church and try to save some of its old sculptures. Just like I would."

"She thought the place was solid! We all did."

Bitterness twisted her voice. "I wonder. What was going through Eric's mind when he cut the House down? Was it the building he hated, or was he using it to strike back at us for how I raised her?"

"No! You can't blame yourself for anything Eric does. Or Terri." He rushed the words out like he could shout her thoughts down. *The first text said the same thing, not our fault,* he found himself remembering. At least that sentiment was true.

"It's not that. I, I really need to know what you think." Zara's voice was clear again, a sudden demand like a hand catching at him.

"What I think? Well..."

He let the moments play in his mind, watching the silver-green shape march through the House library again—had Eric hesitated for anything?

He swallowed. "If you think it was more likely you were in the meeting room? Eric went for the pillar above there first, but he *warned* us which one it was. That gave Bea a chance to brace it up, and that side held." He glanced out at the detective, still on her phone. The same woman who talked about ambushing Eric might have also saved a lot of lives then.

"So that was what happened?" Zara mused.

"Yeah. And then Eric let me get away too. I guess that makes him a murderer and more, but one with some kind of twisted reason for it, and he's not really after us."

"I see. Thank you, I think that helps. I'll try to see him as a menace, not a total monster."

"I'll try that too." It didn't make hunting a friend easier... but at least he could *believe* Eric was following some rule of his own in all this. "Anything I can do for you?" he added.

"No. And I'll keep my head down here."

She still wasn't asking him to stay safe, not quite. "I'll try doing that too."

And protecting himself could start by knowing about the weapon he had. He hung up, and stepped out of the car.

Bea looked up from her phone, but he said "Bathroom," and stepped into the restaurant.

The low rattlings and voices of the kitchen drew a fraction closer when he entered the restroom, and closer still when he stepped into the stall, hidden from the world. At least he could get some practice with the new skein before deciding when to tell Bea.

He scooped Leo's lump of skein from his pocket. His fingers began molding it over his other hand, until it began to stir and flow under his will. It slid around his hand in a thick green glove—more full than what he'd made from the House's skein, less a cestus this time than a gauntlet.

Did that mean he could hit even harder now? Or would that need enough skein to cover his arm too, to strengthen it all?

He gripped the skein with his free hand and pulled, *released,* it to slide off and gather in his palm. Another thought brought it flowing back over his fist, faster now. He had no way to feel its movement like his own fingers moved, but he could still picture that motion and command it to follow.

Because it does *respond to thoughts.* That was the first of many reasons it could never be just some strange, multipurpose armor-plastic. If it really could be magic…

Leo said it was death. But Leo had tried carrying this himself, until he'd ditched it during the chase.

Another thought peeled it off again, then snapped it back into place. A bit more and he'd be ready for Bea's trick of hiding it up his sleeve.

He pinched at one fingertip's skein and drew it out into a half-inch claw. He ran that along the pale side of the stall, with a soft scraping sound—and that sound grew softer as he willed the blade to sharpen, and it dug into the plastic, smoother and smoother.

Time for the real test. He held the gauntlet up, and tried to make it fade from sight.

Nothing changed. Of course—invisibility wasn't a *motion* like controlling some new finger of his own. He filled his mind with the image of his hand beginning to blur.

Nothing.

He laughed softly. Enough skein to hide just his hand wouldn't be much use anyway—

His phone buzzed. He reached for it, stopped as he felt the added strength around his fingers, and slid the skein back into his pocket first.

The message was another text. But the attached recording—

Terri. His sister's own face, pale and wasted with ragged hair. Her eyes, open, struggling to move. Her lips, twitching, making no sound.

There was no sound. There was no background, only Terri's face. She could only just move.

The image filled his sight. Her mouth tried to open... then jerked closed as the image replayed. Stop and restart, what could be a dozen seconds or an hour—as his thoughts spun and whirled around it too.

The text with it. *Get all the skein*, it said... wasn't that what another text had said before? He stared, stared, burning to reach through the screen and touch that face, make it real, rip that pain away from her.

Terri. Terri was alive. So she'd been alive for years. She did look older, but in her state those three years looked like decades.

Something felt stuck in his chest, weighing down his breath. Somehow, somehow it was real.

Find her. He had the file, he'd have Bea go through every pixel on it, find out what had happened. What it meant.

Do something... but his eyes couldn't move. He had to find her, or rip Eric to pieces if he'd made a fake this cruel. But it... it couldn't...

Something crashed and beat against what had to be the restroom door outside.

"Come on—Leo's on the run!" Bea called.

He was leaping up and shoving the phone away, dashing for the door and free of the image's grip. He and Bea dodged around one startled customer and raced to her car, and it roared to life.

As soon as they reached the street, Bea scooped up the phone she'd dropped in her lap. "I said, stay back. Do *not* pursue!" she told it.

"That's the cops we left Leo with?" Colin heard the idiot question bubbling out, even while she split her attention between the car and the phone. "They let him get away?"

"Please, shh!" she snapped at him, and he clamped his mouth shut.

At least they seemed to have a direction. Bea dropped the phone and sped them down the street, with tight control and barely legal speed. In one minute Colin recognized their direction, and in another they moved into view of the same houses where he'd found Leo.

This time nobody could have missed him. The huge man was pounding against the same house's door, shouting, not even seeing as they rolled up.

Bea slid the windows down an inch. Leo's shouts cracked through the air: "You have to listen to me! It's not safe!"

"Leave me alone!" came a voice from inside the house. Across the street a boy on a bicycle slowed to watch, and a face peered out of another house's door.

What was this, Leo going back to Eric's "orders" to scare people, all over again? What had Eric *done* to him?

A black and white police car pulled up behind them, the same two cops they'd left Leo with.

Bea's radio squawked. "Code 415 at your location, possible forced entry."

"Simms, copy. Responding," was all Bea said.

"Nooo!" Leo's yell burst out. He stared at them with wild eyes, then broke away and ran down the street.

Again? Colin leaned back as Bea brought the car into motion.

The boy on the bicycle pulled back, to a safer distance. At least two other people moved at different places on the block, both drawing back but not getting out of sight.

The police car in the mirror cruised up behind them. Leo's bulk drew closer in front, running and trying in vain to keep ahead of the car.

A shape moved. A shimmer, a dim outline in the sunlight, rushed at Leo.

Leo screamed. He flung himself away, away from what had to be Eric swinging a claw at him, and dashed for the sidewalk.

Bea grabbed at her phone. "Officer Ling, you keep Stone back! Understand me?" Then she dropped the phone and snapped to Colin "Watch for him! I'll drive, but you have to spot him."

She brought the car along to keep behind Leo. Colin squinted and stared around the street. Eric's shape had to be somewhere—

A motion drew his eye, like a wisp of smoke swept along in the wind. Rushing at Leo's side.

Leo dodged away *again,* lunged into the street. A car honked and swerved around him, and Leo reached the far sidewalk and ran. Back the other way.

Bea wrenched the car around in a squeal of rubber, making Colin brace in his seat. A sudden thought flashed: Eric didn't need to, shouldn't, cut Leo down himself if he could run him to his death without leaving a mark on him. Nobody else knew Eric was there.

Where *was* he? Colin stared around, but he'd lost sight of that shimmer in the turn.

The black-and-white struggled to reverse in the street, and Bea slid her car past it. They closed on Leo again.

"Don't!" Leo screeched at the air. "I've got skein here, just let me show you!"

Bea brought them closer. Leo twisted away from the car, dashing along a yard's fence.

A masked figure sprang up from behind the wall. In plain sight this time—with one green glove clamping around Leo's throat, and the other raising a green blade.

The huge man went deathly still.

Tires squealed, from the police car struggling to turn. A voice on the radio squawked "Who the hell is that? Hostage situation!"

Eric leaned toward Leo, seemed to whisper something.

Then he released him. Leo scrambled away down the sidewalk.

Bea's window snapped down and she raised her gun, but Eric had already ducked below the wall.

"Hostage is free." the radio said.

A glimmer of light moved, Eric blurred again and shifting position.

"Both of you, stay back!" Bea demanded.

Leo moved up the street, at a clumsy, dead-eyed jog now. He ran past a window where a little girl's face stared out. The block looked familiar... the same one Leo had cut across before.

"He's a dead man." Bea growled it under her breath. "He can take Eric to more skein, but then he's dead. Eric's already too tough for anything we've got."

She was right. *Why is Eric doing this, what does he* want?

"Still no sign of the hostage-taker," the radio said. "We'll get the big guy off the street."

"Stay back!" Bea said. "There's a sniper somewhere out there, you'll never see him."

Leo was only two houses from the gap where he'd left the skein. A blur moved in the yard behind him—Bea wasn't wrong, Eric might as well have him in gunsights. He was marching to his death.

Because I took the skein he hid. The fact crashed down like a brick through Colin's insides, the piece he hadn't fitted to the rest. Leo was leading Eric to a prize that wasn't even there, *because I stole his last hope of bargaining.* Something worse than cold clawed up inside him, something he couldn't vomit out.

The police car drove away past them, on up the street.

Leo turned into the space between the two houses, with the wall between them already in view. Eric could crush him any time—there had to be *something* that could stop this.

Bea flipped a switch, and a megaphone boomed her voice around the street: "Attention! This is the police—please stay inside, away from your windows. Leo! Just run for the street, we can still protect you." Her hands tightened on the car's wheel.

Right, the car itself might still hurt Eric through his armor, if they got him to the street where they could run him down. Leo slowed, glanced back at them, his face washed out with despair.

He turned away. He shuffled in between the houses, started up the wall toward the other side.

Bea muttered something. Her gun was clenched in her hand, useless.

There was no use pleading now. At least, not in pleading with Leo. The car door whispered open.

Bea snapped "What are you doing?"

"Terri's alive. Eric may not know that." The words started slowly, but gathered speed as he spoke.

"Alive? You said that was fake, you said *he* did it!"

He drew out his phone and tossed it on the seat behind him. "Keep this, it's all on here, it's all we've got for bargaining. If it's still just Eric… well, he let me go before."

"Colin da Costa, you stop right there." At the corner of his eye he saw what could be her climbing out, leveling her gun at him.

"Nobody else." His voice had a strange hollowness in it. "Nobody else is dying."

He charged at the wall after Leo. His eyes swept the yards for a hint of Eric shimmering nearby. Bea's footsteps started toward him, but he had no time to wonder if she was joining or chasing him.

"Terri's alive!" he bellowed out.

He meant the words to slow Eric down, but now they gave speed to his own feet. The wall rushed up, and his leap let him all but fly up to seize the top.

For one instant he took in the two houses the space pressed between, both sets of windows still empty this afternoon. Then his feet thumped down onto the dirt between them.

Leo squatted among the trash bags, tossing one after another aside with a frantic crunch each time. A deadly blurred figure crouched just behind him.

"Stop it!" Colin flung at them. "Terri's alive!"

Eric didn't turn. Instead he leaned closer to Leo. "What are the words? The words!" he said.

"What words? It *has* to be here!" Leo said. He shoved another two bags aside.

Colin locked his eyes on them, as he heard Bea landing beside him.

"I mean it, Terri's alive!" His voice came out hoarse. "I've seen it. Or maybe you sent the thing and you knew all along—but if you don't? Then I've got proof it's her, if you let Leo go."

The faint, sun-shimmer gleam of a crouching figure glanced toward him. He had no face to watch, not even a clear enough form to try reading his body language. Colin glared back at the mirage-like shape and knew he was staking everything on his news not being Eric's work all along.

One last trash bag rattled away. Leo whimpered "It's not here—"

Colin's mouth opened, with the words *I took it* rising in his throat. In the same instant, Eric snapped "Liar!"

The blurred hand thrust forward. The end of it, the narrowest, sharpest end, sank into Leo's stomach.

The massive man wobbled in his crouch, toppled over. His mouth moved, it coughed, something dark formed around his lips…

"Stop it, Eric!" Colin flung the words at him, as if they could still push back the sight. "Terri's really alive, I've got video that could prove it! What would she say if she saw you here? You hunted Leo down and terrorized him for what—to help you buy up more houses?"

This is crazy, it can't be all I have left when Leo's bleeding his life away.

But he could only race on with "Or is it you that's got Terri? Or it's all you faking those texts, that *picture,* all just to wreck me? How can you do any of this? *Why?"*

The shape took a step toward him. It spoke, in a soft, fierce voice that wiped away any doubt that it was Eric Rowe:

"Someday you'll understand."

Leo struggled toward his feet behind that blur. "E…ric?" he managed in a spray of blood.

Bea, still off to Colin's side, called out "You're trapped—"

Leo surged off the ground like a rockfall in reverse. He threw himself at Eric's back, clumsy, white-faced, unstoppable.

Eric spun and caught him. He snapped into visibility again, a small man covered in silver-green skein. His hands caught at Leo's arms, his slight frame locked and strained and held back more than twice his weight.

His foot shifted in the dirt. Just a small motion, but before the scrabbling sound faded Eric's balance tipped and failed. Leo brought him crashing down among the scattered trash bags.

Colin edged back, circled a step around. The moment he could see Eric under Leo's bulk he'd…

A shaft of green burst out, through the back of Leo's neck.

The huge form went limp. The smaller green figure pushed him aside, shoved him clear all in the same motion of getting to his feet.

Deep in his chest, Colin felt a *No!* tearing its way out.

A new voice burst across the alley, from its far, open end.

"Get those hands up! Now!"

The police, the two uniforms that had driven on past them, closed in from the back street with their guns leveled.

"Hands, I said!"

The green-suited figure turned toward them. His arms moved in a slow, mocking *shrug,* that angled one hand up and raised the blade on it, still soaked in red—

Colin dove away, an instant before the guns sounded.

He saw the impacts, in how Eric rocked back a step. Heard the shrill bullet-whistles that drowned out all the sounds against skein and wood and brick that must be splashing around the alley.

Eric faded away.

In the next instant the shimmer lunged at them. Low to the ground, swift, a vague blur that no unsuspecting eye could track.

In another breath the two men slumped over, and Eric reappeared with a hand through each's stomach. As they fell, Eric *twisted* his hands in wrenching them free. Any sound from the men went still.

Officers Ling and Stone, Bea had called them.

Colin felt the dirt catch at his shoes as he charged.

He lunged toward Leo and past him, determined to keep Eric away from there. Eric rushed to meet him.

As the blade jabbed at his face he remembered, *my own skein's in my pocket.* His arm deflected Eric's thrust aside.

Too easy, he knew, just as the other hand slashed into his leg.

The force sent him toppling over. The blow felt like nothing, numbness—nothing like the pain as he crashed into the ground.

All he smelled was blood. Too many people, cut down too fast. He lay on the ground, managed to lift his head.

Eric stood in front of Bea now. That second silvery-green figure had to be her, from the way she stood, from the pants that showed where her skein couldn't guard her lower body. From the short blade on one hand, and her gun still ready in the other.

Against all of Eric's strength.

Colin's hand fumbled for his pocket. He *missed* it, touched only the dirt beside him.

Eric shifted on his feet. Hesitating, or just calculating which way to cut her down.

Far away, sirens howled.

The hand found the pocket.

One fingertip's touch brought the skein flowing out, too fast—*no, not* around *my hand!* He willed it into his palm, and planted his other hand on the ground to heave himself upward.

He tossed the skein up, a slow glittering arc in the air.

"Terri's alive!" he shouted one more time, anything for the hope that Eric would look back for one moment.

Eric looked back. The skein arched cleanly over his head, undisturbed, and he missed how it fell into Bea's hand.

In the instant Eric turned again, it flowed and merged with her own skein. Not to cover more of her body, but to add more than a foot of wickedly-thin length to her blade.

The far-off siren, not so far now, swelled to force its way across some street.

Bea opened fire. Three quick, firm shots at close range, that sent Eric stumbling back.

As he staggered, she charged, blade first.

Eric whirled and ran.

Too fast, too fast—Colin pushed off the dirt and threw his weight at him, anything to slow him down. Eric *leaped* and soared over him.

Colin slid to the ground on a leg that refused to support him. He had one glimpse of Eric behind him, landing undisturbed and blurring from sight as he darted away.

CHAPTER NINE

LIES

Don't look away. Colin forced his eyes to stay locked on the street, the yards, the houses, for any shimmer of Eric circling back at them in the last seconds. As Bea stood with him, watching. As the sirens closed in.

He held onto that search as the truth seeped into him: Leo lay flat, still, finished. Officers Ling and Stone were dead.

I said I couldn't stand waiting around for people to die. Now an emptiness yawned in him, and a coldness like the moment between claps of thunder...

"We've got no evidence it was Eric." Bea's voice broke, as she looked at the bodies. Her face twitched and clung on to a kind of calmness. "And we can't take him like this, he'll only kill everyone who tries. You can't tell them."

"I have to." For an instant the thunder rolled in his voice, but then it passed and left him scowling on a clear day.

"Just say it was someone with knives and Kevlar, not who."

He gritted his teeth, clenched his fists, tried to clutch his determination tighter around that silence and roaring within him.

Time broke into flashes.

—The first police car howling up and the first officers emerging, guns out to match the bloody scene they found. Bea waving them down one way and another, but him missing her words. Neighbors edging in from along the street and the houses. Forcing himself to look at the three victims, all still.

—The uneasy sounds when the police looked from the scene to him, as the EMTs looked at his thigh. The smell and the sting of the antiseptic, before they bandaged the gash.

The rush of weakness the moment they touched it, when he realized he'd been holding his weight on one leg all the while. The cut, the pain, the weakness creeping through his body that had to be loss of blood.

The medic telling him how lucky he was.

—The police and the medic, arguing over when he'd be ready to talk or where he'd be taken to. Himself gathering the thunder within to make his voice steady and his eyes clear, and push it into his words about how staying at the scene let him remember more clearly.

The faces, uniformed and not, as he began his story with the raids on the Vargas House, glossing over what the thief had used for them. Himself as a friend of Leo's trying to help Bea find him.

And the moment some of the cops spun away and descended on Bea, for bringing him along. Watching her deflect the accusations and defend his help… he thought she had an answer for everything, and he was learning to see the guilt and pain under her mask as well. He gripped tight to his control, to not let her down.

Him telling them he'd spotted Leo in town again, and called Bea in. Them talking Leo down, seeing his injuries. Leo breaking away from the officers, himself trying to calm him down again, the attacker with his "body armor" and "knives."

—The thunder in his soul falling in time with his words as he met those police gazes: "I heard his voice. It sounded just like Eric Rowe, a friend of ours that Leo was bullying yesterday." Bea wanted to hunt Eric herself, fine, but he *would not* deny how that voice marked the murderer.

—The rage spreading from his voice to theirs, when he put a name to the cop-killer. The police pushing closer, asking again and again what else he'd seen, how sure he was about the murderer's voice. Himself wishing he could say it louder.

—Then the police drowning all the thunder with one question: how Bea had already gone to Gardner to investigate Eric, and she'd taken him with her. Then, his own recent fight with Leo.

The police tightening around Bea, as if her bringing him into the investigation was a worse offense than anything Eric had done. Her facing it all, her answers and apologies.

The police edging away from him, as he slumped against one car trying to stand. Whenever he looked at where three men had died, when he turned back the police avoided his gaze.

—The moment he remembered the whole other side of these horrors, and told them about Terri. Insisting she was alive after all, that she might still be connected to Eric, and saying it again and again until he sent them the recording.

He knew he'd left his phone with Bea, and he couldn't remember who'd handed it back to him now. The police kept Bea away from him, the same way they cut him out of the hunt.

But she did grab a moment with him, one time that the others weren't all watching her.

He told her "We'll get him—"

"Of course you held some skein back from me." She actually smiled there. "I deserve that, after lying to Jordan."

And she passed him a handful of skein.

The flash of trust left a bit of warmth in him, one small thing to fill him when he'd unleashed the truth about Eric and somehow done more damage to Bea than to the murderer. Not enough hope, not nearly enough.

Eventually the police drew him to his feet. He reached out with questions, promises, anything to let him stay on site, but with his leg so weak they simply pushed him into the car.

They brought him home, still early afternoon, wobbling on his feet like some drunk. Useless, helpless, not even worth speaking to.

He almost dropped the keys getting his apartment open.

The aching exhaustion and the failure were all the same thing now, one great wasteland of what he had done, did, and still could do. *I ran up and tried to argue with Eric?* And now Leo and Ling and Stone and Bea's career were all dead.

His body needed fluids, and food, he remembered. He hobbled into the apartment, and just reached the little table before he toppled and caught himself against it. Even in a tiny one-room place, he could only make it partway across.

The table creaked under him. Just a cheap thing he'd got when he'd started here, when he'd said it was only until he could enlist. All his boxes made the little room look almost as crowded as Leo's place now—

Leo. Broken, gone.

A scream and a shove sent the table across the room. All ten feet away.

It toppled, the archive books on it already gone flying. Bound volumes of clippings crashed down, and loose pages in their sheaths thumped to the floor.

Generations old, some of them. He moved numbly to start gathering them up… right, these were here to look for more clues about the skein…

His balance failed again. His leg gave out, and he slammed to the floorboards in a great shameful thud.

Lungs heaved, fingers flexed, wanting to *thrash* where he lay and dig the pain deeper and deeper to drive all the rest away…

The records deserved better. A few lay within easy reach, and he pulled them together first, then pushed himself to sit up.

And *these* were the best clues left for finding a weapon against Eric?

Eric had… he'd simply *left* him after he'd killed Leo. *He faced Bea down, but me he just jumped over like he'd already beaten me with just one cut. Did he* want *to dump me there in the blood and the failure?*

Or...

He leaned to sit against the wall. He gathered up the rest of the records, ready to struggle to his feet again.

Except, the skein lay in his pocket. Leo's skein, or it made no difference if it was—he'd tossed that to Bea, and she'd given him back what felt like the same amount.

Eric's skein made him faster, stronger, because it moved *with* him.

Colin pulled his out, and plastered it over his thigh and on past the knee like a bandage. No, a brace.

Slowly he stood up, starting with the good leg, letting the injured one just shift under him as his weight rose. That muscle moved weakly, but the skein felt stiff, making him fight to move it.

No. *Skein moves with me—or even moves* for *me, any way I want. So move.*

The resistance eased. He wrestled his way to his feet. One step across the room had his leg dragging, still stiff, but supported now. In fits and starts he found the rhythm, making the "brace" flex and pull with his command, separate from the weakness in his real leg. By the third walk to the far wall he was moving normally.

So, he could stand again. He twisted away before he could fall into marching around for its own sake, and settled in the kitchen—that was small enough he could have moved around by leaning against the stove and fridge anyway. He was running low on mac and cheese, one more sign of not having the time for anything else.

His body needed the food, but it kept his hands busy and left nothing to fight the worries in his head.

Eric could tear through them all like one of his knives...

Terri was out there somewhere, or else the whole recording was a fake...

Leo was...

So call Bea, or would that turn the police against her even more?

Call Zara, or would that only scare her?

I hate this, having a moment I can't even try *to work on something.* The most he could do was try to focus on what skein clues they had— more of that could still let them stand up to Eric.

Finally his hands were free to thumb through the images of the Vargas paintings again, searching for more dragons. The dim shapes and painted shadows still mocked his effort to see anything more. And he'd already found the skein was only sometimes under the dragon clue, sometimes separate from them, why was that?

Was Terri really alive?

Could Bea find her, or would the police even listen to Bea now—

He locked his gaze on the records, his mind on the task.

At one corner of the table, he turned one book to the list of the places Vargas had designed himself. He filled the rest of the table space with lists and articles about what he'd advised on or restored, even his list of earthquake-vulnerable sites. But the dragons and Eric's hunts pointed to the House, the bank, hillside statues, the pier...

If there was any pattern, it was lost in the rows of text. The bank pillar and statues were ornamental, the pier was anything but. Three sites were pillars or supports, but not the statue. At least most were lower, later, on the chronological lists of Vargas's work, but...

His chin sank toward the table, and he wrenched himself up, awake, again. *I can at least wash the plates first, I'm not living in a pigsty.*

Voices and cars outside had the louder, fuller rhythms of early evening now. He scrubbed the plates clean, with thoughts of the old man spinning in his head.

Matt Vargas. Local architect made good, artist, traveler. And just how many "travels" had he made... no, most of those records were off with Zara, and if Colin called her now just his voice would give away how much the day had taken out of him.

But Vargas's passion was Rayo Hill and its old Hillside, in spite of all its troubles. And his disappearance, was that part of the skein's secret too?

Colin squinted harder. It *had* to be tied to him—Vargas's painted dragons showed he knew about too many skein sites, and one was his own house. He must have put it all there. Unless he was marking where it would somehow form on its own? No, they were *inside pillars and statues,* he must have put it there.

And Terri said to "get it all away"—if those were Terri's words on the texts. Leo said the skein was dangerous… Colin looked down at his leg, that he'd left coated with the stuff even when he was sitting still. Better not take take it for granted; he peeled it off and set it aside for now.

But, the real danger was Eric. Killing Vargas's grandson and the town's police, destroying the House… if Vargas's championing the Hillside had an opposite, it was what Eric Rowe had become.

So we'll beat him. For Leo. For Terri. To show Bea was right…

He read, and he slumped against the table again as he dozed off. Finally he dragged himself to bed, with the book of Vargas's private notes still in his hand.

*　*　*

Sleep should have been easy. But his wound, his body, ached and gnawed at him. A spasm of pain told him he'd rolled over. His stomach rumbled, even after cleaning half the kitchen out.

He steadied his breathing, smoothed his mind, sank back into sleep.

Still, the pains kept pulling at him. His leg, his stomach, his thoughts, every time he sank back in. Scratching at him.

Then he *heard* the scratching.

At the apartment door. At that exact spot, as certain as if someone had a key in the lock. But this was a softer, fainter clicking that should have been lost in the distant sounds of the night. Someone was clicking and picking at his lock, the same way Eric first entered the House. The night Mike Shane died.

Colin held still, silent on the mattress. Then he reached slowly, quietly, over to the skein and pulled it around his fist.

His phone was still in his pants pocket. *No, I'm not dragging any more cops into Eric's reach.*

That tiny scratching continued. He shouldn't even be able to hear it.

Stillness hung over the room, with the only sound the intruder at its edge. Colin slid to his feet—the book still in his hand, too noisy to set down now—and hobbled through the hush. He glanced around the shadows for other weapons, but Eric's skein could bounce bullets.

The scratching ended in the lock's soft *cha-click.*

Colin edged to the side of the door. It was his only sliver of a chance, that or use the Vargas notebook as a shield.

The door swung inward. Nighttime sounds and breezes wafted in. In with them came the faintest blur within a shadow, crouched and silent and deadly. One step in, two.

Colin's gauntlet crashed down on Eric's head. His shoulder rammed Eric and sent him spinning away.

Eric was already stumbling to his feet, slower but uninjured. Colin forced down his rage and slapped his hand's skein over his leg again, and bolted out into the corridor.

Just get outside, he might *not kill if there are enough witnesses—* every flying step was a moment further away, another slim chance. But his rhythm was off, the skein had one leg slow.

The blow he expected on his back... never came. He dashed past doors and out for the garage, running smoother with every second. Somehow he'd guessed right, that after this bloody afternoon Eric wanted to avoid attention.

Colin's car was a battered, bright orange lump waiting in its place. He yanked the key from his pocket, fumbled the door open. The old ignition wheezed—

struggled—

caught, and he wrenched the wheel into a turn and made for the street.

A block flew by in the night, then a second, suddenly so easy. He drove two more blocks before he felt his fingers locking on the wheel hard enough to hurt, and eased over to the side.

He fumbled his phone out, and called Bea.

The moment he sent the call out, the thought crashed into him: *just like that, I think I can call her, at this hour?*

But she answered it on the third ring. "What's wrong?"

"You okay?"

"Sure. Colin, *what happened?"*

"Eric broke into my place—God, that's what I get for going home at all, Zara was right." His voice sounded ragged. "About Zara, is my mother okay?"

"I can check. We should have put protection on you. Just a second—"

The phone beeped for a moment. A mini-van ambled by Colin in the night, with a family crowded inside the windows on some night excursion of their own.

"What's up now?" Ed Jordan's voice conferenced in, harsh but wide awake. Maybe cops never did sleep.

"What's up is, Eric came after me." His voice was now perfectly steady, and it took only a few words to give them the news. "Tell me you can stop him, soon!"

"It's not that easy," Bea said. "The evidence we've got, even the Gardner video, doesn't count for much so far."

"You report the break-in yet?" Jordan said.

"And if he's still there? Those cops will be slaughtered!"

"So that's it, now you're scared to *look* at the bastard because it'll make him kill more?" The stern control in Jordan's voice hit harder than a shout. "We need this attack on record, so there's a chance we can catch Rowe with no alibi. That'd be *something."*

"Got it."

"I never thought she'd drag you right through the investigation. And endanger you, and her, and all of it—but I never knew she was lying about the 'skein' being stuck to her either," he added.

"Sorry, again," Bea said.

Colin swallowed. So she had come clean with her partner, one consequence of today's trainwreck.

"Now," Jordan rumbled, "I'm trying to figure how to save her career. That and how to report all of this stealth super-armor in a way that lets us trap a cop-killer and make it stick, before some Fed decides to show up and put him in a spy job instead of the hellhole he deserves."

That or doctors will want it, Colin realized. A bit of skein let him walk with an injured leg—

Oh God, could it get Jordan *walking again?* His mouth opened, snapped shut, this was nothing to say over the phone. And it only made the skein more important, when there was so little of it.

The line had gone quiet. Colin forced out "I'll... call 911. But, any news about that video of Terri? Is it a fake or not?"

"The IT squad just got the thing. We'll find out," Jordan said. "So now your sister, Rowe's missing fiancé, might be back? That's one more reason to keep you at a distance from this. Simms is halfway to going rogue on her own."

"Yeah. Sorry." It was all Colin could say, except "I'll make that call now."

A few taps and a few simple words put the call through. Then he moved the skein brace out of sight under his pants, and drove slowly back, watching for the blue lights to gather. Minutes passed, and then the police were there, and heading in to his apartment.

For long, long moments he sat at the wheel, engine ready, waiting for a shout from inside. Or a scream.

Finally the police came back into view. "Nobody there. Nothing's broken, looks like nothing's taken. You want to come up and check?"

He walked in, and as he did he heard the two cops muttering in codes on their radios. About him and what he'd been through, probably—he knew the sad, tight look one of them gave him now, a look for someone they'd *expect* to be jumping at shadows.

Nothing was damaged... but the Vargas archive books were gone. Had Eric even been after him at all?

All Colin could do was set down the one book he'd saved, and tell the police as much as he dared.

* * *

I should get out of here. Zara had been right to hide, Eric had just shown he could reach right into his home...

The thought hung in his gut, heavy and sour, worse than the pain of his wound. In the end, he simply shoved the table against the door and kept telling himself Eric had chosen the books over finishing him.

He held on to that hope, and his pride, lying in bed as the hours crawled by. He even felt his eyes close some.

When dawn had swelled enough to fill the cracks of the window, Colin dragged himself up again. A cold shower and devouring most of the last scraps of food forced him awake.

He still had the one Vargas notebook. And the online archives— but just comparing those with the scattered thoughts in the book reminded him how much of that history had never been digitized. If the devil was in the details, most of those were with Eric now.

That thought was just settling in his head when a text popped up. He steeled himself for another "Terri" message, but this came from Bea: *Heading to Gardner in force to question Eric. Watch if you want, don't interfere.*

He shoved the skein in place and ran for his car. Thoughts of a final arrest, a battle of lawyers, or a literal bloodbath warred in his head—just the last image of Eric slashing his way to freedom wiped out any thought of staying away. And Bea had judged this tip was worth leaking to him.

Then halfway to the Gardner building, a new text came in: *Correction. He's already out at 9th and Sunrise.* Colin swung the wheel around.

The address didn't ring any bells, but when it came in sight he could see why Eric was here. Two houses in a row had the "flat-nosed" look of buildings that had never fully rebuilt their porches from the quake, and a white truck with a construction hammer-logo was dispersing workmen to look at them. A Gardner-green car had brought Eric and two other men in suits to supervise them.

Or they would be supervising, if Bea and another detective and two uniforms weren't closing in on them. Colin settled his car across the street to watch.

A flash of white shone on Eric's cheek—a *bandage,* where Colin had hit him last night? Colin smiled grimly, and walked across the street, angling so the bulk of the construction truck hid him from Eric. *Just like I tried with Leo.*

One cop, the male detective, was speaking now. Colin caught the words "that festival of yours," that had to mean the death of Eric's colleague. The cop waved up the street, as if promising to drag Eric away.

The voice that answered was too low to make out, but Colin knew tones of doubt and denial when he heard them. That might be one of Eric's partners, probably talking about "arrest" and "lawyers."

The detective's answer was louder: "…where you were last night?"

Colin risked one step closer, to peep around the white truck. He could see Eric's back, and Bea and the other cops around him.

Eric *shrugged* at them. His words were a quiet murmur, swallowed by a car rolling by in the street, but most likely some easy denial. Colin ducked back, holding down the urge to march out and accuse him himself.

"How about that afternoon, 2 pm?" the detective snapped. "You want to think hard about that one."

Eric's answer was louder, but unruffled. "I was out on my rounds, a lot like this."

"Buying up more homes like this? Funny how right at that time, a man was killed in the middle of telling people their houses were doomed. And *two cops* died with him."

Eric stepped into view.

It looked like just strolling a few steps away from the cops, but it brought him around the truck into line of sight. And he glanced right toward Colin.

"Am I under arrest?" Eric asked the police, and his voice carried now. "I'd rather answer your questions here, and get back to work if you're satisfied. Or we can drive downtown and wait for my lawyer."

The detective closed in on him. He reached for Eric's shoulder.

Bea pulled the cop back. She whispered something, he snarled back at her... Colin tensed. *Eric wouldn't just tear into them, he wouldn't...*

"...he'd like to stay at work," the man with Eric added. "...offers for other..."

For a moment the cars and the sounds of the neighborhood drifted into a lull. In that stillness the cop said quietly "Like the Vargas House?"

"Of course. We've got just the offer in mind to fix..."

A car down the street drowned out the rest. Colin held his place, watched the police lead Eric off toward the edge of the lot—*not* to their car, not away under guard.

Colin stared after them. Was that all they were doing? And they were out of his earshot, unless he marched right in and accused Eric himself. When they needed all their focus on Eric's guilt.

And the company has plans for the House, that means Zara...

He pulled back across the street to his car. Looking back showed he could still see the police lined up around Eric now, so he could watch for signs of the killer turning desperate. Though there'd probably be no bloodbath here, or else no warning at all before it broke out.

As he watched, he settled in the car seat and called Zara.

Two rings, four, six. His mind filled with the image of her already on her way to meet with the Gardner people, walking right into Eric's grasp.

Then, "Hello there."

"Hi. Listen, I'm watching Eric right now. *Tell* me you're not about to go into business with Gardner."

"I can't believe you'd say that," she scoffed. "Of course I'm not— we can rebuild the House without partnering with the man who levelled it, or anyone with him."

Something in his chest loosened. "Just needed to hear that. Since even going to meet them would let Eric know where you are."

Across the street, the figure of Eric pointed a hand toward one of the cops. Colin grabbed for the door, but nobody moved, nobody fell over. False alarm.

He said "I... yesterday I saw Eric kill again. Leo."

"Oh God. But, you're alright?" she added, a bare moment later.

"He slashed up my leg. I can walk fine now, but..."

"Bastard!" Her rage surged through the phone. "No, I'm sorry for interrupting you. But, is that everything? Please don't start hiding something from me now."

Of course she sensed it. "Eric... came after me after that, last night. I hit him and ran clear, and he let me go." A bit of a smile pulled at his lips at that victory. "Trouble is, he was really after the archive books, and he got most of mine." Eric was still just *standing* there between the police, like nothing could worry him.

"Oh. Is there any good news? Anything about Terri?"

She had to ask that. *I* can't *show it to her. But it's the best sign we've had, no matter how painful it is.*

His throat was suddenly tight, and he forced it to move. "I got a video of her, don't know if it's fake yet. She looks, let's call it, too weak to talk—and you *don't* need to see it, not until we know if it's real. Right now, can you trust me on this?"

"A picture. Or just a fake." Her words sounded dazed. "So. So, is there something I can do? To find her, or track Eric, or anything? *Anything?*"

Her only answer was to keep moving. Just like she'd taught him.

He said "You do have the Vargas books Eric didn't get, and you know the online files better. We need that to find more skein."

"You think we can?"

"All four of those dragons you found, their places were already searched. We need to figure out if there's any more. Hell, we need to know what the stuff is, how to use it, everything. But it's looking like the only way we can beat Eric. We sure don't have much of a way now," and he glared at the police and their suspect across the street.

Two of those police figures *turned away* from Eric, at the same moment. Like they were all done.

"Of course," Zara said. "I'm sure there's an answer in there."

And she still didn't ask him to quit, no matter how close Eric came to killing him—

"Gotta go. I swear, I'll call soon, I'll stay in touch."

"Hold you to that," Zara said.

The lead detective took a few steps away from Eric. Then he stopped cold, to look back with some wide, ominous sweep of his arm. Colin brought the car window down, but he still couldn't make out what he said.

He started the car. This time the old engine turned over smoothly, and he slid the car into place on their side just behind the construction truck. He cut the engine.

"—seeing you again, soon," the detective called out.

"Whatever you need," Eric shot back. So confident now, everything under control. Had he *ever* been their friend?

"You're on one hell of a lucky streak. Someone brings down the Vargas House, and now Leo Tozer was yelling about more places falling?"

Did Eric flinch? Even from up the street, Colin thought he saw his body stiffen.

Then the detective turned right toward Colin. Not some sudden, surprised twist, more a deliberate turn as if the cop had seen him long ago and only put off dealing with him. He marched toward him, face grim.

One of the others, one of Eric's teammates, called out to them. "Sounds like you've got it backwards. If this man Tozer was talking about homes collapsing, we'd be the last ones to want him hurt. You see all this, Detective?"

He motioned around, at the two quake-crippled houses, at the workers eyeing the sagging walls and porches.

"What about it?" the detective said, as he reached Colin's car. From the side of his mouth he told Colin "You get out of here, da Costa!"

Bea was trotting up behind him.

"This is why we're here." That was Eric, louder now and not just confident but fierce, throwing the words right at Colin. "None of the old buildings can stand much longer. Leaving them up won't save this town."

Colin's teeth gritted together. Eric, the murderer, the liar, sounded like he *believed* that. Even when he'd knocked one House down himself.

Colin couldn't pull his gaze from the enemy, from that glimpse of... whatever it showed about Eric. Not while the detective banged on his door, talking about *interference* and *get him away*. Not while Eric turned back to work—maybe more out of reach than ever.

Not until Bea climbed in beside him and told him to drive.

CHAPTER TEN

THE SHORT VIEW

They drove without a word. Colin's foot on the pedal had the car roaring and lurching down block after block. But he couldn't look at Bea, knowing that at any moment she'd be sending him away.

Then she said "In here," and motioned to a chain family restaurant up ahead.

"Finally." *Anything to stop the silence from building.* To cover that he added "I'm starving."

"You've been using the skein then," and one of her smiles edged along her face. "A full stomach seems to fuel it better. Or it could be that the more we concentrate to work it, the more it takes out of us."

"Oh. Good to know." His mouth tried to smile back.

That moment hung between them as they walked in to the place, past the half-full tables of a mid-morning crowd. He hated to let that slip away.

So when they sat down, instead of picking up his menu, he leaned in and whispered "I've been using skein to help move my leg. I bet a big chunk of it could get Jordan walking again. I'm sure of it."

Bea's eyes flickered. That was hope, that he'd given her.

Then she looked over beyond his shoulder. The waitress had just *appeared* there, young, nervous, pad in hand.

Bea took a glance at the menu and ordered their biggest, simplest hamburger, two of them. Quick protein for handling the skein, Colin realized—he got the same.

When the waitress moved on, Bea said "I'll tell him. If Jordan still trusts me." She shook her head.

Then her voice went softer, almost tentative:

"You ever think Eric went after your leg, and Jordan's, for a reason? That he wanted a way of removing threats without killing them?"

"It... crossed my mind." He looked down at the table, at the speckled surface that almost hid the tiny scratches there. "If that's why I'm alive? How do you get comfortable being one of the few people a killer won't finish off, when Officers Ling and Stone weren't so lucky? And it doesn't change what has to be done."

Bea's face shifted, drooped in sadness. For a moment the table was silent, and a child's light laughter sounded a few spaces away.

"No, it doesn't," she said.

Colin looked at her, back to the restaurant wall, knowing she was just a few words away from cutting him out of the hunt. And how that might be what she needed to save her career.

"You getting enough proof on Eric yet?" he rushed out. "Any word on Terri?"

"Going through those messages will take time. I know some IT folks that are fascinated—" She halted, and Colin heard the waitress scurrying past behind him. Then Bea went on "—by the idea of an earthquake victim still alive after three years. They're going through every byte, and keeping it quiet. But, the number they came from has been well-protected."

"No surprise there."

He leaned closer, feeling the varied sounds of the place turning around their little pocket of secrets. All those messages *could* be simply more ways Eric tried to rattle him... but if Terri was alive, with Eric or anyone?

Just hearing Eric say how the town was doomed... a scrap of an idea twitched in the back of his mind...

Bea said "I told the lead detective I'd make you stay out of this investigation."

"I know. But, if that is Terri out there, if someone else knows about the skein—"

"That's not how you plan a thing, based on what-ifs."

Bea's eyes closed for a moment, then looked straight into his.

"I always need a plan, or a way to understand what I'm getting into. A killer with an impossible secret weapon, that I got hold of too? That needed me to go around a few rules, the only way to keep control and move fast enough.

"And then *you* clamp onto my case. But it turns out you know the killer, you know his world, you can stand your ground and you learn fast when you need to..."

Then she heaved out a sigh. Colin saw the pain in her face, before she said:

"And then you had to run right up to Leo and Eric into a hostage situation."

There it was.

"I know," he said. "I couldn't stand seeing another friend killed, but... I endangered everything, my life, your career, the case you were building—"

Her hand *slapped* the table, and it rang like a shout in the close space. "The case is worthless. Or... you tell me, you really think we'll pull enough evidence together to lock Eric Rowe up, the way things stand?"

"I..." Colin looked away, folded his arms over the table as he weighed it all. When he looked back he had to say "I'm starting to think not—"

She jerked a hand up to stop him.

The waitress swept up behind him, leaning past him to pass out plates. The *smell* of meat yanked his head around and set his stomach growling. Working the skein really did take its toll.

Colin could have stuffed the first burger down in a few gulps. Bea took one quick bite of hers, then grabbed for pepper and ketchup and poured them on. Bea, always getting things onto her own terms.

They both tore into their first burger. Colin slowed down for the second, enough to find words for Bea's question.

"Getting hard proof on Eric," he said, "it might never work. I keep thinking what he said today, he thinks the town's already doomed the way it is. Maybe he won't make any more moves if he's got everything he needs, with his new job and the books he grabbed, and all the skein we could find.

"But there's still the skein you've got, and mine. That means he could still come after you. And me again—if he's figured out I've still got some. I should never have gone back home. We have to stay on our guard, both of us."

She said "Never occurred to me," and she *grinned.* A quick, off-center grin that flipped his ignorance around into a joke between them.

She knew. She knew I might be in danger every minute of this; she did keep warning me. That's the same kind of fear I have about losing people, and she faces that down every day, by choice.

He slid the unfinished plate aside, so he could lean in closer. "Look, if you want me to back off, I can try to. You watch Eric so he doesn't go kill someone else."

"I will." But something flickered in her face. She couldn't keep that promise, and she had to know it.

He swept on "And, I'll keep trying to find you more skein. You said the best way to beat Eric was to have enough power to disarm him. We have to gamble that there's more of it, maybe that there's some of it everywhere Vargas needed it. We have to believe that, I'm not letting you fight him without enough…"

His hand was resting over hers.

He stared down, at where his hand had somehow crept out to. Her fingers on the table were warm, strong, callused in a few places. And so still under his.

I can't look up. He couldn't bear seeing what answer might be in her face, but she let his hand stay there, for what had to be three slow breaths now, five…

Her hand pulled away.

Her face had her hard, professional look again. "That is… a bad idea," she said, but something that might be reluctance thickened her voice. "There's too much left to do."

"Of course." Somewhere far away he heard plates clatter. "We have to focus." *We? Right, I was just saying I'd be finding skein for her.*

She said "Focus, yes. But… not on building a case against Eric. That could take months, with him sabotaging it and my superiors pushing me into procedure."

She leaned closer, lowered her voice. He could feel her breath.

"Colin, that still ends up with more bodies, or him *vanishing* and… just walking away. The only solution is to take him down."

"Then we'll find you that power. Enough skein and you can stand up to him—"

"No. Sure, a better weapon helps. But I need to catch Eric and finish him before he can work his skein at all."

"No!"

She still wants to take him that *way.* He stared at those eyes, gone tight and cold now. The way she sat, chair to the wall, but leaning in so close.

"You, you're a *cop,"* he tried whispering. "You're here to protect us, even from our own worst moments and what we could do. Sure you went behind their backs, but you still did it for us. For *us,* so people can come to Zara's meetings and talk about old recipes and feel safe. You can't be a monster yourself." *What am I saying, is that all I have to stop her?*

Bea looked right back at him. "I don't see any other way."

"Just *assassination?* That's not serve-and-protect, it's not being a warrior. My father was a soldier, a real fighter. They, they put him up for sniper training, and he turned it down. Said he'd never seen a problem that didn't get worse when one side stayed out of sight."

"Colin—"

"God! You miss that shot and you're dead, you know that. And if you don't, you really think they won't figure out it was you? You think you can look at yourself when it's done?"

Those eyes still didn't look away. "That's quite an appeal. I don't have a range of reasons like that—what I've always gone by is my view of what had to be done. And the more I look at Eric Rowe, the more he looks like the most dangerous combination of threat. He's been careful and restrained about any reckless moves he couldn't cover up. But then when he was leaning on Leo Tozer, he lost patience and cut him down, all in an instant. So why do you think he did that?"

"We had him outnumbered... no," and he looked at the table. "That was Eric's temper slipping out. But he'd been taking crap from Leo for years, this was the one person he could lose it with. He won't be on that hair-trigger again—"

"But he *has* that temper, somewhere in him. And he's killed police for getting in his way, and your quake inspector too. No, Eric Rowe is someone who knows how to go unnoticed, but every day could be one when he lashes out and someone else dies. Because I let him have that day."

Then the close hiss of her words softened.

"And, I hate facing a problem that makes me *that* kind of police. When Leo was leading him toward that skein, the thought in my head was, could I shoot *Leo?* In the leg, to stop him giving the murderer more power? That's where my head can go. In fact, thank you, for jumping in and at least saving me from that."

And her hand gripped at his. He stared up, felt the squeeze—just for a moment and it was gone.

She said "But, I don't see any other way. Eric Rowe has to go down."

"That can't be it... you just..." Was there anything he hadn't said? How all that could go bad and kill her? What she stood for as a cop?

A voice behind him chirped "Would you like refills?" The waitress, the damn overeager waitress was there with her pitcher—

Not refills. We need more skein, enough to stop Eric cleanly—

Bea said "Actually, we're done here. But thank you." Her eyes edged away from his gaze now.

They gulped the last of their food, Colin eating numbly as his thoughts flailed for any kind of answer. They paid the bill.

Then Bea broke into his thoughts again: "Here's what it comes down to. You stay clear of Eric, and the investigation on him. Period. You can keep researching the skein, though—anything you find might make the difference. And now I have to go report that you learned your lesson."

They stood up, and started through the morning crowd for the door.

The minute she gets to work, she's out of reach, and she'll be looking for ways to ambush Eric. Colin glared at the crowd, too thick to even let him speak to her until they stepped outside. *Find more skein, there had to be enough out there. Where is it, why would Vargas hide it? Dragons, pillars, quakes...*

The orange bulk of his car waited right there in the parking row, why couldn't it be a longer walk—

Bea said "I won't ask you to drive me back." She reached for her phone.

No, one glance *at any messages and she'll be gone—*

"Wait!" He caught at her arm.

She jerked back. "What?"

"Well... the quakes."

And the scrabbling pieces of ideas locked together, and the concept cracked wide open.

"The *quakes*. The thing Vargas always feared would ruin this town. And how we found the skein—look, I know it was here." He raced to the car and fumbled open the door, yanked out the notebook he'd saved.

"What are you getting at?" She edged in beside him, letting a passing car roll by.

Pages flipped under his fingers, page after page of eclectic thoughts from decades past. "The skein. Vargas hid it… or he wasn't just hiding it. He put it where it would reinforce the buildings, see?"

He shoved the book at her, finger on the page heading: *Prominent sites – quake construction flaws*.

Bea glanced at it, and her eyes, her face, grew sharper as she read. Another car hummed by the row of vehicles.

"Possible," she said. "The bank, the pier, listed here with no details. Not his own home, but that could be an early test. This list is close to a match for where skein might have been. Close, anyway."

He sighed "There's St. Mary's." *Did he try to shore that up too—*

"No, I mean the statues aren't here—"

He reached over, pointed at a scribble in the corner. " 'Hope statue, near cliff' it says. But Terri had to be at the one place where it wasn't enough—"

He clamped his mouth shut, tried to start again.

"Never mind that, that's three years ago, and anything there must be long gone. But we've got this one spot left." He pointed to the words.

Liddel Elementary School. And a scribbled note, *needs it*.

"You don't know that," Bea said, but he grabbed out his phone.

Nobody answered. Seconds ticked by, and he filled them by staring around at the cars, the sidewalk, looking for any shimmer of light that could be Eric listening in. It all looked clear.

"Morning," Zara said.

"Hi. We've got an idea: we think Vargas may have been placing the skein where he thought buildings needed reinforcement against the next quake."

"God…" She went silent a moment, then added "So Eric is pulling it out to knock everything down? And there's how much of this under the Hillside?"

"It's not like that," he said, but a shudder crept over him and locked up his jaw a moment. "There's just a few places, just a bit of extra protection, as far as we know. Eric's not *trying* to level the town. Even if he could."

He knew that, but the shudder wouldn't let go.

He went on "So when this is over we put the skein back, or we have the places reinforced." He took one more glance around for any glimpse of Eric, and dropped his voice to a whisper. "Anyway, do you know any record of Vargas being concerned about any one place, besides where he put those dragons, plus St. Mary's and Liddel Elementary?"

"I… the *school?* " Her voice caught. "I, I can check."

Bea said "We can take a look tonight. Yes, 'we'—since Eric shouldn't be onto this yet."

Her words had an energy now, a buoyancy, that he hadn't heard all day. He said "I knew there was a reason I hung onto this book. We'll find a way." *She said* we *again.*

"Or, can I—" She reached to ask for the phone. He handed it over, and she added "Let's keep this private," and she stepped into the car.

Colin joined her, and when the doors shut out the sound of the outside, she switched the phone to Speaker.

"Ms. da Costa? Are you there?"

"Detective Simms? Or is it 'Bea'? Either way, I'm Zara," she laughed. "And you're looking after my son?"

"Trying to. I wonder, are you still in contact with your community?"

Zara laughed again, louder. "You have to ask? Of course I am."

"That's what I might need. If these are the only other skein spots, is there a way you or Colin could *leak* a clue that points somewhere else? In case I need Eric to believe it."

She's still thinking it. Ambushing Eric.

"As a decoy?" Zara said? "Or a trap?"

"A trap. Don't worry, whatever place we pick I won't let Eric destroy it."

"Leaking that wouldn't be hard. I had to ask some friends to help me look for those dragon images—any of us could drop a hint somewhere online, that we'd found another. That's just off the top of my head."

"You're good at this," and Bea smiled. "But on second thought, Colin and I need to set this up ourselves. When he thinks we're ready."

Colin let a breath out, then frowned. Bea was leaving Zara out of her scheme, but she wanted him to approve it? What was she thinking now?

"Alright then," Zara said. "Just, move fast? Because I think those two sites are the only ones. If there's skein there, you can't let him find it first."

"We'll get it," Colin said. "Thanks."

"What do they say—'watch your back'?" Zara hung up.

Bea handed the phone back. "It looks like we agree on one thing. We can search the school, tonight. Now I have to get back to following procedure, and getting that ground-probe radar gear again."

Just like that she had a plan?

"Tonight. Got it," he rushed out, trying to catch up. "You think you can get that radar? I mean, will the police still let you…"

"If I ask Jordan to keep it quiet? We'll find out."

* * *

The afternoon ground by. Bea had to be busy working the system again—she didn't contact him all day, and he tried to think it wasn't from salvaging her career.

He kept the car moving around town. Eric would probably be deep in his own work and not looking for him at all, but Colin guessed the best way to keep an invisible man from following him was not to be spotted himself. So he let the car sit for at most a quarter of an hour at a spot, letting him search through the notebook and what information he had on the school. Then he always moved on.

It was only when evening settled that he drove by the school. Liddel Elementary looked just the same as he remembered, the brick shape between the soccer field and the playground. Colin drove on past it, just slowly enough to see the several cars in the lot—staff working on some late plans.

He parked the car a couple of blocks away and texted an update to Bea. At least in midsummer there'd be no kids here.

As he waited, he concentrated on the skein around his leg, and thinned the brace down so he could peel off a bit and wrap that around his finger. *Now fade, blur out of sight, do something...* Images and commands churned in his head, but nothing made his finger disappear. Instead he could only sit, looking around the street for any hint of Eric's shimmering. While the darkness closed around him.

When summer night washed the sky clean enough to show the stars, he drove by the school again. The cars were gone.

A text to Bea brought a quick *"On my way."* That left him looking at the building and trying to picture where Vargas might have wanted skein to reinforce it.

Or how someone might get inside. The doors and windows seemed the same as ever from a distance. But looking at them now through his years as the House's security, they seemed all too easy to slip through with some of the skein tricks he'd seen.

The skein on his hand stretched out, like extending his own finger, if that finger had been stiff and numb from weeks in a cast. Eric would be faster, whenever he shaped tools like this.

Bea's car pulled up in front of him.

She climbed out, and he rushed to join her. "Did you get a key?"

"Too risky," she said. "We want no traces that we were here, remember? But I do know they've got no security in the summer."

She started for the school.

He trotted after her, his leg clumsy with its brace weakened. "Wait, where's that probe radar?"

"Couldn't get it. We'll have to find the skein ourselves."

And she thought they *could?* Colin gritted his teeth. But, this had been his idea, his hope of heading off her own deadlier plan. He led the way over the chain fence, and to the side window he'd been eyeing. *Serves me right for wondering if I could do this.*

He slid the skein into the window's crack. He stared at the dim shape through the glass, straining numbly to make it move by thought when he could only guide it with his eyes. So he could *break into a school.*

And stand up to Leo's killer, and stop Eric. The skein inched out, hooked around the latch, and swung the window open. Bea made a soft *hmm* that might have been impressed.

They clambered inside, like the start of some distorted kid's prank where he was too bulky and heavy to slip around like he should.

"Where do we look?" Bea glanced around.

"I'm thinking. The building doesn't have any central pillars or supports, just..." He motioned along the corridor, at smooth walls and display cases all clear enough in the single light above its corner. "If the skein's here, it's somewhere important. He can't have it running all through the walls."

"Better hope not."

They moved up the corridor. The cafeteria lay on their left, sending out the ghosts of fried smells that no cleaning could scrub from the air.

He looked up and down the walls for anything that shored it up, or any lingering signs of what the last quake had shaken and what it hadn't. Their feet echoed.

Glass cases stood along the sides—probably half-emptied out, now that another year of kids had moved on.

All the other times I've been here, Terri was alive. These times were *me and my big sister, as a boy who couldn't imagine her not being there.*

And now… he had a sudden image of Eric here again, bringing the whole building down like he did the House.

Halfway down the corridor was the auditorium. Enough light reached it to show a half-dozen folding chairs sprawled around one table there, signs of whatever meeting had let out earlier.

Or were they looking at this wrong? Vargas couldn't *protect* a whole building with a thread of skein, but he might place it more as an act of pride, picking one token thing to make sure it stood through the next quake.

Bea said "Maybe the arch here." She flicked on a small flashlight. He squinted at the sudden glow and saw the beam centered on the little flower-carved arch above the kids' theater.

That might be the center of the whole school, the one heart of it to save. Bea could have been reading his mind.

She handed him a second light. "Look for faults in the wood, or cracks if that's how he worked the skein in."

"Right. Vargas didn't build the school, so he might have had to…"

They looked over the archway inch by inch, starting at its base. If there were a groove or crack here it might be spackled and painted over.

For what chance they had. Colin wondered if Bea had figured out what he had, then looked beyond there, brought him here just to humor him.

He said "No good. Look, I'll walk around, see if something else seems right."

"Sure, if you think so." Bea nodded, with a smile that didn't quite move up her cheeks.

She is *humoring me.* He flicked the light off and stepped out into the corridor, feet echoing and shapes blurring as he began readjusting to the dimness. Did Bea even think they could find anything this way? Did he?

He headed right, passing one short row of classrooms to start up the stairs. He knelt down to run a finger along one step—no, even if there were any skein here, the stairs were too big and broad to search.

Like everywhere else here. He thought of Bea's sad smile again. She could be letting him go through all this to finish out his ideas, use up all his objections to her own plan for Eric.

Footsteps moved on the floor below, Bea moving out to explore.

If she believed that. *She wants to shoot Eric in cold blood. I'm walking these children's halls with someone who says there's nothing left except a bullet in the back. And she still has me counting how often I can make her smile.*

Except, Eric. Eric had wiped out Leo *and* the House, so wasn't Bea's plan what he deserved?

But then, there had been that moment that "Terri" had said not to trust Bea.

The upper corridor stretched ahead of him now, still just more dim blurs of wall and posters and nothing that seemed worth clicking on his light again. Below, Bea's footsteps moved away down the lower floor.

Something in the air… he must be imagining it, but he thought he could *smell* the classroom on his left. That room where he'd spent years with Eric and Leo.

Eric. Always clever, nervous, seeing what the rest of the kids missed. Leo, loud and bragging, and maybe a whole world of knowledge about the skein and a life he'd been living. That Eric had snuffed out, in the middle of questioning him, just for a flash of rage.

Before he killed him, what had Eric been demanding? More skein, or… But those moments of sudden blood loomed in his memory and froze any reaching for the seconds just before them.

Colin forced his thoughts away from that, from the grandson to the grandfather.

If Vargas protected anything here, would it be something conspicuous, or something vulnerable? Instead of left, Colin turned right.

The library nestled in the corner. He pushed the door open, glanced at the mismatched rows of the shelves—all so much shorter than him now. *This was where I'd come to look for Terri. Her place and Eric's, and mine and Leo's was the playground below.*

Leo. Games, stories, songs. Not from down there but…

But the door in the corner… it was still there, the balcony with the fire escape and the slide down. Where there'd always been a balcony, where disaster could drop it straight onto the playground, if anything failed here. It felt right.

Footsteps moved lightly below.

The balcony did look small, with the metal safety cage over it, and the covered tunnel of a slide. He pushed the door's opening bar with a creak and stepped out. The balcony had been cramped for him just by the time he graduated—

The footsteps below had gone quiet. Right at the moment he'd pushed the balcony door open, but that didn't mean…

He stepped out and eased the door shut behind him.

Through the door's glass, something shimmered. A faint mirage-image moving into the stacks.

Eric had found them after all. Colin crouched down, but the kid-sized perch felt too tight for how his heart was pounding.

No use hiding, Eric would remember this door too. But Eric only stood in the room, head turning around the bookshelves. Then he walked in to look among them.

How'd he get past Bea? Did he already catch her and—

Colin wrenched his thoughts from that. Whatever delayed Eric in here was still giving him one chance.

He crept to the far end of the balcony, hunched low, hoping the door between him and Eric muffled his footsteps better than he could. He reached out between the cage bars, straining down to reach the balcony's base.

Fingers flicked over stone. Heavy, solid… he felt a crack.

He clutched the scrap of skein on his fingers and drew it out into a needle. It glided in, but he couldn't *feel* the skein moving, he could only will it to hold strong and not break as he jabbed it blindly in, hoping just his hand behind it could make out some difference in the resistance—

Then he felt it. Not a touch through the skein, but a spark, a recognition. The skein knowing its own.

Up. The motion was as simple as breathing in, to make the skein deposit wake and flow and slide upward onto his hand—

The stone grated, a low, inevitable sound. He remembered, he'd never pulled skein out of rock before, only one handful from a wooden pillar. And waves of silver-green surged up to wrap around his hand, his arm, thickening like a triple layer of coat sleeve…

The door swung open. Eric stared right at him.

CHAPTER ELEVEN

WORDS

Can't let him through the door! Colin rushed at Eric, and the green figure ducked back a step.

Colin caught himself in front of the doorway. *That* made a good choke point, where the smaller, deadlier man would have to come through there, and couldn't trap him in the kids' balcony or dash around him in the open.

The floor lurched. The stone groaned and ground, the balcony *dipped* an inch under his feet—

"I need that skein," Eric said.

And he crouched, a sliver of a man coated in silver-green power, talons ready on each hand. The door should have swung closed, but the tilted balcony jammed it open.

Colin edged back half a step, to keep the door frame between them. His new skein was still piled onto his arm. He raised his guard, trying to make that arm's motion spread the skein around and give him strength. *How'd he find me?*

"I need that," Eric said again.

"And you think I'll hand it over?"

There could be a dozen ways a body shifted, tensed, before it attacked. Colin waited to feel them in his opponent.

An elbow moved, Colin blocked as Eric lunged in with the skein's speed. Force slammed against his armored arm, rocked him back. He swung back as his foot clashed on the flooring to catch himself—Eric darted back again, tentative. A killer, but still not a fighter.

The balcony *groaned* again. Colin shifted his weight, trapped. The safety cage over it barely let him move, the ladder and slide were too small for him to escape. But Eric would cut him apart out in the open.

Where's Bea? Did he already get her?

Something numb gripped his throat at the idea. Began creeping through his chest, his eyes—

He blinked, hard. *Stall.*

"So you're a murderer." He spat the words at Eric, keeping his breathing controlled, ready. "You wipe out anyone who gets in your way?"

Eric jabbed at his face—a feint that he warded off without making contact. The balcony creaked and held steady.

Colin added "This used to be your library. Leo and I played just down there." He motioned with an elbow, kept his eyes *away* from the jungle gym down below. "Now you terrorize Leo into a babbling wreck, and then you butcher him—"

"I need that skein," Eric hissed. "For Terri."

"Liar! Fake all the messages you want, tell lies about the skein or Bea..." Mentioning her brought the numbness seeping into his muscles again. He pushed on "Fakes! You do anything to slow me down, that's all. She believed in you once, but you've slashed through everything else in our lives, so why not our memories too?"

Eric leaned closer, just an inch.

That low voice tightened. "You found this skein. Now you can find me more magic, and the secret for making more."

"More—wait, 'magic'?"

"Of course. What else could the skein be?"

What's he think, that there's some charmed circle or magic words for it?

"So you followed me here. You won't catch me that way again." He kept the thought off his face, how there was still one other place on

Vargas's list—where Terri had vanished. If Eric didn't know that, if he didn't know anything about whatever had happened... she could still be...

Far below, down in the stillness of the building, footsteps moved.

Eric gave the softest laugh. "Following someone is simple. Like Zara, down at the Wyngard—"

Colin struck. The punch lashed out and flowed into a kick as Eric blocked the first blow. The little man staggered back a step.

Don't get lured in. Colin caught himself, saw Eric already rising, unhurt in his armor. Colin stayed back behind the doorway. A moment of emotion could lose a fight faster than getting hit, the instructors always said.

"You're going to find me more skein tomorrow." Eric spoke like he hadn't even felt the hits. "Or give me yours. Or else tomorrow night, I'll come see Zara." And his claws spread.

The room went still. Out behind Colin the scattered rumbles and birdcalls of the night still sounded, but they could have been in another world.

"Don't you touch her! Zara was always good to you, we all were! Now you're threatening her life because, what, she's the only one left you haven't tried to kill?"

As he spoke, Colin edged his weight onto his injured leg. He'd been wrong trying to batter Eric down through his armor—but his own skein was on one arm plus bracing that leg. Perfect to launch one driving lunge and an all-out strike.

Down inside the school's stillness, one faint sound shuffled.

Eric shook his green-armored head. "Throw all the words you want at me. You still need to bring me that power by tomorrow. Midnight."

Words. I wish I had something to say that could cut him. "Bastard," he flailed. "You slaughtered Leo—"

Leo. Leo said, his grandfather had—

"I told you, it's for Terri."

Eric lowered a hand. His skein slid back from his waist to let him hold up a phone.

The tiny face on the screen was Terri's.

"More fakes!" *Why didn't I hit him as he reached for it—*

Eric's phone audio was perfect. For one moment Colin was in the same room and catching every strangled tremor of that voice: "Colin? That... you, with... skein..."

She saw him. A live feed, Eric had the real Terri alive. Real, all along...

His leg sagged. Somewhere far away from that *face,* he knew his leg and skein had lost the focus to move, and he was tipping against the door frame...

Her face clenched, spasmed with pain.

No, she drew in a breath. She wheezed "Have... to... stop Eric..."

The screen turned away, its spell loosened as Eric's clawed hand twisted it around to stare at it. Even with his face hidden under the skein, he moved like someone remembering he was human, like he could *hurt.*

His head rocked sideways and he crashed against a shelf.

Gunshots were roaring. Rapid, relentless firing hammered through the room, and Eric jolted where he lay.

Bea stepped into the room, covered waist-up in her skein and blasting round after round into the enemy. Alive, she was *alive!*

Eric wasn't bleeding.

Colin saw that as he stepped back from the barrage, as he felt more than heard the balcony creak under his step. Eric didn't bleed, he didn't go limp. Instead he staggered to his feet.

Eric lunged. A single blur of motion that spun away, deflected away when Bea blocked, ready. The force sent her staggering back, but she slashed as he swept by. Her claws must have landed, the way Eric jolted away.

Eric dashed on, spun around, still moving like nothing had reached the man under the armor. Bea pulled back, sidestepped, to put one of the waist-high bookshelves between her and Eric. Safe from blitz charges for now.

Eric blurred and shimmered from sight.

Colin threw himself at him.

One surge of will for the skein on one leg to fling him across space. One flailing step with the other leg to keep that momentum going and hold him almost upright. His fist rocketed into where Eric had stood.

His punch sank into empty air. The last of his balance failed and brought him down, but he twisted as he fell. A slash came down on his arm, blocked.

He crashed down on a table—*keep rolling!* He tumbled on, caught a glimpse of Eric stepping toward him, visible again.

Back outside, the balcony *creaked* and began to tip.

Eric turned away. He turned away from Colin and rushed at Bea. He closed with her as Colin got to his feet, and those claws jabbed at her waist. She blocked, but he followed up and slashed low again—

He was going to kill her. Eric had full armor in his skein, while Bea's still left her lower body as easy meat. She had the skill to fend him off, but nothing they did had scratched him, and he only needed one moment. Any moment now.

Colin drew back his arm, but their fight's speed mocked any thought of throwing his skein to her. Eric had seen that move too.

Instead he edged forward. One more charge might still hit Eric, might be strong enough. He braced his leg again.

Eric drove Bea back, back between the undersized shelves. If they'd just move another step apart...

What Leo had said. A thought, from the frantic moments before the fight, snapped into clarity. Leo chanting, messages from his grandfather, and now Eric calling the skein "magic."

Bea fell back one more step. Eric slashed again.

Magic had to get its power from somewhere. Like, a spell.

"Night and day," Colin breathed, *"gratshay kodo va—"*

The skein seared into his arm.

All wrong. He knew it as the scream ripped from him, as the agony tore at his arm, turned his leg helpless and dropped him, the skein burning and biting and fighting against all his need to make it *let go.*

One moment, he saw Eric staring. Another, Bea charging, blocked.

Let go let go, stop stopstopstop... Willpower beat at the skein, as pain ripped at him and tore his strength to shreds, the stuff clamped on deeper and deeper, all wrong, white flashes tearing across his sight, fist pounding against anything, anything, to feel something besides the pain—*won't let go—stop—*

One moment between the flashes. Eric swinging, Bea getting *hit* and sent crashing away—

Vision vanished. Skein burned. But, *can't let her—*

One last wrench of will, and the skein went quiet. Too late.

The ghost of his strength floated him up, hollow and raging, standing on his good leg only.

"Eric..."

That figure whirled, the other shape in skein. Colin rushed, staggered, toward him.

Eric *looked* at him. He didn't move one fraction, just stood watching as Colin forced himself closer, closer. Steps came steadier now, stronger and faster, and even his throbbing right arm began to rise.

Eric hopped away, clear over one shelf and dashing away. Colin twisted after him.

Motion caught the corner of his eye. Bea was sitting up.

He drank in the sight, for a moment, then another.

Eric darted away out the balcony door, leaving it swinging shut again. Colin reached it in time for one last glimpse of Eric leaping down the fire escape from the still-crooked balcony, and blurring to vanish in the darkness.

Bea's voice sounded behind him, close. "You alright?"

"He's getting away..." The inane, useless words slipped out on their own, no reason to say them at all. He swayed, slumped over.

Bea caught him. He felt her wedged under his arm, holding him up and bracing him against the wall. Ignored pains roused up and down his flesh, one arm felt like it had been too near a furnace. But on his other side, all he felt was her strength.

"I saw you go down." His voice came out hoarse. "I thought…"

"Shhhh."

She drew him closer around her. Her skein armor was long gone now, and his cheek lay against hers.

Breathe. He sank into the moment, just sharing the space with her. Safe. Alive. Close.

Her voice vibrated against his cheek. "Wha… what happened to you?" Her words were clear, but her breath sounded weak.

"Something he said." Saying that much helped him line the rest up. "And what Leo said when we found him. I tried a guess, but my skein went crazy. I think I got control again—"

Bea's lie to Jordan, that she couldn't get the stuff off. What if—

He twisted away from the wall, swung his skein-coated arm up and at the ground, begging the stuff to *let go.*

The silver-green thing sloughed away and slid to the floor. Like tearing off a bandage—his arm looked red and burned underneath, but the skein obeyed him again.

Bea looked from it to him. "And then Eric ran? You think what you set off scared him?"

"I guess." Or… Eric liked ducking out of fights and choosing his moments, his power made that easy. So any good surprise made him pull back. "I got the idea from what he said. He called the skein magic, so maybe this is some spell for it that Leo knew. Or more like a charm against it."

"Magic?" Bea shook her head, he could feel her motion against him. "There's no such thing."

"How would we know that? After all this, you're so sure?"

"I know one thing." She slipped under his shoulder again. "We can't stay here. Those gunshots must have been reported by now."

And they couldn't leave their weapon, even after it had backfired. He leaned down, dug his fingers gingerly into the skein, and pulled it up again, holding it back beneath his grip like some half-liquid bowling ball. Bea helped haul him upright again.

They stumbled out of the library. Colin took one glance back, hating to leave some of the shelves' books lying on the floor after all their crashing around. *Books? I left the kids' whole* balcony *hanging crooked when I ripped its skein out. This time I'm the one who did that.*

Bea helped him balance as they climbed down the stairs. Once they reached the first floor his feet moved faster, echoing more smoothly with every step. Though he still hung on to her arm.

So many changes spun in his head, coming so fast. Threats to Zara. Seeing Terri. Eric. The skein. And his hand clinging to Bea.

As they stepped outside, one thought pushed out through the swirl: "Wait, your bullets! You don't want us found here, but they'll trace the bullets to your gun."

"They'll try. That wasn't my regular weapon."

Of course she'd planned for that. A smile tugged at Colin's lips... but no, Bea would really be keeping that gun for any chance to catch Eric with his armor off. *And that* can't *be the only way.*

They made it to their cars.

Colin sank into his, forced his eyes to focus and his hands to work as he guided it through the night streets, block after dim block. By the time Bea slowed down and pulled over ahead of him, he knew what she'd worked out next: his car was the one they had to leave behind. His pumpkin-orange rattletrap might be what had helped Eric spot him all along.

He settled into Bea's simple black car, book in his lap and skein lying at his feet.

She let the car idle. "What happened with you? My side was simple: I was looking around, and I went to check what might have been a footstep. Skein out, watching every corner and all. Not sure if I missed Eric or he was leading me away from you. Then I heard you upstairs."

"He didn't jump you, though. Guess I look like an easier target. But he could have *killed you.*" His hand went to her shoulder, and she let it stay there.

Except, Terri said not to trust her—

No, he'd seen the real Terri defy Eric. That made everything before that Eric's own tricks, just as fake as they always felt—

"Terri! She's really out there, I saw her." The words tumbled out. "And, Eric knows where Zara is, he could go after her any time!"

"He would." Bea pulled out her phone. "He *could* go after her, or he *is* now? I can get a squad car to her in minutes."

"He... he said he'd come after her if I didn't get him more skein. Said he could always find her. I don't *think* he'd go after her right now, but..."

"Right. And we're close enough to the hotel."

She twisted the car into the street and wrenched it around, throwing him against the door, right against his singed arm. Then the motion steadied to push past the dim lines of the streets. The siren stayed off, but she still drove faster than he ever went by day.

Colin shot a call to Zara. The phone rang, rang, useless.

Because it's the middle of the night. He watched the buildings slide by in the dark, telling himself all of this was just worry tipping into panic. Except, Eric had a way of bringing the worst case to life.

Then Zara answered. "Colin? What happened, are you alright?"

She went straight into worry. Not panic, but assuming it was the only reason he'd call.

He pushed the thought down. "I'm fine. I'll tell you all about it soon. Listen, we're coming to pick *you* up. Eric knows where you are, and there's a chance he's closing in on you now. You need to..."

Get out? Hunker down? If Eric did show up, which was safer?

"Lock yourself in, and stall if anything happens. We'll be there soon."

"I will. But you're—alright, I'll be waiting. I'll keep the line open."

"Okay. I hope I'm wrong."

He tapped Mute, and turned to Bea. "Eric said he'd find us anywhere. Do we even have somewhere safe to put her?"

"Of course." She picked up her own phone from her lap. The car slowed for a moment as she made the call, then surged back to full speed.

Jordan's voice rasped through the speaker. *"Detective* Simms—if the word still means a thing to you. At this hour? Just how deep are you in now?"

Bea cut right through the warning. "You still have that security up?"

"So that's it." Jordan coughed. "Sure, cameras, sensors, automated warnings. Hell, I could spot an invisible man if one walked in here."

Colin snapped "No jokes! You know that *is* what Eric keeps doing... oh." *That video we have, of Eric's almost-hidden killing on camera.* "You would spot him, wouldn't you? You'd record him, shimmers and doors moving and everything. Real proof of what he does, to go with the Gardner video. And if he lets you get that, he loses his best weapon, that nobody thinks there *can* be an invisible killer."

"Not bad, not bad," Jordan said.

"Well, that's what we need now. Eric just threatened to kill Zara. My mother."

"And Colin too," Bea added. "They need real protection, now."

"So you're out there with da Costa. Chasing our suspect, again." Jordan sounded each word out, clear and hard, more like a prosecutor than a cop.

"Not looking for him," Bea said. "And it was a lead that Colin found, that nobody else would believe. It seemed worth trying, so I made a decision."

"With da Costa," Jordan repeated. "That's always your 'decision,' isn't it?"

A scowl tightened over her face. "I'm chasing a killer, the man who put you in that chair. Go on, judge my choices for how they work, or how they go wrong—I'll defend them any time. But *don't* you tell me my thinking's being dragged around by some girly crush and say I'd let it get *personal.*

"And no," she added, "I'm not sleeping with him. I haven't even kissed him."

Jordan coughed again. "There may be hope for you yet. Get them down here, we'll try to salvage something."

"Right." And she hung up.

Not a word of thanks between them, just two professionals sparring over the next step. And over how far off track she'd gone, because of being around him, and so she told Jordan all those moments Colin had felt meant nothing.

Bea's lips moved. Without a sound, but the words she shaped could have been *more lies.*

About him, and her.

She didn't look at him, might not have known she'd said it. Colin sat quiet in the seat, letting himself believe.

Then the car slid to a stop in front of the Wyngard Hotel. The place looked as dead as the rest of town this late, except for the bright red neon sign across the top.

He still had the line open to Zara. He unmuted and said "We're parking now. Still okay?"

"Still okay." She could have been checking in about some random, ordinary event. They just had to stay ahead of Eric a little longer.

He reached down and scooped up the skein. It should make his skin crawl after it had attacked him, but it still *obeyed* him like a numb, flexible limb... he tucked it under his shirt and drew it around into a vest. So much more of it now. If Eric was there, he'd need every scrap.

Bea led the way in, with a fluid stride that kept her head tilting slightly, unobtrusively to each side as she walked, watching everywhere. The night clerk gave them a nervous look, then fell back at one look at her badge.

When they entered the dim, carpeted corridor, her hand went to her gun. They walked with constant glances over their shoulders and around corners. The speckled wallpaper on all sides *might* help show Eric's shimmer against it.

Then at last: "We're at the door," he said, and Zara swung it open.

She was dressed, ready, gaze darting around the corridor. "There's no need to waste a moment." She hoisted a small bag and a tall stack of archive records in her arms.

"Got everything?" Bea said.

"Everything important," was all she answered.

They headed back, Zara hauling the books and Colin and Bea watching the corridor and then the parking lot for last-minute trouble. Finally they sank into the car, with Colin taking the back seat beside his mother, and they glided away safe.

As they gathered speed, Zara twisted toward him and rushed out *"Are* you alright?"

"Alright, yes. Just some close moments—we found some skein at the school, but Eric spotted us again. And this time he threatened you. Either we find him more skein by tomorrow night, or he comes after you."

"But you're okay. No, I know, I'm not going to hold you back now. We'll work something out, all of us."

"I'm sorry. For all this." He forced himself not to look away from her, from the trembling that only showed around her eyes. There had to be *something* more he could say.

She said "But, we're out of ideas about finding this thing, and that was the last spot on your list. Except the church, and the old building's not even there anymore. Whatever it was that happened there."

"Yeah. About that..."

He drew in a slow breath and met her eyes.

"Terri's alive, I'm sure now. Eric showed me a live feed of her, and she looked right at me. She spoke to me, a couple of words."

"So. They aren't fakes." Zara's words were clipped, her voice straining as if the emotion could rip her apart. Her eyes clenched shut. "And Eric, Eric really has her."

Bea spoke up, soft but insistent. "She said a couple of words? How much did she say, before we start assuming what it was?"

"Assume? Oh, it was her alright," Colin laughed. "Why would Eric make a fake that told me to stop him?"

"Then it's true. She's alive." Zara clenched her eyes tighter. "With Eric, and Eric has been killing... what's he doing with her? You said she was in pain, in that other image. Did *he* do that?"

"To Terri? Maybe not." He tried to think, how Eric had been talking. "He kept saying he wanted the skein *for* Terri, like he still cares and he's trying to help her. Except he's after something else too, some other thing that she told me to stop."

"I see."

That was all she said. She didn't look up, only huddled in around herself.

They drove on through the darkness, on toward Jordan's house. *That's going to be awkward, the way he is about keeping Bea away from us.* He tried to keep his thoughts on survival, and keeping the smile Zara needed, and not the hostility they were driving into.

Still... something about Zara tugged at his mind. The way she kept asking about his safety, that didn't sound like her losing the battle with fear. And with Terri back from the dead... He knew his mother.

They pulled into the driveway, with Jordan's tall little house as a wall of shadow against the headlights—but only for a moment, and then lights sprang up all around the driveway. Part of the security system they'd be hiding under.

Bea tapped a speaker button at the front door. "We're here."

The door clicked.

They had just stepped inside when a voice, some recorded male voice, announced *Attention, your image is being recorded—*

It shut off, and Jordan rolled into view. His face looked as sharp and alert as if this were only the start of a day. A hard day.

"I've got it all automated, so it should keep you out of trouble. We'll see if you return the favor for us." He shot Bea a glare, making no secret of his disapproval.

Bea only turned to face Zara. "My sergeant, Ed Jordan. Taking time from saving my badge to try protecting you."

Zara glided toward Jordan. The smile didn't *form* on her face, as much as seem like it had always been there—typical Zara. She said "We're both beyond grateful to you, for opening your door at a moment like this. We'll follow any boundaries you want to keep out of your way and get us out of here soon. And I *insist* you set out a few, since it's the least we can do for you."

"Ma'am." Some of the lines on Jordan's face eased.

She only nodded, didn't even insist on him using her name. Of course she found the right note to take with him, with one glance.

"You have everything?" Jordan asked.

"They do," Bea said. "You two ready to get some sleep?"

Not yet.

"I was thinking," Colin broke in, smooth and confident as he could, "that Zara and I are up to us all comparing notes first, if you are."

He caught a cold look from Jordan—*did I just imply he might be too tired?* Then Jordan only said "Come on, sit down."

The next room had its table and chairs ready, the same as it had last time. Zara looked comfortable enough; the most uneasy one there was Bea, from the way her eyes avoided Jordan now. That could be about to change.

"Let me start," Colin said.

He talked them through his idea about the skein's locations, and their late-night visit to Liddel Elementary, facing down Jordan's glower for that bit of breaking and entering. He told them about the skein, and the whole encounter with Eric. When he mentioned the "magic" words he'd used, Jordan glanced straight at Bea with *Is he crazy?* written all over his face, until Colin went on to what those words had done.

He even managed to cover their escape in a few words, without his voice catching as he skipped over how he and Bea had clung to each other. Just a simple brush with death.

When he finished, Zara shook her head. "I think I wish I never knew the details."

"I'm still okay," he said.

"He said he'd—" She stopped.

"He said he'd come after you, unless I helped him get more skein." He steeled himself, opened his mouth to press on.

Bea cut in: "A direct threat. Now that Eric's made that, he'll have to follow it up, if he can find you here. If he does, the cameras should be the best thing to make him back down. He's still got more to lose than to gain here."

Zara folded her arms around herself. "But... we *don't* have another clue to this skein. Except St. Mary's, and that's all rubble and cleared out long ago. We can't get you any more strength to fight him."

"And," Colin grabbed the moment, "it means we can't pay him off either. There's just no way left that I can buy you out of this."

Carefully, gently, he added:

"Or, anything for you to trade for my life?"

"What?" Jordan's jaw must have fallen open; Colin couldn't see.

He kept his eyes on Zara. "It's just... something, in how you've sounded about whenever Eric got too near me. Like you were checking on something. And he did knew where you were. So, has he been telling you he'd kill me?"

Zara's mouth opened. No sound came out.

He pushed on. "It's just, when he killed Leo, he only gashed me a bit, like that was a warning of what he could do. And tonight he tracked us to the school—"

Like my mother sent *a killer after me? What am I saying?*

He gasped "Sorry, I've got it all wrong, forget I ever tried guessing at this…"

He stared down at the table, trying to lose himself in the grain of that simple, wooden blankness. But he *had* said it, he'd taken everything his risks had made her endure and he'd used it to stab her, all on a sheer, stupid hunch…

Jordan said "You need to look up now." His voice was barely above a whisper.

Colin glanced up.

Zara's hands covered her face.

"I *didn't* tell him where you were tonight," she breathed. "I didn't. It was before that. I found the same list you did, and I told him that."

She looked out. Her eyes glittered tears.

"Before you found it, you see? This morning. I didn't know you'd be out there too. And he made me the same deal he offered you—I find him skein and he lets you live, so you had to be alright. And he had Terri too."

Colin tried to move, to touch her. His hands couldn't stir.

"He *showed* me. She almost spoke to me, I know it was her. All I could think was… we could still get out of this, if I could just keep you both alive… I couldn't, couldn't tell you…"

His hand reached her shoulder. She crumpled, and he drew her into a hug.

CHAPTER TWELVE

HIDEAWAY

He woke up slumped in a chair. Stiff, tired—the padded seat had looked so much more comfortable when there'd been no sunlight pouring in through the cracks in the window shades.

Colin held up his arm in the light, squinting. The pain from last night clung like a bad sunburn... but he could make out tiny marks or gashes all along his flesh. The skein that had done it lay in a mound beside him.

His stomach grumbled and ached with its own need.

Shower first, though. He forced himself down the bare corridor toward where that room would be. Some of the layout and Jordan's security system stuck in his head, from what he'd been able to learn last night. Faint rustlings and footsteps came from another room, someone else awake.

Jordan rolled into view.

His eyes were as hard at this hour as they were last night. "Your mother's digging a hole into her research. And Simms is back on the job."

How late did I sleep? "Where'd she stay, here or... Eric could still be after her."

"She can take care of herself. You? You still have to prove it," and he waved him on toward the bathroom.

Colin held his steps steady, and made it to the shower. The water was cool, soothing out some of the knots in his muscles, but he gritted his teeth when it touched his arm or leg. *Keep moving, back to business. I know we didn't do much real planning last night.*

When he was dressed again, he headed to the kitchen. Jordan sat there waiting. Instead of another word, he simply motioned Colin to the shelves.

Bowls and cereal lay in plain sight; that'd be fine if he just got enough of it into him. He poured out a bowl on the counter.

Before he dug in, he said "Look, I never thought I'd land Bea in this kind of trouble. Is she out there tracking Eric now?" And planning to shoot him? "Or looking for Terri?"

Jordan didn't say a word. He only lifted a hand and motioned at the food.

"I'm *sorry,* I mean it," Colin tried again. "I wanted to help chase a murderer down, and I couldn't stand knowing anyone else could die. And it turns out Terri was never dead, Leo got cut down right in front of me, and it's someone I called a friend who's doing it all…"

Jordan still didn't speak. Sure, excuses based on guilt and an empty stomach were no way to reach the sergeant.

Still, he went on "Just remember, Bea already wanted to cover up the skein and keep this off the record. Before I even met her—"

"So she turns her back on her badge and sucks me into it too?" Jordan didn't move an inch closer, but his tight-leashed anger made up for that. "All to keep this thing secret. And let *you* in on it."

And if she shot Eric in the back? Would that be going rogue or just removing the problem?

Colin flinched away from that question. Instead he said "She's trying to think what it would do, if you just dumped the skein out for everyone to see. The magic's got too many tricks not to wonder about that."

"Magic." Jordan's lip curled at the word.

"Look, whatever you call it, it keeps us alive! And it can—"

Talking wouldn't be enough.

Colin spun and scrambled away, dodged past a couple of rooms to the chair where he'd left the skein. He scooped the stuff up, like palming a pillow filled with liquid, and headed back.

"I just have to think it, see?" He held out his hand, palm up with the skein sprawling on either side. Without moving a muscle, he made it wrap around into a gauntlet and on up his arm.

"So?"

"So I had it brace my leg where it was hurt. It doesn't just support me, it moves when I want it to." He looked straight into Jordan's eyes. "Something like this could make you walk again—"

"Shut up!"

Jordan slammed a fist down against a counter door, and wood splintered.

"That thing is what's tearing the town apart. That's the thing that *took* my legs, and now you say it can give them back and leave thousands of other people stuck in their chairs? What makes me so lucky?"

"Sorry—"

"It patches up one person, and lets the world fight over who gets it? Now *that's* dangerous. *That* could be worth playing this case quiet, so we can finish up by dropping that thing in a hole so dark that nobody ever knows we had it!"

The words buzzed, hung in the air a moment.

A door creaked. Zara walked in—refreshed and wide awake, of course.

She turned to Colin, with a smile that simply ignored the storm Jordan had turned on him. "Ah, you're up," was all she said.

"Yeah. Listen, I'm sorry again for pushing you last night—"

"No, I should have told you about Eric."

"Yes, you should have," and the anger in Jordan's voice throttled back in mid-sentence, toward a simple warning. "But you," he added to Colin, "shouldn't be dragging confessions out of your mother."

"I know." Colin sighed, then turned back to Zara. "But, one other thing came out of last night. If Eric comes after you here, I found a way you could defend yourself."

Zara tilted her head, smiled. "Now, what have I told you about over-promising?"

"I know. But this one did a real number on me."

He set the skein down, and let it slide free to pile up on the counter. Zara watched, and Jordan narrowed his eyes in distaste, but Colin knew he wouldn't look away.

"All you have to do is remember this. You say—"

What was it? He'd only heard the charm once, and Leo had sounded too crazy to pay attention to. And that one memory was all he had...

"Got it. 'Night and day – *gratshay kodo* – far away – *gratshay kodo va.*' And I didn't need to use all of it." He touched a fingertip to the skein.

Nothing happened.

But, the effect could have come and gone. He kept the finger in place, and tried not to look at what Jordan's face must be showing about childish chant. "I think that's all it takes, to turn this against whoever's holding it. Try saying it."

Zara looked at him, and her eyes turned to his bruised hand. "And that's what burned you? Those words?"

"Please. This just might save your life."

She swallowed. *"Gratshay... kodo... va."*

Nothing changed. Not even a hint of pain, only the dry, flexible texture of skein ready to obey. What did they have wrong?

Jordan's voice broke the silence, and this time it was gentler. "Have you ever seen a hypnotist tell someone they were holding a hot poker? Enough belief can do very real damage."

"It wasn't *like* that. I was thinking the words might make the skein stronger, and I never considered that they could attack me instead. But that's what they do, it's some kind of a charm against the skein."

"A 'charm' that you got from Leo Tozer? But Leo never used it against his killer. Think, why would that be?"

"I don't know, Leo was babbling. He could have remembered the charm but forgotten what it was..." No, something about that didn't fit. "Or I've got the words wrong. *Gratshay kodo va—*"

Pain licked his fingertip, and he yanked back.

"What?" Zara gasped.

"It's not the wrong words." He grinned, held the finger up. His flesh shone angry red, but no worse than that. "If I'd had the whole skein on, it would have knocked me flat again. We're starting to get it."

Was it me, and all my practice? Did the charm need the kind of concentration he'd developed from shaping the skein? Or was it some other difference? Anyway, it could work.

It worked. A way to stop Eric... A different kind of jolt, a tingling, floating sensation welled up in him. They could shut Eric down, disarm him, deal with him without Bea turning assassin.

"We're going to do it," he breathed. "We're going to win."

"Cool down," Jordan said, but a crack of a smile showed on his face. "You keep talking about the weapon. The case is still about the man, and what Eric Rowe's after."

Zara laughed. "Except the weapon is what he's after. But, it might not be as a weapon. He's got Terri, and, the way she looks in that video... he could want the skein to heal her."

"He... could," Colin said. "Last night he said the skein was for her, and he even wanted to know how to make more of it, so helping her might take more of it than he's got. Or he could just want more for himself." He looked at Zara—Eric had threatened her too, but she still wanted to find a good side in him. "He's also killing, and he bullied Leo into telling people their homes were doomed... he talked like he thought they all were... he killed his teammate at work, that has to mean something."

"Simms is looking into it," Jordan said. "Myself, I think there's two things you keep missing."

"Alright, what?" Colin reached for his bowl of breakfast, and his stomach gurgled. Had he really let that blessed *food* just sit there?

"One is your sister." Jordan leaned forward in his chair. More softly he went on "This part I understand. She disappeared, and it turns out he's been hiding her, and she shows signs of abuse..."

Zara said "You don't have to tiptoe around it. He could be healing Terri, sure. But he's kept her hidden for years, and he could be the one that hurt her in the first place. That's not love, that's... something else."

"And it means he has a *place* to keep her." Jordan pressed a finger on the countertop, like pinning someone to a map. "I have friends taking that recording apart, and what we can trace from those messages. Terri was last seen at that church, so what happened in that quake? Someone must have seen something. The man's only invisible, not untraceable."

Zara nodded, slowly, deeply. "Thank you—"

"Don't." He flashed her a small smile, like he was powering through a moment of embarrassment. "This is the job, that comes with the badge. If you need something to be grateful over, try this after-hours protection you're getting."

"Believe me, I am—"

"The other question," and Jordan pushed right on, "is what's wrong with those dragon pictures? Vargas knew something about this skein, but half the times you've found it the clues have been in the wrong place. Someone does that, it looks like they want it *harder* to find a thing. So why still put the clues so close, or have other spots with none of them? Why mix it all up?"

"I know," Zara said. "I keep trying to put myself into his head, and I can't. It could simply be there's another code somewhere, about which dragons mark the spot and which don't, and we'll never know what it is if we don't find that key. Or there's some other reason—"

Colin's phone chimed. He grabbed it out, to see Bea's name on the screen.

"Yes?" His word shot out, too fast and too eager.

"I've got a lead on Eric. I wanted you to see it."

"Oh?" Her trust had him grinning—even though that sunk Jordan's face into a fresh frown.

"I could use your strength if it goes bad," Bea said. "And your insight. I'm almost at your driveway."

"I'll be ready."

When he hung up, Jordan shook his head. "Another off-the-books lead? And she's taking you along, *again?*"

Colin nodded. He thought of arguing that Bea still made her own decisions, or saying that none of them could keep him from going— Jordan could probably push a button and lock every door in the house. Instead he let the silence hang between them, nothing more to add.

Zara glanced between them, silent as well.

Bea knocked less than a minute later.

Colin scooped up his skein, and spared one glance for the bowl of cereal he'd barely started. Then a longer look and nod to his mother, hoping she'd be safe. And he was out the door and settling in the car before anyone else could speak.

Once they pulled away and settled onto the road, he glanced over at Bea. "Jordan hates it when you do this. Not that anyone could miss it."

"I can't apologize for how I see the case."

Her eyes stayed on the road. But, he could make out a twinge of regret in her tone, tucked away where most people might miss it.

She added "I'm hoping this is one time your presence won't be a problem for either of us. We're meeting Eric's boss Dennis Fields again, and I made it clear we can't have Eric walking in on us this time."

"Or anyone reporting that I'm still tagging along," Colin nodded. "You think he's got something good?"

"Could be."

And if Eric did find them again? They weren't ready to face him, not when they knew so little about the charm. They couldn't even risk it without disarming themselves of their own skein.

The streets glided by in the morning sunlight, half still like they usually were by now.

Colin wrapped his finger in skein, and glared at it, willing it to fade from sight. *Blur, hide, shimmer away*... If he could just find the key to invisibility, he could work on Bea's trick of looking *through* skein to spot a hidden enemy. But no matter what he pictured, the most his thoughts did was make it tremble.

His head ached. And his stomach shifted and burbled loud enough to hear over the car.

Bea reached down into her car door, and pulled out a packet of jerky. She handed it to him without a word.

"One more point for the planner," he grinned, and tore off the first piece. Skein work really did need fuel, magic or no.

He knew their destination at first sight: a small apartment complex that was being wedged in among the houses, still a fenced off, half-finished shell. He would have known it even without the green Gardner car parked alongside the work truck out front.

Dennis Fields stood near the entrance, talking with a woman in a suit and a man in work clothes. Bea drove past them at a steady, easy pace, and Fields's head glanced toward them once and then twisted away. Bea kept the car moving, and Colin had a moment to glance around at the houses along the street—how were those people so comfortable with Gardner buying up more space in their midst?

Bea pulled them around the turn of the block, out of their sight.

"What now?" he asked.

"We'll give him a minute." Her lip twitched in a smile. "I'm thinking it won't be long."

It felt longer than a minute, before Fields strolled around the corner and moved toward them. Just taking a typical walk, no reason for anyone to follow, as long as Eric wasn't there to notice.

He climbed into the back seat, and while the door was open Colin heard a drill whining back at the project.

"Thank you for seeing me." Fields could have been at just one more of a dozen business meetings in his day.

Bea started the car up. "You called me. And Rowe won't be anywhere around here?"

"That's right. You know…" In the mirror he shook his head, slowly. "I hate to think anything bad about one of my team. And Eric is one of our best."

"But you called me," Bea said again.

"He's the best. He understands, what we do depends on the willingness in each community. We find people who want to partner with us—did you see the reaction to the building we're putting up there?"

Stop stalling. But Colin kept his mouth shut.

"But Andy… Andy was the one who had the highest standards. 'Never take a deal any side is going to regret,' he'd say. When he was mentoring Eric, he had them turn down a few properties—until the owners found some damage in some of the beams." Fields wiped some sweat from his forehead, and a bandage flashed around one finger.

Colin said "Eric did it. That's what you think."

"Andy didn't say what he thought. Before his… accident."

"Accident?" The word was too much. He snapped "You look at the kind of *accident* that happens to people around Eric. And this is the girl who was going to marry him!"

He brought up Terri's recording and held the phone out for Fields to watch, in all her withered, fumbling horror.

Fields swiped away more sweat, and cast a nervous look around the street they moved by. "That's… I… I started wondering. So I asked about Andy and Eric, and those properties. And then… my car went out. It could have been much worse. A leak in the brake, they said it could have been a stone I kicked up."

Bea said "Or someone cut it, with just the right tool. You know where Eric was when it happened? What kind of schedule is he on anyway?"

"A busy one. But a lot of flexibility in it. He's even taken on the day-to-day work about a whole block on 12th Street until we move forward with that."

"Hold on, 12th and Rey?" Colin said. "That graveyard of fallen houses is yours? *His?*"

"Sure. We bought them all together after the quake, but our plans haven't started…"

"So," Bea said, "there's an actual deserted warehouse—or empty houses, anyway—that a kidnapper is supervising."

She pulled over and grabbed for her phone.

Her first words were "We've got a coworker of Eric Rowe's, who just dodged a suspicious accident. And Rowe's been managing some condemned property on 12th and Rey. How's that location match up with the phone data from those texts?"

For long moments there was silence. That had to be Jordan on the other end.

Then she added "The property's out of use now. Do we have Rowe's supervisor let us in, or can you get a warrant and make this airtight?"

* * *

A graveyard, he'd called it. At least if putting up a few warning signs and cheap chain fences around partly-collapsed houses counted as a decent burial. Colin stared out the window at a slumped-in roof here, a surviving but silent place beside it… They'd sat there for years, but he imagined he could smell the dust even now.

If Terri was in *there*…

If. He looked from one house to the next, trying to count the number of buildings on the block. Each one he set foot in could be its own deathtrap—but they couldn't be that bad if the town allowed them to sit there. He could race through and search them all right now. If she was there.

He glanced over at Bea, sitting silent in the driver's seat and watching her phone, probably checking for updates from Dennis Fields. She wanted them to wait, for the warrant and some reinforcements to sweep the block. Jordan went out on a limb to get this, she'd said.

I'm not waiting for his *sake.* Colin forced his fingers to stop drumming the door handle, his body to try resting with the same tireless patience she showed. They could be wrong, they could all be wrong about this place.

Instead he struggled with the skein around his finger again. Somehow, there had to be some command that made it fade away, instead of just ripple or sit like a useless lump, but all he could do was drill the headache deeper between his eyes...

He groaned. Of *course* he was trying to master this trick himself, all to impress the driven, fearless—beautiful—woman sitting beside him. *But I should know better than to try this the hard way.*

Before he could hesitate he said "You can make it invisible, right? How do you do that?"

One of her smiles crept over her face, and in that instant none of his pride mattered.

"Hard to describe," she said. "I give the skein a sort of twist inside it. I figured it had to be bending light to pass around me."

"I see. But, that's what I'll have to change," he added, and heard her chuckle.

He eyed the skein on his finger. Put a twist inside it, that bent light? He pushed, fumbled, strained his will at it, and it only clung to the same stubborn silvery green.

Instead he turned back toward the block ahead. A whole block of people's homes, that had all been cracked by the quake or sold for sitting next to those scars... would there be squatters lurking in some of them? Up here on 12th Street he could barely see any life in the blocks that did have people. Like too much of the Hillside.

"You really think Terri's here?" he asked. Like that *emptiness* could have its silver lining.

Bea barely looked up. "He needs a place for her, besides his home. Fields says this block isn't on record as his responsibility—"

The phone in her hand pinged.

A different kind of grin touched her face, something fiercer. She tapped the screen, then switched the phone onto speaker.

"There's your warrant," came Jordan's voice. "Don't make me regret this."

Colin's hand was on the door handle when understanding broke in him. Bea wanted the warrant instead of just Fields's permission, to protect her career, and to keep finding Terri a full police operation. *Without* him complicating the search.

But I'm her brother, we'd still find what we find if I'm there...

He slumped back against the seat with a wrench of breath. Down the street, a police car came in view, then another.

"Almost ready," Bea said, and her hand touched his arm.

She froze, looked at it. Colin searched her silent face for some sign, any sign, of what was passing behind those eyes.

She turned away and strode out to meet the officers.

Colin cracked the window, so he could at least hear some of what went on. Bea corralled the four uniforms with a few gestures, and commands so low he couldn't make them out. She sent two of them to keep watch around the streets, and led the other two straight into the first house.

The back of his hand brushed the car door handle—he'd never really drawn it back. He stared around the street for any sign of Eric, then held up his finger again and simply told it to fade.

The thought *sank into* the skein, sank partway and twisted. The green sparkled, glimmered, and his finger faded away into a shimmer of light.

He stared, afraid to blink, afraid to move his finger or shift his will from just how he'd touched it... The finger flickered and settled back into sight.

Outside, Bea and her team emerged from the first house. Alone.

The moment of disappointment pressed him down on the car seat, heavy and helpless.

—That was still just the first house, though. Colin clutched at his memory to recapture that sense of making the skein fade, to separate that sensation from the next instant's sorrow.

Bea neared the second house.

She stopped her team there. One sound burst through the morning air: a dog, no, two, more, savagely barking together. The search team moved on to pass that house.

What's she doing? Those can't be feral dogs or squatters in there, someone would have heard that much noise before and complained— Gardner would have them cleared it out, unless... And Bea was just moving *past* it?

In the next moment he wrenched the door open, dashed down the street. A part of him saw the police sentry on that side looking the other way for now, but he was already closing on the house. A simple one-floor place with a damaged, shoulder-high fence, and the clamor like a beacon from inside.

One of the police with Bea started to glance back. Colin ducked down, down behind some of the scraggly brush along the sidewalk.

Crazy, this is crazy, but they can't stop me—

When the cop looked away, Colin vaulted the stubby fence. A broken window peeked out on the side of the house, where the dogs' havoc spilled out into the air. One twist of skein caught the latch and wrenched it open.

The sound raged on, but one triphammer of rapid barks sounded like a repeat pattern, a loop of sound—the same false front continued unchanged even while he slid inside the house. That *had* to be what it was, and every sign of it drew him in faster.

Light seeped through the windows, enough to show plain empty rooms and cracked yellow paint. A musty thickness pressed at his nose, too late to fool him now. How could Eric be keeping her *here?*

He stopped just for a few breaths, to call out his skein and wrap it over his arm and torso. He wrenched open one door, a closet, and raced through the next room, the next.

The sound guided him. Even thundering within the closed space, the worst of it came from one last door, and he yanked it open.

The noise smashed at his ears, but nothing more. Instead he saw stairs, leading down, down to a basement. He pulled out the flashlight he'd gotten from Bea.

Bea. The thought shook through him: the police were waiting up there, ready to take this over and do it officially. *And drag me away for coming close, before I found a thing.*

His light touched a gray shape at the foot of the stairs. A loud-speaker, next to a squat little security console—the source of the "dog" pack sounds. A door stood just beyond it.

Teeth clenched, he pushed down the steps through the trapped, echoing essence of the sound. He stabbed at a button, and silence crashed down.

For one blessed moment he held his breath and hoped the echoes would fade from his skull.

A step creaked behind him. He whirled—nothing, no motion, no shimmer of Eric coming to trap him here.

The door inside was locked. An armored fist smashed it open, but it swung in with a whisper like foam sliding over foam. Sound-proofed.

Light shone from inside.

A *groan* touched his ears. One weak, half-coherent sound that could have been "Who…"

He rushed in. Feet stumbled over clean, clear carpet, but none of that mattered, nothing mattered except the voice and the glistening shape.

The figure lying there, with the chain to the wall.

So thin. Wrapped, *coated* in skein with only her face showing.

Terri.

CHAPTER THIRTEEN

SHELTER

He reached her side. Her head moved, lolling back to follow him, and he knelt down to let her see him. Her mouth stirred, but all he heard was her breath.

Her eyes... they shone, with something too bright for their layer of tears to hide. Sheer, piercing joy.

He opened his mouth, and no words came.

Somehow he looked away, enough to take in the rest of her. She could have been a bundle of sticks wrapped in green cloth, from what he could see of her. Why was she so thin, so weak—with *so much* skein?

A heavy chain ran from the wall to her upper arm. But the manacle glinted, lined with marks and scratches all around the metal, some of them cutting halfway through it.

She's still fighting. His eyes blurred and he wiped them clear, then tightened the skein on his fingers into claws. They slid around the metal shape, over and beneath it, and bit deep.

Eric put her in chains—he let that explode through his fingers. The surge of rage clamped his skein's grip shut. Metal tore, broke, fell away.

Now he could finally look around. The basement was nearly as empty as the rest of the house, but cleaner, brightly light by a single bulb set in a battery pack in the corner. He even caught a hint of air freshener, pine. Mostly faded but still lingering.

And the skein.

"This stuff comes off, now!" He shifted his claws, thinning them down to hooked shapes that might be delicate enough to peel Terri free.

She moaned. A single fierce gasp that left her head slumped and helpless, her eyes dim. A warning.

"Okay, sorry. Come on."

He hoisted her up on his back—*no, no, this featherweight* can't *be all there is to her!* She made one more sound then, a sigh that he felt against his body more than he heard it. A sigh that went all through her.

The steps stood just ahead, but he could have gone miles and not cared. He was at the top before he thought to look around for shimmers of danger, and he still caught no sign of Eric.

When the front door opened, he felt Terri's arms try to tighten around him. How long had it been since she'd seen sunlight?

One of the uniformed cops stood right outside. That cop turned and shouted, some meaningless words that had to be a call for help—a roaring in his ears swallowed the sound. Bea ran up, with a shocked, jagged look on her face.

Slowly, gently, Colin laid Terri down on the sidewalk, beside one of the black-and-whites.

Two uniforms closed in. One was younger, black, and he stared at Colin as he moved in to crouch by Terri. "You got her. Damn, you really got her!"

Far up the street, a voice called "Is she—"

"All of you keep back!"

The other uniform bellowed it at an old man standing up the street, like he could push him away by sheer volume. Then he marched right at Colin, tall and red-faced:

"Who are *you?*"

Bea spoke on her phone: "We found her, get that ambulance—"

Colin wrenched his gaze back to the taller cop. "I'm her brother."

"No, you're the goddamn civilian who walked all over a crime scene. How'd you even get here?"

Bea said "He's the reason we're here at all." Then back to her phone, "You tell them, keep Eric Rowe under surveillance—"

"You even think how much evidence you stepped in? How are we ever going to prove you didn't put her there yourself and this was your last chance to cover it up?"

The younger cop said "Ease up, he saved her. But she," and his voice broke, "she looks bad."

Colin spun. "How bad? How is she?"

"All wasted away. Conscious but nonresponsive, I think. And she's got injuries, I don't know what. Maybe you shouldn't have moved her."

"Oh God—"

A hand grabbed his shoulder and the taller cop spun him around. "Yeah, you might have killed her. Or killed our chance of getting the sonofabitch. What did you do, *roll* in the goop he kept her in?"

He slapped Colin's arm—the skein that coated it was still in view.

Colin waved an arm back at the house. "All you need is right back there! The chain he kept her on. The soundproof room. The recording of those dogs that scared everyone away. And your *witness!* Terri can tell you everything."

"Or she kicks off right here and we get nothing. You even think about that?"

"I *know*, but…"

He stopped, his lungs full of empty breath and no words, his head moaning *It was three years! Three years we thought she was dead— and now she's right here, I can't have blown it all…*

Figures moved at the corner of his eye. The old man standing up at the far corner, the woman staring from another side.

The younger cop was prodding at Terri's face. "Come on, can you hear me?"

Bea stepped forward, between Colin and the tall cop. "Enough. There's still a case here, and we're going to pull it together."

"We can *try,*" the officer snapped at her. "This is on you. My report won't cover for you, how you brought a victim's family here and he contaminated the evidence." He turned away.

"You do that," Bea said.

"Okay now, miss," the younger cop said. "I'm going to try to cut some of this off you…"

Bea turned to Colin, disappointment thick on her face. "You were going to let us handle this. I trusted you."

"Look, I *tried—*"

He choked off his rising roar as the younger cop's words penetrated. That man was bending over Terri with a knife and his other hand on the skein.

"No, don't—"

A blur of motion, out from behind the police car. A footstep ringing within a hushed instant. He began to turn back, too late, too late.

A shimmering form slammed into Bea.

She tipped, toppled, crashed to the sidewalk. *Not again, not again*—blood sprayed from her face, nothing from her chest, but the mirage blur swept on past her. And he dropped, Eric simply dropped himself flat to the ground.

"HANDS! Hands up, get away from her, now!"

The tall cop's face was beet red, as he clawed out his gun and aimed it right at Colin.

"No! He's there, see—"

He waved to where Eric lay, just a shimmering patch on the pavement. A dim shape, no more to draw the eye than if he were the sheen of some oil spill.

Bang!

"I said get your hands up!" the cop roared, and he swung his gun down from firing in the air to cover Colin again. "I got you cold!"

"I told you he's—"

The cop's eyes never left his target. Instead he stalked around behind Colin, shoved him forward, and slammed him against the house's chest-high fence. The force drove the wind from him and rocked his chin down to bang against the top of the bricks.

"Easy there!" called the younger cop.

"You check on her, call it in! I got him!"

Colin struggled to twist his head and keep Eric in view—the monster still just *lay* there letting it happen. The cop wrenched his arms back and broke his sight of the enemy.

"Officer down!" the other cop reported. "Unconscious, unknown injuries. Yes, not like the other person with unknown injuries."

Colin gasped "I never touched her! Will you just look—"

"Shut up!"

Colin went still, let the officer haul his arms down, and focused on keeping his head toward Eric. The faint shape was moving, pressed low and scuttling away up the street like a bit of vapor in a breeze.

If he gets out of sight before anyone looks, they'll never believe he was here at all—

Handcuffs snapped around Colin's wrists, biting into flesh and closing on the skein-coated hand.

"Done. Now, who's back there?"

And the cop pulled his hands away and spun clear of Colin. He stalked up the street, staring around.

Eric was gone.

But the cop advanced on the corner of the wall, gun out. "If you're there..."

Colin shouted "Don't! You two stay together—"

"I said shut up!" the cop snapped with one look back. Then he crept around the wall, hunched low.

Colin took a step after him, arms still locked backward. If that idiot cop would just *listen* instead of walking into his death—

No. Eric wasn't targeting their lives, he wanted his enemies locked up in a way that had nobody looking any further. If the cop decided he was chasing shadows after all, Eric won.

Bea lay limp, sprawled on the sidewalk. Still no blood except on her head. *I don't have a knife, so he made it look like I hit her.* But with that much blood on her skull... And Eric could come back for her and Terri later...

Terri moaned.

"Alright," the cop with her said. "I'll try to get this off you."

Terri moaned a warning. The cop's hands only pulled at the skein.

From around the corner, the other cop called "Nothing here!"

So that's it. Eric's trapped us all, and I can't let him.

Colin reached his right hand's fingers around the handcuff chain, and squeezed them shut, with the strength of his rage and his skein. Metal crunched and split.

The younger cop looked up from Terri at the sound, but Colin was already charging. He struck straight for the solar plexus, with just an extra nudge of skein force around his arm. The cop folded up and top-pled back.

He crouched down by his sister. "Eric'll be back. Can you stand being moved?"

"Yes."

Not some nod, not a moan, she could *talk*...

Sound scraped on concrete. He looked up.

Bea stared at him. *Toward* him, with her head just raised clear of the sidewalk and weaving from side to side, her eyes out of focus. But awake, alive.

"Bas...tard..."

The cop he'd hit dragged himself to his feet, fumbling for his gun.

Colin wrenched Terri up and threw himself toward the police car.

"Hol' on..." That slurred voice had to be Bea. Warning the cop, or him?

He dropped down behind the police car, the same cover Eric had launched his attack from. Terri's frail body still had some weight, even if his legs throbbed like they could run forever.

My legs. He sent the skein moving, sliding down from his arm and chest to fold over his legs. *All moving like a part of me. Now when I need it most.*

He leaped clear of the car.

The louder cop roared "Stop there!" but he was already running.

It was like riding a horse—and the one time Colin had tried that, the brute had gotten away from him and galloped clear down the corral with him fighting to hang on, to sway and match his own balance to all the jolting, thundering power in that gait. Except this time his body was the rider's but part of his *mind* was the horse. His mind shaped every step that pistoned him forward to crunch down on the pavement and fling him onward. While the rest of him fought for balance, and clutched the limp form in his arms.

Just a form, his sister. Thoughts of how much jolting she could take rattled away and fell behind, along with what and who he'd left back there.

An engine roared behind him. He twisted away to dodge through a yard, squeezing between trash and a pile of old boards. Junk and gravel twisted under his feet, but he danced clear and held his balance. The other side of the block lay just ahead.

When he burst out onto the street, another police car was already rounding the corner.

He raced on, eying the half-empty blocks ahead. So, find a place to dodge through again before they ran him down—but what then? He could hear more sirens moving out there. Bright morning sun washed away every shadow in the broad, open streets, and streaked his face with sweat.

The car engine roared behind him, closing in.

Hopeless! His arms felt like heavy, thickening concrete, carrying Terri with no skein to support them. *If I only had enough for invisibility... Terri's soaked in the stuff and I can't use it...*

A gunshot screamed by, so loud and high-pitched it must have torn right past him. He slammed a heel down to kick him sideways off the street, scrambling for the next space between houses.

Brush sprawled in his path. He rammed his strength down to fling him into a leap. *There've been no more gunshots, they remember I've got Terri, but they could forget again.*

He came down on open, clear dirt beyond the bushes and dashed between the houses. Faster, faster, any corner he turned could have Eric behind it—

His steps faltered, and he sagged over against a car parked in the street. The *same* street, the same row of houses he'd left. Dodging that bullet had him running back closer to the cops, deeper into their net. No police cars in view now, nobody in sight, but any second...

The little rust-brown car he leaned on was locked tight. He grabbed at his leg, scooped off a handful of skein, and hardened his desperation into a blade that he stabbed into the door's crack. Metal creaked, groaned against his resolve, and split. One more heave swung the door open.

He dropped down on the back seat's floorboards, falling on his back with Terri clutched to his chest. Something hard dug into his back, but he dragged his legs inside and pulled the door shut.

It barely fit.

The car had no room. He struggled, twisted, pressed the backs of his shoulders against the street-side door to bend his head just below the window—but his legs still sprawled out and stuck up in plain view for anyone in the street. Terri's limbs strayed everywhere.

A car engine moved outside. This car must have a window cracked somewhere—he could hear the shape gliding toward them, a slow prowling speed that could only be a police car. Trapped.

"Sorry, Terri..."

Focus.

The thought was all he had left. He shoved his thought, his need, at the skein that already coated his legs. He'd made this work once.

Heartbeat pounded.

If I'd just kept my head and broken into a house—

But he locked his control onto the skein and saw his legs flicker, fade from sight against the window. He spread the same command through his grip into the skein around Terri, and she faded as well.

He held it. Cramps twitched through his legs, and some tangle of metal that could have been a whole toolkit dug into his back against the floorboard. He could ignore all that, to just *make* their skein work as if it could turn all their trouble away.

The cruiser crept past them.

When the sound faded, he forced in a breath—in what room his chest had to breathe, anyway.

Terri's chest moved too, so shallowly he could only feel it, not hear.

"You holding out okay?" He spoke to the exposed patch of her face, that hung in midair among the weighted shimmer in his arms. She had to be okay, she'd *said* he could take her…

Her eyes stared back at him. They trembled half-open, almost swallowed in the dark circles around them, like someone holding on after days and days awake.

Her eyelids steadied. They lowered in one slow, deliberate blink, and the lines of her nose and mouth dipped down as well. A nod.

Colin forced another breath, and waited for his heart to stop pounding. Desperation had chased him into this trap, but now he needed a plan, a place to go.

He wriggled up a fraction and peeped across at the opposite window. A huge, round young man stood hanging clothes at a clothesline—right beside the car.

Colin squeezed his head down again, low as he could. As he moved, he heard another car rolling by, this one faster and pulling on past them before the fear could dig in.

His nose twitched—some kind of fruit, gone bad, just a trace of the smell in the cushions.

How many police were out here, hunting them down? How long before they had cops walking around, knocking on doors and looking in every corner?

But even if they got away... they had nowhere to go. The larger truth pressed in like a storm front, looming dark and *everywhere*. The police would hunt him—with so many of them searching now, even shooting at him, Bea must be too hurt to tell them who'd really hit her.

And he'd left her.

He swallowed an ugly, sour taste in his mouth, and dug underneath him for his phone. If he could reach her, or Jordan, they could start to dig their way out of this, some way that didn't put him and Terri completely at Eric's mercy—

"The phone. They could be tracing it, idiot!"

His fingers fumbled and dropped the phone once, but it only had a few inches to fall before he caught it up again. Then a bit of skein pried it open and he pulled out the SIM card and the battery.

Or they could have already traced it... *No.* He crushed that down, no use worrying about what he couldn't change and falling into just reacting again. Time to think forward.

Still, his fingers twitched. It would be so easy to click those back together and call, just long enough to ask how Bea was. *To know it's not all on me.*

Another car rolled by, at slow, searching speed. And right past their hidden, half-invisible shapes.

He looked at Terri's face hanging in front of him. "I finally get you back, and I can't even tell Zara."

Her eyes stirred with a spark of... amusement.

She got it, she was awake and *with* him. That made this tiny, rib-crushing cell of a car *their* place.

"Sorry. We'll find a way out. But all I can do is listen for them, if I try to look if they're right outside I'd have to stick my head up again—"

Oh. His head.

"Right. Of course I can hide my head, the same as Eric did." He grinned, wished he could get enough breath to laugh. "We'll find a way out, sure. I guess we'll find you a hospital, and I'll try to find a doctor who'll keep you quiet so Eric won't track you down."

"Nuh... no."

Her word jumbled—a clear breath through a mouth that struggled to shape the sound. Too much like Bea's dazed words after Eric hit her head. He pushed that thought away.

Instead he asked "No? No hospital?"

"Skein... keeps strong."

Strong? This *is Terri being strong?*

Colin stared at her. She was speaking and hearing him, awake, but she dismissed her own condition as long she had this stuff? What had it done to her?

But, it was Terri. He had to trust his big sister. He already had, when she'd told him he could get her away.

He sighed, and shifted back to the immediate problem. He scooped off a handful of skein from his leg—it left a patch of his thigh visible, but this wouldn't take long. It smeared down over his head and flowed to fit, *around* his eyes and covering the rest of him down to the jaw. Then he twisted slowly around and up to the window.

Another black-and-white prowled down the street, right at him.

He froze, locked the invisibility tighter. The car rolled on by, slower than any of the cars before. And a second police car crept along behind it.

Too many. If they had that many cops out, they'd be searching house to house soon, and car to car. Because they'd had two cops die already, and this time they'd never let someone get away with attack-ing another cop. Or him "kidnapping" Terri, when they didn't know how her real captor could reach through ordinary protection.

At least the cops drove *past*—but if he crept out now they'd be too close. If he stayed put, they'd tighten the net and catch them, or Eric would find them.

There had to be a way…

The police car turned.

Colin locked his will on the skein's effect, but the car turned, and its engine roared and it raced back and on past their hiding place the way the police had come. The other car raced behind it.

"They're *leaving?*"

Then he saw it, far up the road: a column of smoke puffing up against the sky.

Fire. Back where he'd found Terri.

"Damn him!" he said to her. "Eric's burning the place he kept you—*that's* why he never came after us. Burn all the evidence and he might get away with this. And I can't even go help fight the fire."

He took another look around the street. It looked empty now, but every minute would only bring more people to watch. They had no more time.

"Here goes."

He pulled the skein from his face and legs, and tucked it out of sight under his shirt. Then he slid around Terri and clicked the door open.

Just as the door of the house opened, and the oversized man with the laundry basket stepped out to look at him.

No, no, no… The sheer *luck* of it froze his brain, left him staring helpless. A young man, half of him swaying as he lurched to a stop. Startled eyes under the broad hat, blinking and staring at Colin and the car.

"You do that fire?" he said slowly.

Colin couldn't move. *Remember, remember days ago when I wasn't on the run, when I had no secrets. When I was someone like this, and I only wanted the trouble gone.*

"No. The guy who did it is after me," he said.

"Oh." The wide face nodded, and split in an awkward grin. "Better go, then."

Colin nodded back, knees suddenly weak.

His glance fell on the clothesline. One more trick Eric had used...

"Can I borrow that shirt on the end?"

"Sure. Too big for me anyway," he mumbled.

More like too small, Colin thought as he pulled it from the line. When he turned around, the big man held out his hat too.

Colin tried to pour a world of gratitude into his smile. He swathed himself in the huge, long-sleeved shirt and set the hat on his head.

When he reached into the car—*I'll send him the money for that broken door, I swear!*—and gathered Terri up, she blurred away at his first touch. Was that him controlling her skein now, or her?

He started away down the street.

One step at a time, that had to be the trick to making the change on the open street. With every step he spread his arms a fraction wider around their barely-visible burden, and hunched forward. The skein under his borrowed shirt crept outward, into a slowly spreading framework that stretched the cloth folds over him. By the end of the block, Colin's build was swallowed in the huge shirt and his shuffling gait, with the hat hiding the lines of his face.

He turned toward the edge of town. Two fire trucks and a police car screamed past him, but nothing slowed to stop him.

* * *

It took more than an hour, while the summer sun rose in the sky. With all his skein spread out to bulk up his figure, Terri's weight dragged at his arms and made each slow step its own battle. She hung there limply, breathing softly. He held on to that sound and told himself she was only asleep, as he trudged uphill toward the scrub trails.

His brain refused to stretch any further; he only knew that getting off-road had to be an advantage against more cars, to keep them safe until nightfall.

The open air filled his nose, a cooling breeze one moment and a whiff of dust the next. The hat sheltered him from the worst of the sun. Buildings and people thinned away and the road turned to gravel, until all he passed was a repairman up on a phone line.

Finally the road was clear. He stepped in among the scraggly trees and let the shirt fall limp, as the skein slid down to his legs again.

And he ran. Pounding over hillsides, weaving around carpets of brush and watching for trees, for cover, for clearer paths that would let him run and *run*...

Somewhere a mile into the hills, he sagged to a stop along a dried-up gully, where a handful of gnarled trees fought to hold onto life. He laid Terri down on the least rocky patch of soil he could find.

Hunger clawed through him. *I could have pocketed that jerky Bea showed me—*

Was Bea even alive?

The thought slammed down on him. The weight of it, and every other change he'd taken on, he'd been carrying them all the way up and fighting not to look at them as he went. He tried to sit down and his knees wanted to slip from under him.

No. No shutting down, not now.

He looked over at Terri, thin as a skein-colored shadow where she lay. One of her arms slid an inch along the pebbles, as if that was the most she could arrange herself.

He crouched down beside her. "Are you alright?" *Stupid!* "I mean, do you need anything? There's got to be water somewhere, that's safe enough. I think." He tried to remember what he'd heard about the streams up here. "Or I can find you some real food, if you need it now."

"No."

The word puffed out softly, clear. He swallowed, looked at her again. Whatever she looked like, his sister was *there,* aware of everything he did. Tired, struggling to shape her words, but aware.

"It's really you. It is. We lost everything when you died... and there was Eric looking right at us all the time and *lying...* "

He turned away as his voice broke. His fist flailed at his thigh, once, twice, he rolled away and drove that skein-coated fist into the ground. It sank straight into the earth, in up to the wrist, and wedged there until he worked it loose.

Terri breathed "Showoff." Her mouth curved.

Something lodged in his throat, that might have been his heart. *My God—she can't even move, and somehow she's* teasing *me.*

He rolled over to sit beside her, staring out across the hill. "Eric did it. He was looking for the skein—he tore down the House..."

The whole story began gushing out of him. The masked intruder. The skein. Leo—his voice broke again there. The texts.

When he got to those, Terri said *"Mine."*

"What?" He shook his head, he must have heard that wrong.

"The first." Terri's hand flattened against the dirt. Her shoulder hunched, her face contorted as she pried her head up from the ground.

Colin couldn't breathe. She could still move, she could—

Her elbow folded, at some angle no arm was meant to. A gasp tore out of her, and she thudded back down.

He caught at her, fingers desperate to hold her, to share the pain any way he could. Pain lay all over her face, gritting her teeth and making her breathing harsh.

It took forever. Or the longest, coldest minute of his life. Before her face eased back to something like peace.

"You're okay, you're okay," he said. "You don't have to talk. I think I get it—you said 'first,' so that's the first text. The one that said your dying wasn't my fault." Yes, that was the one.

"He… said." Terri's whisper could have been speaking around a mouthful of broken glass. "So… crawled to phone."

Her breath faded away. He blinked, blinked again as he felt the ideas coming together. "You mean, you did that? A phone, Eric left a phone where you could see it. And you tried to escape."

"Yes."

The gashes on her chain. That he'd had to chain her at all. After three years worn down like this, she could still…

"The first text was yours, you said," he heard himself babbling. "Not the others, then."

"No."

"You got out and contacted me once, so Eric sends all the rest to confuse me? Even sending your own picture."

Terri didn't answer. Her eyes still followed him, still awake, but she seemed to be saving her strength.

He laid back on the rocky ground beside her, and began telling her the rest. The Vargas House collapsing around him. All the ways Eric had lied and tricked and murdered.

And Bea. Every time Bea came up, he found himself saying more, a few words more about her, and then catching himself and trying to cut that short. Terri couldn't have missed that.

It all finished with their escape, and leaving Bea to bring Terri somewhere Eric couldn't touch her.

"So… I have to stop Eric. He started all this and he's tearing the whole town apart. You'll never be safe until he's finished. Somehow," he added.

He glanced over at her. Twig-thin, too weak to even scream when she tried to move…

He rolled over to face away. Bea's plan of blowing Eric's head off felt too good for the bastard.

Then Terri said *"Me."*

"What?" He twisted back to her.

"I started it." Her every whispered word sounded in perfect clarity. "Not him."

"What? No, no, you don't mean that." He reached toward her, jerked back from the fragile look on her face now.

Her lips trembled, more of her strength used up. "Qua... quake."

"How is that your fault? You didn't start the quake, you know that." He tried to laugh, but the sound came out shaky and nervous.

"No. I went in."

He frowned. "You went in. Into the church, when the quake hit, right. They said you were trying to save some sculpture. I knew that wasn't like you."

"I did." She stopped, drew in a slow breath. "Then... pillar. Cracked." Her lips stumbled over the last word.

"What pillar?" He leaned closer, chill spreading over him. "The original pillar at St. Mary's? What cracked it? You mean Eric did that?" *He can't, he* can't *be that monstrous...*

Her eyes went still. Her lips trembled, a motion that might have been "No."

"You did it? Or, did it crack on its own—"

She lowered her eyelids, twitching her face down. A nod.

He let out the breath he'd been holding. So, the church coming down had been natural after all.

Then she breathed one more word: "Skein."

"Huh? Skein was... was it inside the pillar? Holding the place up?" She nodded.

"I guess. Vargas kept doing that, we think. He had some good guesses about what places needed it most. But you just had to be there on that one spot, where it wasn't enough, and the place just..." He slapped a hand down on the ground.

"No," she said. *"Not till I touched it."*

His mouth opened, but he couldn't breathe. He snapped it shut, coughed, tried again.

"You... The skein was holding? Until you saw it, until you disturbed it? And that brought the church down—"

She moaned, twisted her head away, moaned again at the motion.

"Sorry!"

He brushed her shoulders with all the gentleness he had. She didn't flinch, and he held her there until the pain left her face.

"I'm so sorry," he said again. "Here, you want to rest a while?"

She nodded, one of her tiny eye-only nods.

"I won't go too far."

He stood up and crept away up the gully, thoughts whirling.

Terri had... she'd found the skein holding the church up, and her touch had brought it down?

Onto her, and the other nine people that had died.

And she'd *lived* with that, and her own mangled body...

Locked away by Eric. Eric must have found her in the ruins, gotten her out...

Of course. He found her and the skein, and that's all that's kept her alive. While he's locked her away, and hunted for more skein and said it's for her, while he cuts down everything in his way...

Colin stomped up the hillside, slamming his shoes into the dirt that was all he had to hit right now. It did nothing to beat down his rage— by the time he halted he felt more like he'd shaken off all his hopes instead and ground them away.

Terri's form was a thin figure far down the slope, just close enough to still make out among the sparse trees, when he stopped.

He yanked the skein off himself and dropped it to the earth. For a moment he wondered if even this was too close to Terri, if he could risk any chance at all of disrupting her own skein. But, just sit and do nothing?

He touched the pool of silver green. *"Gratshay kodo va."*

Pain flared and he yanked his finger clear. The skein seemed to be rippling where it lay. He brushed it again and it still stung, weaker this time. But he'd seen that if he said the spell first, the skein would already be normal by the time he touched it.

The spell worked—but why hadn't it worked when Zara said it? They had to get it right.

He swept his gaze around the slopes, miles of open space and patches of brush and trees, all baking in the sun. Hiding up here like an animal was all he had left, him and what Terri had become. Because of Eric.

Eric. There was no way back except finishing that murdering bastard. *Disarm him and lock him up, rip his head off from behind... maybe I don't care which, if it just stops him.*

His breathing rasped in his ears, too harsh and too quick. He fought to pull his thoughts back into line. Deal with Eric, yes. Get Terri to a hospital where Eric wouldn't find her—or stop Eric first. They needed help, they needed *Bea,* or Jordan or Zara. And Eric could be stalking them all.

His fist slammed down onto the skein. *"Gratshay kodo va!"* The pain tore into his knuckles, and he drove his will against the stuff: *stop, stop, shut it down!* He'd done that before too, did that mean Eric could...

The pain faded away, the skein calmed by his touch.

Oh. Touch.

Understanding broke through him and spilled out in a laugh.

"Of course. I have to touch it to control it anyway, so of course the spell only works on skein I'm touching. Idiot."

That could be the key... and he'd only guessed it *now,* when he had nobody with him to test it, nobody to try the spell on him at a distance except the person who didn't dare mess with her own skein. He barked laughter again, and the sound sent a bird fluttering out of the trees.

Even if that was the answer, using would mean disarming himself and getting his hands on Eric. If he could even find him, or get near him without being locked up...

He trudged back down the slope to where Terri lay. Her frail arms stirred against the ground.

He leaned down close, and her eyes moved to watch him.

"How are you doing? I keep thinking we should wait here for night, if that's alright. And then slip back into town."

Her lips twitched. "Yes. Find Eric."

"What?" Surprise made him jerk back. Of course he had to settle things with Eric, but hearing the battered Terri think the same way shook him.

She said "Bait."

"No! Don't you think like that, you just got away from him! I'm not letting you anywhere near him."

Somehow, her weak voice sharpened. "You? Your choice?"

So determined, when she couldn't even raise her head from the ground, and she was giving him orders? *Because her choices are* all *she has left, that and hoping that I won't take them away.*

"But I... I can't... you need a hospital!"

"He'll come."

"A hospital! We'll hide you there, we'll keep you under guard. If we haven't nailed Eric first."

"You'll try," she said.

"We'll do more than try, we'll get him! I've even got a new weapon—"

He stopped. In the sudden silence, a puff of wind rustled the tree above them. This made twice in a few minutes that he'd missed the obvious. Being on the run must have him more rattled than he knew.

"I'm trying to figure out this weapon," he said. "And you know about the skein, don't you?"

"Some. From Eric."

Some. If she had the strength to talk normally, he'd have picked her brain from the start. "What I've got is a, a spell, I think. From Leo. I say the right words and the skein, let's say, burns me, until I can

command it to stop. I think it only works if I'm touching the skein."
He swallowed, and said "You know anything about that?"

"Burns you?" she said.

He held up his hand. The fine crisscross of welts on it had new
gashes where he'd been testing.

Terri stared at it, stared, her eyes growing wider. Some kind of understanding had to be pooling behind them.

She said "Don't. Never use it on him."

"*What?* But—I almost did once, I tried it without touching him,
and it twisted my own skein. He still ran away!" Colin knew he was
babbling. But if Eric came after Terri again? If he tried to kill again?
"If I get the chance to hit him with the words, why wouldn't I?"

"Then he could use them. Worse."

Colin squeezed his eyes shut. Terri made sense: the last thing they
needed was to give Eric one more weapon.

He'd have to survive it first...

They sat quiet, waiting for the night.

CHAPTER FOURTEEN

FIGHTING MONSTERS

The minutes ground by and slowly sank into hours. Colin sat with the skein next to him, unwilling to even practice with it—not when his stomach already rumbled and tore at him, with nothing but more waiting to fill it.

What he did was wrack his brain for what he might say, to Bea, to Zara, to the police, to anyone he met, or for ways to start again with Terri. Like *As long as you're alright,* or maybe *Can we just get Terri safe first?* Plotting out different conversations was the only way he could scrabble for some advantage in what would come, and every time he tried that much, his imagination derailed after a few words.

A few times he saw people in the distance, strolling or exploring the hills for whatever reasons brought them there. Colin watched each of them, ready to grab the skein and pull Terri away if they got too close.

The sun was just touching the horizon when he saw a young couple below, with backpacks and an easy pace and all the other signs of a hike.

It was one chance to act like Zara's son again, instead of a failed wannabe cop. He trotted down to meet them.

Not too fast... the trick had to be not making any dangerous or odd signs from the start, if they were going to trust a stranger out in the wilds. He gave them a wave and his best smile. "Hi."

"Um, hello." The man, thin and older than he'd looked, edged back half a step. The woman stood behind him, so small she almost disappeared there.

"Really, I don't mean any trouble. It's just that my phone died, and there's someone I *really* need to check in with." Understated but true—he hoped it worked. "I don't suppose I could use yours."

"Well. I suppose."

The man held out his cell, but as he did he flinched back. His gaze locked on Colin's hand and the fresh marks on it. The woman gave her partner a nudge, and he handed it over.

"Thank you, believe me."

They might be bugging Zara's phone by now. Instead of calling he sent her a quick text: *Hope you're alright. When you wrap up the meeting, I hope you're in a place where you can look around and face what you thought you lost first.*

That ought to get the message across. If the police even saw that text, they wouldn't know it was from a complete stranger's phone. And they wouldn't know Zara normally finished her last meetings at nine at night, or that "face what you thought you lost first" meant Terri and the church she'd disappeared from.

He held the phone back to the couple. As he did, it rang in his hand.

He took a step back from them, catching their surprised, suspicious looks as he took the call. "Hello?"

"Who's there? Is that you? You're safe?" Zara's voice shook, fighting to hold in its eagerness.

"I'm fine. And, I'm with Terri."

"Oh *thank God...*" Her joy surged into his ear, fierce as a sudden kiss. Then her voice steadied. "Now: Bea is recovering too. All the same, the police aren't listening to her about you. And... I've gotten some other secret messages, that have to be from Eric."

"Eri—" He clamped his mouth shut to glance at the hikers, and lowered his voice. "So he's still free? You mean there's no evidence left on him, nothing?"

"Not much, and he's got lawyers. But this is the problem now—"

"Careful. You know they could be listening. The police."

"I wish they would! You see, Eric's boss Mr. Fields wants to meet me about buying the Vargas House site. Tonight. And after he called, Eric said I have to meet him or Eric will go after him next."

Blood pounded, hammering in his temples so he could barely hear. He saw the hikers flinch back another step, and realized his face had gone to a snarl.

Even after all this... Eric's still trying... "Is there *anything* he doesn't want destroyed?"

"I'm not sure he even cares," she said. "It lets him draw me out, and then he can threaten me again for whatever he wants. But if I don't come, somebody else pays for it."

"Well you know you can't go! Or, you can't go alone."

* * *

In the end it was just walking down the road at the edge of town, as the night deepened around them. No coded messages or sneaking through the streets, not when Zara had insisted they could simply arrange their meeting. Colin stood back in the brush with Terri, watching the darkness for any sign that he'd have to dash away.

Then Zara drove up.

Then she climbed out.

Then the control in her face crumpled, and she sagged to the ground sobbing with her daughter in her arms. Colin hugged them together, and Zara cried as if she'd never stop.

Until she did. Until she lifted her head from her children's shoulders and gasped out "We... we have to go. Eric, he just changed the meeting... it's soon. And he wants it right at the House."

Meeting at *the place he'd destroyed?*

Colin's arms tightened around his family. "Damn, damn that ghoul! He just had to double down on scaring you?"

"Or…" Zara heaved herself to her feet. "It could be in case Bea and the police are watching their office after all. All that, all of it, could be to throw them off. That and scaring me anyway."

She wrenched open the car door and they tumbled in. Colin remembered to buckle Terri into the back seat and sit beside her, instead of holding her on his lap. Zara handed him a breakfast bar before she started the engine.

Bless you forever. For endless moments the whole world was simply his teeth tearing into the oatmeal-nut energy his stomach craved, and watching his mother steal dazed, blissful looks back at Terri.

"I think we're alone in this." Zara's voice still had a choked sound to it, that she tried to talk through. "Unless Bea can convince the police that Eric's last-minute meeting change is really happening. They've been keeping a close eye on her, and they act as if they'd rather think that attack knocked all the sense out of her."

Colin's appetite was gone. "But you said 'they think'? Have you seen her? You're sure she's alright?"

Zara… chuckled.

"What? What's so *funny* about what happens to the best defender we have?"

Zara slid him a sideways grin. "She's fine. The funny side is you acting as if that's all she is to you."

"What—"

Terri whispered laughter with her mother.

You want to do this to me now? He sighed "Don't you think we've gotten her in enough trouble?"

"I don't know," Zara said. "How much trouble do you want her in?"

He shook his head. "Bea Simms is the best, bravest person I've met in years. Will you stop trying to distract me—"

The word made him glance out: The streets around them were wrong. Too many lights glimmered in the darkness.

"Stop trying to *distract* me," he said, "from where you're driving! We're not heading for the House."

The little glances Zara had stolen toward them were over now, and her eyes stared straight ahead. "We will. As soon as we stop at the Hillside Clinic."

"To drop Terri there, you mean."

"No!" Terri hissed.

"You need help!" Zara said. "You need—"

"NO!"

Terri's voice rose and lashed at them, though her body still sat limp at Colin's side.

"You can't do that," she said. "Eric kept me... locked up like some prize possession, for years—I never im... imagined," and she wheezed for breath, "that you'd treat me the same way. I *know* how much I can take. But, how long before you miss that meeting and he kills that man?"

"Terri..."

"How long?" she snapped. "Before you get someone killed, for me?"

Zara stared down the road, her face still. She sniffed back a sob. Then she whispered "When did you get so brave?"

The car swung around.

A moment later she added "But this is just so I meet their deadline. You stay out of sight, understood?"

"I can help with that," Colin said. *When did I get pulled into bringing Terri so close to her kidnapper?*

He shifted in the seat, to fish out his phone and the pieces he'd removed. He fumbled them back together; this was no time to play it safe.

As he worked, he muttered "You really think Eric will kill his own boss, if you don't give them the House? That's just... vicious, and reckless. Is he really pointing at *everyone* and saying they're his hostages now? How do we fight that?"

"The text seemed like he meant it," Zara said.

Terri added "Have to think he could." Her voice was hollowed out, after the strain of saying so much—a better proof of Eric's menace than any words.

Colin added "Does he really want the Vargas House that much? It could all be a plan to get at us. And at Terri, to get her back. So whatever you say to him, all we really want is to get you out of there safe. I'll be watching you, I'll try to catch Eric if there's a way—"

Right. He should have mentioned it sooner:

"And we may have a way. Remember that spell? I think it works on any skein you're *touching.*" He looked at Zara up in front. "That means if he makes a grab for you, you've always got one weapon."

Terri added "Only if you have to." The words sounded torn out of her, whether that was from her exhaustion or from mentioning the risk at all.

The Vargas House loomed on the shadows of the hillside ahead. If that silhouette could ever be the House, with one whole side of the shape and their lives just *missing.*

Zara stopped the car, well short of the shattered building.

"Okay," Colin said. "I'll move in from here. And tuck her out of sight."

He stepped out and scooped up Terri. He shut the door, but paused beside Zara's open window.

"Oh yes—and, there's a man near that burned block who needs his car door fixed. I... cut it open."

"We'll help him," Zara said. "But if you let something happen to me here, you may never get that car repair off your conscience—"

She broke off the joke and reached up, leaning out through the window to touch their faces, and pulled herself up to hug what she could reach of them.

Then the car headed on toward its destination, and he stepped off the road and made his own way toward it. Terri's blur melted into the darkness as if he were holding a bag of tangible night—a reminder that made him sweep his gaze through the shadows again and again, hoping Eric wasn't setting his own ambush.

Up ahead, Zara's car settled beside one of the Gardner-green vehicles. Lights shone just inside the entrance of the... ruin.

Terri gave a shocked jolt of breath. Colin eyed the half-shattered structure as he drew closer. *Eric did this. Just to cover his escape, or had he always wanted to wipe it out?*

The entrance rooms were intact enough for Zara to step through the door. Colin crept up when it closed, and drew skein over his head to hide him while he peeked through its undamaged window... Eric's trick again.

"—very grateful to you for seeing us. And I really apologize for the... overdone setting." That was Dennis Fields, and he cast a nervous look at Eric behind him as he waved Zara deeper into the foyer. "I never expected you'd agree to meet here, or now."

"That's quite alright." Zara's steady voice carried all too well, with all the gaps in the building.

"There should have been one more person here," Fields went on. "But it looks like our lawyer's been held up, so it will only be us." His eyes moved again, like he wanted to keep an eye on Eric but wouldn't risk turning around.

"I imagine so. Your lawyers must have their hands full these days." She looked straight at Eric, and venom seeped from her voice.

Colin pulled back. He looked around him at the damaged, half-clear pieces of the House... over by one corner lay a tarp over a pile of something.

He crept toward it, silent as he could. He lifted up one corner to reveal a mound of collected wooden fragments, and laid Terri on it, gently as he could. "I'll protect her, I swear."

She nodded, and he set the tarp over her. It would be better cover in the darkness than trusting everything to that shimmer.

He moved back to watch through the door.

Fields stood over a small table in the foyer, where he'd set up a light. He had a bundle of papers under his arm, but he ignored them as he spoke. "Of course we're talking about property held by your Foundation, so this wouldn't be a simple sale." He smiled to her, and it looked honest, even reluctant. "We're more hoping you can cooperate with us on this."

"Of course," Eric added. "You're always the person we'd prefer to work with. Leo Tozer would never have listened. But then, I expect his share of the trust has reverted back to the Foundation." His toe tapped a briefcase by his feet.

Because you *killed him, no matter how polite you sound—*

Standing this far from Eric was useless. Colin needed to get in closer, behind him, ready. He spun away and crept around the side of the shattered building, picking his way in the night through the debris and the forest of warning markers.

When he reached a clear patch, he stopped and yanked out his re-assembled phone. Bea's number went straight to voice mail.

All he could do was whisper "We're here at the Vargas House— me and Zara *and Eric!"* and hang up.

He reached the House's back door and moved in. Closing the door should have shut off the light from outside, but the shattered ceiling let it stream in, enough to pick his way along the corridor without sending some bit of debris rattling ahead of him. He needed to be in position to grab Eric.

The battered House lay still, tomblike. He could just make out the words ahead:

"—not be taking over anything," Fields insisted. "Our interest is in rebuilding the Vargas House as it was."

"And why would you do that?" Zara said.

Colin eyed a fallen bench sprawling in the corridor. At least the light from above was enough to step clear around it and keep silent.

"We believe in cooperation here," Fields was saying. "We'd welcome a chance to partner with the most respected people in Rayo Hill. On your side, you'd have some obligations to us, but I think you'd find them quite comfortable."

Something *creaked* above—Colin froze, but the sound went still.

"And if I'm not so comfortable?" Zara said.

Eric spoke more softly. "Then we'd enforce those obligations. But all we want is to work together to improve this town."

Colin moved toward a pile of rubble ahead, crouching low. But the nearer he came, the higher the pile looked. Too high to leap, too noisy to crawl onto.

He blurred his head and peeped over, to the room beyond.

Zara said "I've heard your promises. What is it you really want?"

"Improving this town *is* our mission." Fields brushed the table he stood at, as if that could keep the conversation professional.

"Is it *yours?*" Zara looked straight at Eric. "Which Eric Rowe am I talking to? The family friend, or the Gardner buyer, or the one with Terri or…"

"All of them." Some kind of hidden pride peeped through Eric's voice, like a glimpse of a blade. "The one who saves people from themselves."

And he took a step, a small step, behind Fields's back.

"By destroying it all and taking over?" Zara said.

"More accusations. You might want to be more careful."

Eric's smirking tone made Fields shoot him a warning glare. But when he turned back to Zara, Eric flexed his fingers out in one claw-like gesture, hidden from his boss. A reminder for Zara to see, a ready threat.

"We are trying to negotiate here—" Fields began again.

Colin wrenched himself away from the barrier. He needed to be *in reach* of Eric, not stuck back here listening. He turned back toward the corridors to move in from the other side.

"Yes, let's negotiate," Eric said. "And bring some more of the most respected leaders in the Hillside into our plan. I wonder what the Gardner partners would think about your soft-pedaling this..."

Step by step, Colin crept back between the dim shapes and objects that lay scattered on the floor. The voices behind him grew fainter, but their volume and passion were all he had to mask any sounds his feet might make. The smell of dust lingered in his nose.

"...my department... successes..." Fields was saying.

"Of course... but they've been taking an interest... I think they see my potential."

And Colin reached the foyer's second doorway. The skein around his head hid him as he peeked around.

Eric, Fields, and Zara stood all of ten feet away.

"You're disappointing me, Eric," Fields said. "You force your way into these negotiations, and now you antagonize the person we want to impress?"

He moved away, a step out of Eric's reach. *Good for you*—Colin crouched ready, hoping against hope they could still get through this without him having to lunge in.

Fields turned back to Zara. "I hope you can ignore him. We do want to support your place in the Hillside. But, I have to say that re-building all this would be expensive."

"When destroying it is cheap?" Zara said.

"I'm... sorry that you believe any of us could do this." Fields made a slow glance around the crippled building, and Colin ducked his not-quite-invisible head back. "But I suppose the simple fact is, you can't restore this on your own."

"Don't be so sure."

Fields laughed. "Yes, I could be wrong. But, can we get past some of the ugliness, and let me ask you to *consider* your foundation working with us? As a partnership, for all of us?"

"Partnership?" Zara said. "You really don't believe me, how much that man next to you took from me?"

Eric growled *"You took more."*

His flash of rage stabbed at Colin, tensing his legs, clenching his skein-coated fist. One move, one move from Eric and...

Fields snapped "Enough! Eric, be *quiet.*"

"No, let him talk," and Zara turned to glare at her enemy. "You have something to say?"

Eric only folded his arms, back under control.

"Again, I apologize," Fields said to her. "I should never have let him come, no matter how he... insisted. I just hope we can still reconsider talking somewhere else, someday."

As he focused on Zara, Fields took a step behind him.

"Consider it?" Zara said. "Of course I never thought much of your offers, but now I actually might think about it. If I knew the terms were under your control."

"Well... of course they would be." Fields looked at her a moment. "I'm the project head, and we'd offer full transparency—"

"I mean *that creature,*" and Zara leveled a finger at Eric, "stays out of it. No hanging around sneering, no voice in the agreement. And none of your lawyers fighting to shield him from what he's done. Then I'd consider it."

Fields laughed. "After tonight, I think we'd be happy to. Our legal support for any team member is part of our policy, but only as long as he's with us—"

He stopped. He stepped away, toward the front door.

Colin heard it too, from how Zara had left the door cracked open. Cars, driving up outside.

Fields opened the door. "Police? This might be a good time to have them around."

He walked outside, waving them up as he moved out of view.

Something *snarled.*

Colin turned back to see it—Eric rushing at Zara, his hand clamping over her mouth.

Time froze.

Colin's fist and skein clenched, but he stared at Eric, looking for his target's own skein.

Something silver-green shone above Eric's sleeve, on the hand that was only *clutching Zara's arm—*

Skein, ready to kill them all.

If I used my fists.

Colin tore free of the frozen moment, and reached up and yanked the mask of skein from his face. It and his gauntlet fell to the floor.

He charged.

Eric still faced away from him, struggling to subdue Zara. That face was just beginning to glance around, when Colin locked his hand around the skein on that wrist.

"Gratshay kodo va!"

Pain flared and burned under his fingers, stinging him and stinging Eric. The killer wrenched at his hand, but Colin squeezed tighter around the pain and snarled the spell again.

The little man flailed—still too able to move, but weak, too lightweight against his fury.

Sounds, voices, moved beyond the door.

Zara wrenched free and smashed a kick at Eric's leg. Colin twisted their enemy up, and swept him across the room to slam him into the wall with a fierce, joyous *whack.* His foot knocked over the briefcase Eric had left.

He pressed Eric against the wall, and stole one glance around. Zara stood safe.

Bea charged into the room, gun in hand. His mouth opened to call out to her.

She raised her gun and took slow, careful aim. She fired.

Eric's hand, his free hand where it flopped against the wall, split open in a shower of blood.

Colin stumbled back. *Away.*

Eric slid down the wall, slumping toward the fallen briefcase, without a sound. Bea fired again to spray his upper arm with red.

Her gun moved one more time, to cover the back of his head.

Then she swung it up and stepped back, leaving Eric curled up on the floor grunting in agony.

A cop, a huge figure in black, rushed up behind Bea and wrenched her gun away. Colin stared at Eric—*he really kept most of his armor off, he never thought Bea would pounce on one weak spot, whatever it cost her...*

He reached Zara, caught her shoulders and traded a rush of *I'm alrights* with her. Other cops swarmed in, and joined the first in dragging Bea down.

"Don't hurt her!" Colin yelled. "She was saving us!"

Bea snapped "Eyes on *him,* the prisoner! He's still a cop-killer!"

Another officer stepped in front of Colin. "Alright you, back away. Aren't you the one—"

Zara said "He was protecting me, from that killer! They both were!"

One cop knelt over Eric. "His hand's ruined, but he's conscious. You let me see—"

Bea yelled "Cuff him now! Watch him—"

Two cops hauled Bea up and dragged her outside. Colin stared after her, turned back to what was left of Eric.

Eric's hand moved.

Teeth clenching, he brought his remaining hand into a pocket and slipped out a taser prod. The cop on him spasmed, grunted, collapsed.

"No!" Colin started toward them.

The cop in front of him stumbled into his path, staring back and forth between Colin and Eric but still stuck right in his path.

Eric's hand flipped open the latch on his briefcase. And thumped down inside it into a mound of skein.

Colin slammed the cop aside, but the officer twisted in his grip and spun him around. Colin had one glimpse of silver and green power surging over Eric's body—

Something smashed into him. The world fell away, he hung in the air, drifting, drifting...

He crashed down along the floor, numb and weak and *I never saw him charge at me.* Swirls and flashes danced through his sight.

The monster in skein, seizing Zara, hand over her mouth again.

No police left standing.

Then the enemy leaned in close, through the haze in his sight. Pain clawed and twisted at Eric's voice, as he said:

"You took her! Now, you bring Terri to the church."

And he and Zara were gone.

CHAPTER FIFTEEN

BLOODLINES

No, no... pure need shoved Colin to his feet, faster than his numb legs could push him along. He heaved himself down the corridor, the way Eric—and *Zara!*—had vanished. Gone, no sound but the dazed, angry voices of the police behind him.

His skein lay on the floor where he'd left it to launch his "rescue." He scooped it up, splashed it over his legs, grateful for one thing that still did what he needed. How could he let Eric get away? And that *voice* before he left, was the man even sane any more?

"You... you hit me!" one of the cops behind him said, swaying on his feet.

Colin waved down the corridor. "Not me, didn't you *see* him? And Eric's got my mother!"

"You were the only one there. Not that tiny little cripple—"

"But," the other cop cut in, "that 'little cripple' pulled a taser on me! And where did Simms's gun go—"

Colin rushed past them out the front door. Plunging into the night left him blinking, trying to separate the shadows of the steps under him from the glaring lights of the police cars, and the figures clustered around them.

One figure stumbled toward him, with Fields's voice. "What is *happening?* Talk to me, someone!"

He saw one cop pacing up the street looking around, and another speaking on his radio. Not enough, not nearly enough.

Colin charged for the cars' pool of light. Bea stood there, hand-cuffed, in the midst of a milling knot of other cops—staying near her but not sure if she was still the threat.

I can answer that. He looked straight past the others to Bea and said "Eric grabbed Zara! They're gone!"

Bea's head slumped, silhouetted in the cars' lights. "So he *could* still get up."

One cop, a woman, grabbed at Bea's arm. "You mean after you blew his hand off?"

"Look, he got away!" Colin said. "Bea—"

"Colin da Costa, here again," the cop said. "You already attacked her and ran once—"

"That was Eric! Bea tried to stop him this time, but now he's gone!" Colin waved his hand around the dark streets.

Another officer growled "We're bringing both of you in—"

"Bea!" Colin stared past the others, uniforms and detectives, to the hunched, unmoving figure in their middle. "He's... got... Zara! I need your help!"

The second cop stepped in front of him. "She's not going any-where."

Fields's voice came from the rear. "Will somebody please explain what's going on here?"

"Him."

That was the cop Eric had taken down with Colin—he still had his hand to his battered head, but his voice was firmer now.

"Da Costa there was fighting Eric Rowe. Then 'someone' shot Rowe," and he paused a moment, like he was afraid to say her name out loud, "and da Costa must have changed his mind and covered Rowe's escape. It's the only way they could *hit* us like that—"

"Eric did that, Eric! Bea—"

Colin cut himself off. The cops had seen Bea shooting a prisoner, he couldn't keep talking just to her. *And we're wasting time!*

He turned to face the officer Eric had hit. Calmly as he could, he said "You all came out here because Eric's a suspect, right? To protect Zara and Fields? Well, now he's grabbed Zara."

The cop leaned in to glare at him. "With two bullets in his arm? *How?"*

Colin looked at the cop standing behind that one. "And you, you're the one who got tased even after Eric was shot, right? That didn't stop him then." He turned to Fields. "And you saw how Eric was tonight— he's cracking, isn't he? Didn't he force you to meet Zara out here?"

Fields looked at him a moment, then nodded. "He did. And I would call him unstable, yes."

"Unstable. And he threatened you?"

"Yes." Fields's voice was firmer now.

"And, he held my sister prisoner for years. And you're investigating him for murder. You *know* all this."

"He's right," Bea said.

She drew herself upright. She looked straight at the woman cop, the tall one who'd challenged her first.

"Of course we know how dangerous Eric Rowe is. You got tased?" She glanced at that officer, then back to the woman. "He did it, and now he's gone with Zara da Costa. And you're still standing around here."

The cop Eric hit rubbed his head again. "You keep saying he—"

Colin snapped "Because she knows what Eric can do! Just let her go—"

"I don't matter now," Bea cut in. Firmly, evenly as if she were some lawyer pushing through a jury's resistance, she said "Zara is the one the clock's ticking on. You saw me shoot a prisoner, yes. So take me away or let me go... but at least ask yourself what kind of man would be *so dangerous* that I'd choose to shoot him. And he *still* got away! So, can you just lock me in a car and go after Rowe already?"

"Yes!" Fields said. "Just go get him!"

The tall woman stood still, her face blank and hidden in the cars' lights.

Then she gripped Bea's arm, and waved the other cops toward Colin. "That's enough from both of you. We'll find Rowe, and get the whole story when you're all locked up—"

"He's got a gun! Up there!"

That wild howl of a voice could only be Terri.

And if she shouted right at that moment...

Cops crouched or stared around. "Where?" "Up where?" "You take the—"

But Colin scrambled toward the shout. He dove between the scattering ranks of cops, skein driving his steps further than any legs could move.

A dim shimmering lay across the steps up to the door. Colin dashed for that shape, forcing back any thought that he might have read the timing wrong, that that shape could be anything except...

Terri appeared. She blurred into sight as he dashed up, and melted away again when he scooped her into his arms. Two figures in black, cops, closed in behind him.

He kicked off and ran. He leaped past the upended tarp he'd left Terri under, sliding as his foot came down on some loose thing in the dark, but leaping clear and catching his balance to reach the street.

"You lied?" he hissed to Terri.

"Lied," came the word against his chest. There was no gunman out there, she'd only given him the distraction he'd needed.

The police must have seen that too, from the number of figures behind him and the car lights pulling into the street. He flung himself down the pavement, then twisted away behind one fence. Then around a tree, past a corner, out onto the next street... the blocks around the Vargas House were almost his back yard, even with the darkness lying over it all.

One block after another flew by at skein-powered speed, and what shouts and sirens he heard fell further and further behind. He twisted again and again, always heading back toward his destination.

St. Mary's Church. Eric.

Why couldn't they listen *to me?* he wanted to yell. But no, the police had tried to listen, they'd just had too many guesses flying around and insisted on sorting them out in their own, grindingly slow way. And he and Bea had kept so much hidden from them.

All the time I was begging them to go after Zara, I never told them where Eric said he'd be. Did I ever think I'd get through to them?

His phone was buzzing in his pocket.

Bea could be calling him. Or… Eric.

He eased his hurtling steps down to a walk, and crouched in the shadow of a wall to get the phone out.

Ed Jordan's voice blasted into his ear. *"Tell* me that Bea Simms didn't try to *murder* a prisoner—in front of other *cops!"*

"She didn't. She put those shots where she wanted them: in Eric's hand and arm." Was Jordan furious because she'd shot him, or because she never tried to hide it? "I guess she thought they'd slow him down," and he lowered his voice and stole a look around the wall's corner. Terri shifted on his shoulder, far too light.

"You with her now?" Jordan said.

"No. And Eric has Zara, how many times do I have to say it? I have to go after them."

"Listen to me…" Jordan slowed, then went on, low and insistent. "You have to come back and tell them what happened."

"I did! But you didn't hear how Eric was—he's losing it, and he wants Terri back. God, I think that whole meeting might be just about trapping Zara and Terri all along…"

A trap. Eric hadn't even worn most of his skein, because he'd seen the spell at the school, he was ready for that too.

"He trapped us," he said again. "And he got trapped himself, Bea shot him where he left himself open. She always said she might have to shoot first... now Eric's wounded and he wants Terri and he's got Zara, and *I have to help her!"*

"What you have to do," Jordan said, "is come in. This isn't your job, Colin. Think about it, you take one step wrong and you can get that woman killed. So you come in right now, or I won't be able to defend you."

Colin laughed, a small, bitter sound in the night. "Bea turned herself in. You going to defend her?"

"Of course, everything I can. But she crossed a line, Colin. And if she did it, what do you think you're heading in to do?"

He paused. Somewhere a breath of wind moved over the town.

"You were telling us you couldn't stand anyone else getting killed. But you've seen how this works now. Who's going to break this time because you got in the way? Who are *you* going to hurt?"

Colin sighed, shook his head.

He answered "You know... the more I remember it, I think after Bea shot Eric the first time, he was still reaching for his briefcase. That's why she shot him again—and she could have stopped him, if the other cops hadn't grabbed her."

How many times had Bea said, she wouldn't give Eric any chance at all? And she still stopped short at shooting his head.

Against his shoulder, Terri said "Come on."

He swallowed, tightened his grip on the phone. "Look, if any of you want to stop Eric or save Zara, he said he'd be at St. Mary's. If you'll even take an answer when it's handed to you," he added.

"Just listen to me—"

Colin cut the call. Then he stared at the dim shape of the phone, and used touch and memory and a bit of skein to slide its card and battery out again.

He broke into a steady, loping run down the street. Only a handful of streetlights glowed along each block, more like oases within the dark than guideposts. For him they were barriers that burned his night vision and hid where police cars might roll into view... but the street was quiet. Except a dog barking from a house he passed, shouting into the stillness.

"You told them," Terri whispered.

"Where I'm going? Sure. I mean, we're dodging them now because they'd try to take me in, yes. But at least now we can all *get there*. This is saving our mother, I have to try everything."

"Do they help? Or get in the way?" she said.

He only jogged on, one step at a time.

"You have a plan?" she asked.

He glanced down at her—just a face and a blurring to his eyes, but still a weight in his arms. Like arguing with his own conscience, if his conscience only knew part of what he'd been through.

"I know it'll be a rescue, whatever else it is," he said. "So I'll be looking for a chance to move fast and pull her out of there. Or if Eric spots me... I've got enough skein to stand up to him. Besides, he's still not a trained fighter, just someone used to having the edge and using it. As long as I protect the spots I can't armor."

A car rolled into view around the corner. Colin eased back to a walk—not that anyone on the street this late would blend in anyway. Bumps in the sidewalk caught at his feet.

The car moved on past them.

He drew in a breath, and went back to his answer. "Or there's the spell, if I get a chance to grab him. Maybe I just free Zara and then he can't touch either of us. I've got the skein to hold him off at his strongest, and she's got none so she's free to turn his own against him. When one man takes on a whole family, it *should* matter that he's alone." That thought spread a smile over his face.

Softly, Terri said "Think he'll let her live?"

His foot slid on the pavement, for one step. "Sure he will."

Except that now Eric was fighting off kidnapping charges, he'd used that meeting to taunt her... *and he's had his hand shot, so now he's a wounded animal...*

He forced that thought down. "Eric wants Zara as a bargaining chip. She's not one of his targets."

"Yes she is."

His throat tightened. "He, he *wants* her hurt? Zara, and I guess me too?"

"Oh yes." Terri's soft voice was certain as steel.

The car was long gone. The whole block was dead silent, except for a strain of party music from one house across the street. Colin pushed back into a jog.

A block later, he tried breaking the silence:

"Eric is so far gone... I'm sorry. He's murdered one man for spotting him in the House, another for suspecting him at work, then he *killed Leo* and a couple of cops... he crippled Bea's boss, he smashed the House... He's destroyed so much, just to get his hands on more skein—"

Trying to fix Terri. Colin cut off his rambling before the damn thought could reach his voice. Terri had to be torn up with guilt, and now Eric had pulled their *mother* into the line of fire too.

Terri said "He didn't do it for me."

A car moved, far ahead. Colin stood deep in the shadows between the streetlights—and just to his side ran a low brick wall along one house. He whispered "Hold on," and pushed the skein at his legs to a quick hop, to let him crouch down behind the wall.

The car rumbled closer.

Terri said "That's why you need me with you."

"No!"

The word was out before he thought. He fumbled for a way to soften it.

"Terri, this is a rescue. I'll set you down somewhere safe, so I can focus on Eric."

"You don't *know* him," she whispered. "He wants... so much," and her voice trailed off, like she'd never have the breath for it all.

"But you... we just got you free. I just need to find somewhere safe, and I can focus on Eric and Zara." *I said that before. I mean having her there only distracts me, she has to know that.* But how could he say it?

Terri said "He sees me, he focuses on me. If not, he explodes."

Beyond the fence, the car had driven by, but he heard another drawing near, holding them in place.

"So you have to be there?" he hissed. "You're saying we have to trade you for her?"

"I'm saying, hide me somewhere close. Let me hide and look for a chance. *Use* me. Whatever it takes."

Now she was talking like Bea? "You think I'll let you play decoy?"

Terri didn't answer.

The car sounds had moved on. He peeped over the wall. Clear.

One jump took them back over it, and back to a jog forward. The blocks looked too alike in the dark, but the church had to be near by now.

"Or," Terri said, "if he gets me, I use the words on him."

He stumbled, slowed, scrambled to stay upright—and keep his grip on the limp, fragile bundle of skein-wrapped limbs in his arms. She'd be almost more skein than flesh, if she were visible.

"You do that and it'll kill you! Hold on," and he laughed. "That's a bluff. You never *heard* what the spell is."

She laughed.

"Gratshay..."

The one word faded away in the night. Terri's unseen body lay as still as ever, still breathing softly after saying the first word.

Damn you... Of course she'd dragged herself out of the tarp where he'd left her, she'd heard him use the spell on Eric. Of course she had—it was Terri.

His run was slowing to a stop, all interest in moving gone now.

"You can't!" he said. "Don't you tell me you can *survive* that spell, not the way you are. Don't lie to me."

She didn't answer.

He went on "How is that going to help Zara? Is that just throwing your life away because other people didn't make it? What kind of crazy debt is that?"

She said "Look who's talking."

No! His eyes widened—what had Jordan just been telling him? That his fear of losing people was pushing him too far, and only adding more risks? Was that it?

No. He shook his head, let the tangle of needs in him settle and fall into place.

"I am *not* trying to get myself killed," he told her. "This isn't guilt or pain or any of that. I just can't stand holding back, if there's anything at all I could do to save them. You... you talk like you can't stand being left out, period."

"Not that."

The word forced him to look down at her face, pale and taunt with pain, and glaring right back at him.

"No," she said. "But *I get* to choose if I can. Not get shoved aside."

"But..."

This was Zara's life, right in Eric's claws now. Just having Terri there would take whatever hair-trigger balance of a rescue he tried and start shaking it...

Except, those determined eyes had endured *years* as Eric's prisoner, watching him lose his mind, helpless. Ignoring her need and forcing her to stay back now would... it wouldn't destroy Terri, no.

But it was more than he could bear to do.

He drew her in closer, and started forward again.

They had to be only blocks from St. Mary's now. The streets still had no police in view—and their station wasn't much further. Were Jordan and the other cops still struggling with what to believe?

Or they could be already here, out of sight and watching for Eric. They *should* be. Unless he'd burned his bridges with them too.

Is it just that easy, to cut myself from everyone—just one threat of Eric coming after us and I'll pay any price to keep me *in the action?*

No wonder I can't refuse Terri either.

If he could just see one cop, one figure in the shadows watching for him and Eric, one sign that now that he was here he wouldn't be facing Eric by himself... *Bea, I need you now.*

Terri stiffened in his arms.

The shell of the church peeped through the buildings ahead.

First, scout that perimeter. Colin slipped off the street to make his way behind and between one silent house, and in along the back wall of another. Any flicker of shadow back here could be Eric, watching for him—he wouldn't just sit in the church and wait, would he?

But they found nothing: no Eric, no Zara, no police, only the scattered pieces and refuse of the properties to step between in the dark. Nowhere to go but in.

He looked at the silhouette, broad walls with a ghostly ripple in the moonlight that had to be its layers of plastic sheeting. He glanced down at the blurred outline of his sister and searched for some word of caution, some joke they could share. Nothing came to mind.

The front had no door yet. The back door was unlocked.

He slid them through that door and closed it behind them, shutting them into the dark. Moonlight outside shone dimly against the windows' plastic—he blinked and stared around, for any shape that could be Zara, any shadow that could be Eric. Sawdust, and something *else,* tickled his nose.

The church was silent. The floor looked clear in the dark, like a pool of blackness waiting for one step to disturb it, one betraying sound. The wide pillar rose from it down toward the far end like an island.

Some of the shadows resolved—the floor did look clear to walk on, and it was only along the base of the walls that irregular shapes lay scattered or piled up.

That other smell was *blood.*

He took a step forward, then caught himself and crouched down. He laid Terri down by the door, and her ghostly outline was lost in the dark the moment he looked away.

He crept forward.

Then he saw it: a patch of paleness lay by one wall. A face, above an outline in a black uniform. Spatters of darkness hid part of that head. A second officer lay beside her.

More of Eric's kills. The police *had* looked here.

Colin took a step toward them, but a motion caught his eye. Some irregularity ran across the back of the pillar... moving... and a muffled sound...

He edged around toward its other side. The line moved again, a rope stretching around the pillar. Fastened to a hand.

Zara stood splayed against the front of the church pillar, staring wildly at him, bound and gagged to it like some horrific crucifixion mockery—

One chance. Colin crept toward her, pulling a handful of skein from his thigh to clamp it around his finger for a talon. One slash should cut her free.

A shadow lunged out of the dark.

The flicker of motion sent Colin leaping away with the skein boosting his jump. He flew clear of the attack, too far, landed struggling for balance.

Eric's kick slammed into his leg. Its power sent him spinning away, crashing down—the world went gray. A moment later it cleared, and he lay with the bloody face of one cop just in front of him.

Colin spun to his feet. Eric only stood back, a dark-covered figure eyeing his enemy. *And he only went after my leg, where I'm armored.*

Eric had two bullets in him, and a crippled hand under that skein. And he still kept going.

Eric motioned to the bodies. "I made them report I wasn't here, so we won't be disturbed for a while. But, I *told you* to bring Terri."

So he'd missed her in the dimness. Colin gritted his teeth, reached for anything to distract Eric, stall him, for some opening.

"You never cared about her," he snapped at Eric. *One step to the side... work for one chance to leap to Zara and free her, if she got her gag off Eric wouldn't dare touch her...* "You just killed two more people, and all you want is the power to kill more!"

"This is for her," Eric hissed.

Colin edged another step over. "So you wipe out everything else? Even Terri's family?"

"I'm making something better!"

And Eric crow-hopped to the side, into his path, and reached a claw backward toward Zara. Colin froze—*I just* reminded *him about his hostage!*

Soft as a shadow, Eric said "Now, where is Terri?"

Colin locked his gaze on him, away from Terri. At least the dark could hide whatever was in his eyes. "She's safe, of course. She needed real doctors. She's out of my hands now, so there's no way you'll get her through me or Zara." That *had* to be convincing, it was what anyone else would have done.

Eric edged back, closer to Zara. "I told you to bring her!"

"I can't," Colin shot back. "But you say you're doing this for her? You're not just drunk on destruction and forgot you cared about her? Then *prove* it—that's her mother you're threatening. Let her go."

Eric laughed. "You think I'm bluffing? This woman is the worst of everything that's wrong here!" He nudged the claw toward her.

"Don't!" *Just let him look away from me, and I can move—*

"*Her* fault," Eric said. Then he drew his hand back and waved it around the shadows of the church. "This is where Terri almost died.

Because *she* kept her tied to the past, until even when the ground shakes she runs in here trying to save some bit of painted clay!"

"We lost her too—" He cut off. Better to let Eric talk.

"And look, they're trying to put this place back up. All surrounded by empty houses. At least Gardner tries to clear them out and make something that has a chance—all you two do is turn the clock back."

Eric raised a hand to his ear.

"You hear that?"

Police? But no, there were no voices outside. Barely any sound at all, nobody around to call the cops, even with their voices rising. "What?"

"Emptiness. That's the sound of a doomed town. It's had two earthquakes in a couple generations, and all you do is wait around for more!"

Colin kept still, not one motion to draw Eric's eye. One more glance away and he could jump for Zara...

"I've been saying it all my life. I thought you wanted out too." Eric took a step toward him, cutting him off again. "But no, you end up following Zara and the memory of old man Vargas right down the same dead end. But Terri understood—until the *one moment* the world was proving us right and she still listened to you! Well, all that's coming down... now I can erase all this, fix Terri, and get her back. What were you thinking, that you could make me hesitate now?"

He stepped closer, raising a claw.

"Where is she?"

Colin didn't answer. He glared back, knowing the look must be swallowed in the dimness.

"Tell me!" And he charged.

It was the sound of Eric's breath that gave the attack away, more than any shift of his balance in the dark. When he lunged, Colin pitted strength against strength, using the skein on his legs to lunge to meet him.

Colin blocked while those arms were still sweeping around, his hands catching that bruising power and twisting to spin that momentum around and off-balance. He wrenched at the arm Bea had shot.

Eric screamed.

Then he shoved back, and sheer skein power flung Colin away. Something slashed pain along Colin's arm as he fell back—too weak, too much of him unarmored. Colin spun away toward Zara, raising his one talon.

Eric slammed into him, knocking him away again.

Skein speed is useless, he's got more and he's lighter. Colin tumbled, rolled, to his feet.

"Where is Terri?" Eric snapped. "I can cut it out of you or her. I only need one to save her!"

Colin caught at his legs' skein and wrenched at it, willing it all to come loose and thicken around his hands, shapeless globs—

Eric advanced, claws whirling—

Colin flung all his skein down to the floor.

He grabbed at Eric. *"Gratshay ko—"*

Eric's hand crashed down over his mouth.

Shock, the taste of blood... the grip swept him back, mere muscle outmatched. He twisted for a desperate throw, but Eric shoved harder and kicked to knock his leg away. He slammed to the floor, still pinned by that grip across his face.

Haze filled his sight, and the skein mask loomed through it over him... he stabbed fingers at its eyes, but the monster twisted and his fingers slammed against something hard as stone.

The vise-grip tightened on his face.

"Stop!"

A voice, Terri's...

"Eric, what's it take to make you stop?"

CHAPTER SIXTEEN

POUND OF FLESH

The skein-mask turned, toward Terri's figure sprawled in the back.

Colin tried to twist his head free, useless.

Eric gasped "You can *talk? Really talk, real thoughts?"

"Can you *listen?" Terri said. Hollowness whistled through her voice, and pain—pain like bones jabbing in the wrong places, as she forced out "Did you ever... stay, try?"

"You're just, just rambling again." Eric's grip clamped tighter on Colin's skull.

Colin stretched a leg out, behind where Eric crouched over him. The skein he'd dropped had to be back there.

Terri started again. "You... you'll destroy him, and Zara and... everything... for me?"

"All this is already dead! I'm clearing out the corpse, and all their useless denials! They're what trapped you!"

"Vargas tried to... save, save this town. You're using his work to... undo that?"

"*Save it?" Eric laughed bitterly.

There! Colin's heel brushed what had to be his skein—

The motion must have given him away. Eric flung him savagely aside, himself diving clear the other way. Colin tumbled away but as he rolled he dug his heel and his *will* into his fallen weapon.

He settled to a crouch with skein gathering around his foot, his hand.

And Eric only watched him. His masked face and stance stayed focused on Colin, but he held back and spoke to Terri.

"He *saved* this place? If you think you can call it that. You mean you haven't figured it out? How Vargas made so much skein?"

"You think…" Terri's voice faded as her breath gave out again. If that was her breath that faltered.

"I *know* it, now. I know we're all damned."

Eric drew back a step, never turning from Colin. Another step, sideways—he was circling back toward Zara.

Colin charged, forcing the half-settled skein on his leg to move. His balance slipped, and Eric's claws slashed across and forced him back.

Eric settled in behind Zara and the pillar, where his gaze could look past her to watch his enemy. Colin eyed them, and began pulling his skein around his arm and chest. *I have to get him clear, cut her loose so she can run, and then I can try getting Terri away…*

Eric slid Zara's gag down. She gasped in the dimness.

"You're the historian," Eric said. "Tell us, where did Matt Vargas go?"

Colin shouted "The protection spell, use it!"

But Eric had already pulled back from touching her, out of the spell's reach. He said "What happened to Vargas in the end?"

Zara coughed for breath. Then she spat at him "You want rumors? You know nobody knows where he went."

"Nobody?" Eric's laugh was a whisper with a high, shrill edge. "So in the end all your history comes to nothing, doesn't it? But you still taught your daughter to run into a falling building to save a statue—for nothing."

He jabbed a clawed finger toward where Terri sprawled.

"You see what you did to her?"

"Yes." Zara had to strain against the wood to reach her head back around, but the pain in her voice left no doubt that she saw.

"Shattered bones, ruined body, all of it? Nobody else could have kept her alive, but I did! You see that?"

"Yes!" Zara's voice echoed around the chamber, as if its volume could wash away Eric's accusation. "Terri, I'm sorry."

"Sorry?" Eric laughed. "That's an easy word. How about some harder ones: would you *heal* her, if you had a way?"

Zara turned to glare at him. "If I believed you for one second? Of course."

"You'll believe. You can see it—the skein's keeping her alive. With more of it I can pull all the pieces into place and give her the support to stand up and walk again.

"And now I know how to make all the skein I need."

No—he's got enough to be unstoppable already— Colin wrenched his own skein into place around his fist. There had to be something, some way...

"Terri!" Eric called. "When the original church pillar collapsed, what did you see tangled up with the skein in it?"

The shadows of the corner almost hid the motion, of Terri's head slumping. She sighed, "Bones."

"And whose bones were they? What did all the hints I found say they were?"

The sound whispered and spread across the room. "Matt Vargas."

But... no... why... Colin felt his breath gasping, his thoughts spinning in uselessness. He stared, stared—

Eric's hand held a gun.

He'd slid his skein back enough to draw it from his clothes. A stray memory flashed *The cops were looking for Bea's gun.* Eric leveled the weapon at Zara and slid her gag back up into place. Then he turned to cover Colin.

Eric shook himself, one motion. And his skein peeled off him like an unzipped coat and fell to the floor.

Colin blinked. But Eric really was standing in just the same business clothes he'd worn before—soaked with blood from Bea's bullets. A slash of pain across his exposed face showed the weight of his wounds crashing down on him without skein to carry it.

"And you think those words are a protection spell."

Eric spoke through gritted teeth now. His unhurt hand kept the gun on Colin, as he slowly forced his other arm to rise up. One patch of skein still lay over his misshapen hand.

He dropped that skein onto Zara's bound hand, and brushed his own hand over it for one moment.

"Gratshay kodo va."

Zara screamed against the gag.

Colin started for her, but the gun leveled right at him.

Even in the dark, he thought he saw Eric's eyes on him glitter in fever.

"It's only pain, Zara," Eric hissed. "This is how you save your daughter."

Zara's face shook, spasmed... then went taut as she glared at the skein on her hand.

The green shape slid away and dropped to the floor. Her will had fought it off.

The pool of skein had grown. The spell made it *feed*.

Eric scooped it up, so slowly—his gun never moved from Colin, and instead he labored to lift the stuff with his wounded arm. He dropped it onto Zara again.

"Gratshay kodo va!" He glanced at her agony, just for an instant before watching Colin again. "Don't you get it? The old man that you kept your shrine for, this is how he must have grown his skein! How many people did it take, to make all this, to prop up pieces of this damn *town* against the quakes??"

His voice rose to a shriek. Colin gathered himself to charge, but even that motion made Eric's gun stir in a twitch of warning.

"Until he saw what he'd done," Eric snarled. "Until he tried to give his own life for it—and he had the sheer arrogance to seal himself up and die in a *church!* As if there's ever any forgiveness for what he did, all in the name of a town that never deserved it.

"None of you deserve it. Just Terri and me saw through it, and now we can—"

Zara threw her gagged head back, and the skein sloughed away again. The church fell silent.

A lower voice, Terri's voice, cut through that moment: "Eric. You're not saving me."

Eric laughed. "Yes I am! As many times as it takes."

"Not. Ever."

The pause between her words wasn't pain or weakness. It was her taking a full breath.

She said, *"Gratshay. Kodo—"*

"No!"

Eric spun toward her.

Colin flung himself at him. The gun swung back toward him, shaking in Eric's hand, but evasion and waiting were finished now. Something kicked hard against him as he rushed in, through the booming echo, and he slammed his skein arm around to knock the gun from Eric's grip.

Took it on my armored chest, he realized.

Eric scrambled for where the gun had fallen. Colin stared around for it in the dark and kicked out to send it further away. Its clatter against the floor broke through the deafness from the shot.

Eric had already veered away, running on past where the gun had been as if it had never been his prize. Instead he ran for his discarded skein, and one motion scooped it up.

Colin crashed into him. His fist slammed down at full force, crashing into the dark mass on Eric's hand. He shoved in to heave Eric off his feet—the little man wrenched and wiggled away.

When they rolled to their feet, Eric's skein was already sliding to cover his head, his chest...

Got to stop him, until I can do something for the others! This might hurt him more than me— Colin rushed at him, hands spread to grab. "Gratshay—"

Eric leaped back. He tumbled in the dimness and crashed down along the edge of the wall. Colin charged after him.

A shape reached out of the darkness below Eric: Terri grabbing at his foot.

Eric leaped clear. "You can't—"

Colin charged at him. Eric spun, slammed a fist out.

Colin's punch glanced off Eric's armor. Eric's caught him in the stomach.

He flew backward through the air, with perfect clarity feeling the place he'd been struck and knowing he'd barely felt it...

The world went white.

My head, got to shake my head awake, move... He stirred, and the spots shook away and those legs thrashed against something, like his head had hit a wall, he tried to move or roll or anything and down the room Zara sawed at her ropes with a bit of skein in her hand but why couldn't he move...

"Traitor!" Eric yelled.

Then he saw it: Eric's claws closing around Terri.

Digging in, too easily, too delicately, as if he'd done it many times before—and Eric shrieked and *wrenched,* and her entire coating of skein rippled and flowed at his command. And peeled away.

Terri gasped, a broken sound that might have been a scream if she'd had the strength. The outline of her darkened.

That's not all blood, it's got to be shadows, got to be...

"See what you made me do?" Eric's hands were swollen with skein, already shrinking as it slid over to thicken his arms. "If you don't want it—"

He broke off, turned away.

Toward Zara. As the rope around one of her arms parted, under the skein fragment she must have hidden when she shook off Eric's torture.

Eric stepped toward her.

Then he halted. Something fastened onto his foot, and a shattered voice moaned *"Gratshay ko—"*

His foot lashed out. The blow sent Terri tumbling away.

Colin dragged himself upright at last, head still spinning. *He's too fast, too strong, he'll hit any exposed spot I have. We can't even risk moving Terri now, so we're trapped with Eric and there's just not enough power...*

Colin gasped *"Gratshay kodo va."*

Pain blasted through him, erupted, burning away even the difference between his uncovered flesh and the skein over the rest, where it began eating into him. That sound, that had to be a wail of pain, that motion was himself swaying on his feet.

That shape, Eric. Attacking.

He flailed out at his enemy, too clumsy—but the green figure shied away, away from his touch. His feet shuffled trying to keep the motion from toppling him over.

It's nothing. Nothing like what Terri's enduring.

Eric edged back from him. Hesitating, retreating. Afraid.

Colin flung that thought against the skein to squash its hunger away, and lunged at Eric.

His punch exploded out—Eric spun away and crashed down, and Colin knew he'd connected. *Strength* pulled when he moved, stronger than ever, even if that power had to slide over missing skin and raw nerves. He dove at his enemy.

Eric shimmered from sight.

Colin halted, swept his gaze around the shadows of their battlefield. One dark, slowly stirring shape on the floor was Terri. Zara—*free!*—ran toward her.

Something blurred at Zara.

Colin leaped at that shadow, and it twisted away into the dark. Zara spun away from them both to race out the back door.

Shouts for help split the stillness outside.

Another shadow moved, darting toward Terri—*like the bastard can help her now!* Colin charged, smashed a punch into Eric and wrenched him around, twisting at his injured hand. Eric caught his leg with a kick and pulled free.

Colin dragged himself up, through the pain and the blurring in his eyes. His thickened skein needed to spread out—still too many exposed spots on him. Eric had enough to be stronger, faster, but at least the killer was keeping his distance now.

Eric blurred away again. Colin stared through the flashing in his vision, the darkness, for the bit of motion where no shadow should be. There, edging toward Terri—

Just hold him off! He lunged at the shape and the spell rose on his lips. Eric ducked back again.

Something thin and deadly speared out of the dark at him. His arm deflected it and he tried to grab at it—Eric yanked it clear of his grasp. He staggered on his feet.

Again, again, the enemy rushed at him.

From one angle, from another. One shadow lunging out of another, and falling back.

A few running steps to chase that shadow down and trap it—no, gone again. Terri groaned, one soft sound, the only one that mattered. All other noise faded and fell away under the leaping, whirling steps of the fight.

Any shape, any direction. Crouching low, creeping behind him... that voice faded under the rise of twisting, split-second lunges in the shadows, fighting to drive back shape after shape after shape.

On the left, in the dimness.

Then—there, crouching low.

Along the wall, brighter now.

Left and right. More crowding in...

He was *squinting*, staring through a flashing in his vision. The darkness fell back—people were here.

Two or three hanging back from his reach, with bloody faces or injured arms. A cop in a black uniform lay sprawled in front of him, bearded face staring up at him in rage.

Others wore white, paler than the lights they'd brought. Their lips moved. They motioned, past him, to Terri behind him.

Medics. Zara stood at the back of them.

What did I do? Breathing thundered in him. His armored fists were clenching, still rising to fend them all off.

Two more men stepped forward, in black. One cop, they had to be cops, raised a gun.

The shot struck his armored chest—unhurt, again. But the momentum shoved Colin away and started him running, out the door and into the night.

*   *   *

Slipping around them at night was almost easy. Skein at his legs let his steps give him some distance, far enough away that any parts of him still visible were just a few shapes to hide the darkness. Distance was the only thing that didn't tear at him now.

When he circled back, it only looked worse. The same police that had shot at him, that he'd lashed out at before he noticed, were swarming around the site and waving their guns in every direction.

At least that might keep Eric away. He watched them hold back what civilians had come out to watch. Finally the EMTs brought Terri out to an ambulance—she was still holding on, from what he could see of Zara walking beside her. From what he could see.

When the ambulance pulled out, he followed them long enough to know which hospital they picked. He knew where its ER waiting room was.

And climbing the wall up to that second floor let him draw on the numbed kind of strength he still had. Sharp spikes he formed over his elbows and toes could dig into the brick, and the skein's hardness held his weight as securely as a ladder's rungs. Even falling once meant nothing with its power to let his legs catch him.

But looking in the window… that hurt.

Zara sat in the waiting room, three uniformed police beside her. Colin glanced at the room, then off at the building entrance below him—watching those two ways for Eric and waiting for Terri's fate was the most he could manage now. If he could bear to look away from his mother's dazed, subdued, *lonely* face.

The three cops around her tried to pull her out of the room, once, until she seemed to talk them down. They kept their hands by their guns and their eyes looking for trouble—the same men he had found himself fighting in the church, he realized. Ready to shoot him again when he came in.

A shape formed against the glass, his own face slipping into visibility again. If that could be his: even the reflection was pitted with scars along his neck and above, where the skein shouldn't even have touched him.

He blurred that face away again, and tried to wipe his thoughts away too. Not Terri and her wounds that the doctors must be struggling with, not what could be going through Zara's head, not what Eric could be doing here or somewhere else… only clinging to the brick and each moment, watching. Waiting.

Until the woman in white walked out to Zara. Until the doctor lowered her mask, and they saw the smile.

He watched Zara sink back in her chair—alert, guarded, not the boneless collapse of someone whose daughter was truly safe yet. But the sight freed his own bruises and the ache along his skin to flare through him.

Time to go to them… or not quite yet, just let me rest…

He watched Zara try to talk with the police. Maybe, maybe, she'd glance at the window and he could wave to her.

The doors opened. Two people strode in, with *Bea* between them.

She walked without handcuffs, was the joyous first thing he saw. But the other two kept close around her—one the tall woman detective who'd first had her seized, the other a rail-thin older man. They closed in around Zara.

He saw it again: their nervous looks around, their demanding motions trying to push Zara out of the room. Away from her daughter's care.

At least they still kept Bea with them. In spite of her keeping him in the hunt, even after her seeing how vicious Eric could be and trying to eliminate him…

I have to explain. And tell it to the detectives, not get hauled away at the door.

Colin crept to the ground. He moved around to the entrance, hands shielding his scarred face from the few people in view.

One quick blur and a dash brought him inside. The receptionist glanced up a moment, but in the next he was out of view and she did nothing more. After all, one fleeting glimpse of only *part* of a body had to be a trick of the eye.

The rest was simply walking up, and grabbing a set of scrubs and a mask to cover most of his scars. They even got him past the cop at the stairs.

The waiting room looked different seen through the inside door. But he peeked through that, watching for a chance to signal Zara. If she or Bea could get a moment away from the two detectives and three uniforms.

They'd settled at chairs almost at the door where he stood, and the uniforms looked as jumpy as ever. He could hear the oldest detective speaking:

"—but who really had your daughter? Since Eric Rowe and your son are both missing."

"Just tell them the truth," Bea added.

"The whole truth," the taller woman warned, face twisting in a scowl. "Not just how nothing your son did could ever be suspicious."

"That *is* the truth," Zara said. "Eric kept Terri as his prisoner, then he took me to get her back. Colin's not the one you want."

The man chewed his lip. "Plausible enough, on the face of it. The problem has been sorting it out..."

Colin took a deep breath. He reached for the door.

Something moved at the room's far end. A faint reflection off the fluorescent lights—or a crouching, shimmering form edging closer.

Colin's teeth clenched. Eric could creep in, pull back, wait for his moment...

"What are you doing here, nurse? Where's your station?"

The voice came right behind him. Soft, demanding. One of the cops glanced toward the sound.

Not now. Feet shuffling, Colin turned to face his accuser—a small, sharp-eyed woman clutching a clipboard. She looked at his face around the mask, and drew back a step.

Behind him the man's voice rose. "Maybe you can explain, Detective. How one man had armor that shrugged off an officer's weapon, and another took bullets without protection and still disappeared. I'm waiting."

Colin eyed the tiny woman, and whispered the only thing he could think of. "Intruder in there. Get Security." He spun back to peep inside.

Bea sighed "Sometimes body armor works. Or they've simply got the magic touch."

Beyond them, the room looked clear. *Where had Eric gone—*

"Enough," the senior detective said. "You shot a man in custody—"

"Who still dragged *me* away!" Zara said.

He looked right past her, to Bea. "Actions have consequences," and he held out his hand.

Bea handed him her badge. Colin stared, tried to search for Eric.

The last detective, the tall woman with the glare, reached out and began *searching* Bea. Her hands only probed for a moment before she lifted the coat away from Bea's unresisting form. A thick vest lay beneath it, and she pulled that away too.

"Speaking of armor," she mused, "what's this thing? Standard vest with some kind of foam underneath it?"

Her skein—Bea had already found a way to camouflage it. For now.

A shape moved behind them. Eric, moving closer.

No, he was watching Bea. He knew she was disarmed, he could strike at her now or pick his moment any time—

At Colin's back the nurse hissed "You come with me—"

Zara looked up. With the police busy milling around each other, Zara glanced up toward the door.

Colin nudged it open another inch. He jabbed a finger toward the blurred shape behind them.

Zara turned to follow. Then she screamed "Look! There!"

Police whirled, staring at where she pointed. The mirage-form that was Eric leaped away as they moved, and by the time they looked he was far across the room and dropping to the floor, posing as a trick of the light again.

"Up here!"

Bea dashed after him. The tall woman and the uniforms moved after her—more to cut her off than to follow her, but Eric darted away down the hall. Anything to keep them from getting a good look at the shimmer they should be watching for.

And Bea's vest, with its secret, lay abandoned on a chair.

The only power that could stop Eric when he came back.

Colin lunged forward. Before the others could look back—he reached the chair, slapped a skein-touched hand to the inside of the vest, and the "padding" slid away onto his hand.

He looked up—

The old cop was looking right at him. He'd merely bent his head around, a simple, *casual* glance, like he half expected Colin there.

The surgical mask I grabbed, it's slipped down below my face—

The cop gave him a wink.

One perfectly clear wink, on that weathered, sharp face, right to him. And one hand twitched in a tiny *shoo* motion, back toward the door, as Zara began to turn.

Colin took one breath to take in the sight of her—not nearly enough, as relief and concern burst across her face as he spun away, but it would have to do. For now.

The other police were glancing back now, and Bea with them. *If I had another moment... no, never enough...* He dove back out the door.

"Slow down, could be a distraction!" the lead detective yelled. Smart.

Long steps flung him past the nurse and down the corridor. A hospital was no place for running, even this late, but he only had to dodge past a few figures before he reached a closet door.

Once he swung that shut behind him, the skein flowed. He slid his, and now Bea's, skein around him and found it more than covered him. He blurred himself from sight and nudged the door open.

One of the uniforms looked in, gun ready. Then he raced on.

Finally Colin lay still. Silent, resting... just a patch of glimmering in a closet. When he stood up and worked his way out, he felt some of the tension finally easing from him.

That detective, the senior one that seemed to make the decisions, had let him go.

He still had hope. Zara and Bea were safe. Terri, *Terri,* was still alive. Whatever else happened, nobody else in his life was lost. That was the win that mattered.

He began working his way around the corridors, checking if Eric was still lurking around—and not surprised that he seemed to have pulled back for now. The bastard should.

Eric might be more powerful than ever, and more dangerous. After all this, he seemed to be on the run too.

He's got more power. I've still got something better.

I'm still not alone.

*****

Colin's adventures continue in:

Weighing The Scales

from WEIGHING THE SCALES

Miss nothing. He could be anywhere.

Colin crept down the broad, bright corridor, searching the walls for that one faint mirage-blur in the fluorescent glow that could be Eric's outline. If the bastard tried again, he had to spot him.

Colin's sister was out of sight ahead. They'd wheeled Terri out of surgery, but he had to move softly and hang back or crouch down in hopes none of the doctors noticed the faint shape of him—all while keeping his concentration on controlling the "skein" that covered him.

Eric's had more practice with invisibility, and everything else this magical substance does. And he was here trying to take Terri back just minutes ago.

Colin slowed his tired feet, stared through the gauzy haze over his eyes at the junction of corridors ahead. Two, no, three nurses stood talking with a doctor at some kind of station: "watch for any reaction—" "if those cops get in your way—"

And two uniformed police stood behind them. Of course they did, just when Colin felt the urge to reappear and simply talk to them, take his chances to work *with* someone again.

Bea wasn't stationed among the cops. She wouldn't be, anymore.

Instead Colin edged around the intersection—his foot scraped on the floor once and he saw a cop glance up, but he froze and the cop looked away again. There was nothing but "a trick of the light" to see, if they had no idea his glimmer could be more.

Colin moved up the corridor to the side, away around the staff. The hospital's mix of sounds and stillness in the night sounded almost peaceful, so there had to be a way to work around the crowds and catch up with Terri.

Make no sound. Keep in the corner of every eye that could notice me. Hold onto the concentration twist *that makes light blur around me, and spot any outline that could be Eric...* Bea had used skein to help her *see* their hidden enemy, but Colin could only search every pattern of light he saw.

The next intersection was clear, free to let him turn back toward where Terri had gone—

Something twitched at the intersection beyond it, at the edge of a corner. Colin blinked, started on the wider circuit toward that. It looked like simply a shadow, but he couldn't ignore it.

And how many shadows and detours would it take? Did he have to check every inch on Terri's floor, and then check it again, just because Eric could be here? Tiredness blurred at his vision.

A doctor stepped into view at the junction, then another. Colin pulled back, back toward the more direct way around. He had a sudden image of his sister lying alone in some room and Eric simply coming in through her window. The skein's strength could tear right through glass, or iron bars.

Even the intersection he'd passed up had a nurse standing in it now. But she stood off at the corner staring at her tablet, easy for Colin to slip past her and her cart and on toward where Terri should be.

A foot scuffed on the floor behind him, where no person had been.

He whirled. A *motion,* a huge skein-bulked blur lunged at him.

He flung himself clear, far as the skein could let him leap. In mid-air came one thought: Eric should be faster, staying invisible was slowing him down too—

Colin slammed against the wall, glanced off it and crashed down against some clattering shape—the nurse's cart.

And even that impact didn't cover the *crunch* of Eric's fist gouging into the wall.

Colin looked up, saw the nurse whirling toward him. *Can't let go, have to keep the skein hiding me from light.*

Eric sidestepped her. That blur took a slow pace to move out of the nurse's line of sight, and began stalking toward her.

No! Colin sprang up and advanced on his enemy. Eric hadn't lunged yet, she wasn't his real target...

Footsteps raced up in the corridor. A woman charged into view, short blonde hair and watchful eyes and no fear at rushing into the scene. Bea wasn't really a cop anymore, *and* she'd lost her skein, but she was still here.

Two uniforms pounded up behind her, and a doctor at their heels. Colin froze, watching Eric—the blurred shape was already crouching down, letting their gazes pass over him.

"Ma'am? You alright?" one cop said the nurse.

"That son of a bitch trying to get to his sister?" the other growled.

They still think it could be me... oh. These two were the same cops that had walked into Colin's last fight with Eric, the ones he'd attacked in the confusion...

They all looked right past them both now, staring around and missing the two mirage-shapes. All except Bea looking in Eric's direction, no doubt watching his every move.

Eric edged back, away. Colin let out a hushed breath; of course Eric wouldn't risk so many witnesses seeing the not-quite-hidden outlines they ought to be watching for. And Bea let him go.

A motion up the other way caught his eye. Another uniform stepped out from a doorway, with Colin's mother behind him.

If Zara—she was always Zara, to everyone—had just been in that room, then Colin had found Terri. He moved toward them.

"So you just knocked the damn cart over?" one cop was saying behind him.

"No! I wasn't anywhere near it—"

Colin edged away, smooth and silent as he could move. One officer up ahead walked a few steps towards him but never glanced over as he slipped by.

Zara stayed at the doorway. Colin heard his foot scrape on the floor now, and she blinked and stared at the approaching shape.

"It's just me." Somehow his whisper was enough to distinguish his blur from Eric's, and the hardness that had been tightening on her face eased away.

He slipped into the room.

The space was small, too small. But it had room for the unconscious Terri da Costa.

His sister looked odder than ever, as pale and wasted away as when he'd found her, but now surrounded by medical tubes and wires instead of the skein she'd been encased in. She'd survived the Rayo Hill Earthquake, and Eric had kept her prisoner for three years with the skein to keep her alive... and then he'd ripped the stuff away when Colin rescued her.

And he still wants her back. To take her away, or prove he's right, or something.

"The guy's long gone." Words from one of the cops drifted up from outside. "We *all* going to stay here all night?"

"Eric Rowe has already killed four cops," Bea said. "Any time you want to look away, you keep that in mind."

"I get it. But look, you shouldn't even be here, *Miss* Simms."

Colin shook his head. If the police did pull out, if he had to keep watch for Eric all alone—and they forced Bea away too...

He looked at Terri again, so still. Hours ago she could barely crawl, even when she was coated in skein, and then Eric had taken that and she'd still defied him. The doctors must have stabilized her, but they'd just gotten her back.

Soft feet behind him showed Zara stepping into the room. Her gaze went right to him; his control over the skein must have slipped, but she didn't even blink at the silver-green-sheathed figure of her son.

Instead he stepped into her hug.

One warm, sheltering moment after so many hours chasing Eric and trying to keep Terri—and Zara herself—out of his claws... For one moment Colin wondered how she'd talked the hospital into letting her stay this late with her long-lost daughter. But then, saying no to the heart of the Hillside community had never been easy.

"They say they've sewed her all up," Zara said. "As best they understand all her half-healed injuries. They think she's good. Or, alive."

Zara was doing it again. Refusing to show her fears for her children's sake, and almost succeeding.

But Terri had a whole church collapse on her...

"Don't forget, she spent years wrapped up in what has to be the perfect bandage." Colin forced a smile, though she wouldn't see it behind her shoulder. "And I've got plenty of skein to give her—but wait, it's no good until she wakes up to control it."

And she *had* to wake up. This was just the anesthetic, not some sign that she'd bled out the last of her strength. It had to be.

The door moved.

He'd forgotten the police out there. Now he had one instant to clutch at the skein's power and step out of Zara's hug, before the cop looked in.

"Looks like it's nothing, ma'am—'Zara,' sorry." The man looked at her, frowned, but made no real reaction to whatever faint silhouette he saw behind her. "And... when we find your son, we'll try not to hurt him. We just need his whole story on how he found your daughter, and all the rest of it."

You mean lock me up while you bury me in questions, Colin thought. He held his breath until the cop had stepped outside again. *And I let my guard down, stupid!*

The door was closing, but it halted and Bea stepped in.

When she'd shut it fully behind her, he let himself reappear.

She didn't even blink at that. She only said "I'm sorry, Zara. I keep telling them Eric's still a threat. I suppose it's hard to believe."

Colin slipped forward a step to her, enough to keep his voice from the cops outside. "And you're so sure you can't tell them what they're up against."

Bea only looked back at him. That same controlled face, really almost as young as his, that he'd been just learning to get a smile from... She'd taught him to hunt Eric, tracked down Terri beside him, but she'd always been so certain they had to hide the skein from her superiors.

And now Terri was here, helpless, and the police still had no idea what they were guarding her from. Was it really a surprise they were talking about reducing her protection, or ready to suspect Colin himself?

He glanced at Zara. His mother stood so *quiet* now, when it should be her fire and insight pushing them and making every step ahead clear. That she kept still meant that they'd reached a point with little left to say—or no choices at all.

But we survived. He looked between Zara and Terri again, both alive. Except Eric could be stalking back toward them right now, or else watching for some time tomorrow or later, simply waiting for the police to let their guard down. A few of those voices rattled out in the corridor, dry, scattered sounds that felt as restless as drumming fingertips.

While Eric was... something cold slid up Colin's spine. Eric was far enough gone to lash out at anything, and now they knew the price for making even more skein was simply *human flesh*. Did Eric even have limits now, to how far he could build up his strength or what lives he could toss to it?

He was our friend. *But he blames the family and the whole town and its history for Terri and more—*

Colin looked down to see his hands trembling, shaking with rage and just too tired to hold it in.

Bea broke the silence, with a sudden, confident "I'll stop him. The whole department's looking for him now, and I can still use that. It has to be done."

"I hope you're right." Zara barely stirred as she spoke.

"And while you're searching?" Colin said. If the police let their guard down watching Terri...

A voice pushed through the sounds outside. Calm, soft, and stilling the fragmented noises from the police: "What happened here?"

"False alarm, sir," one of them said.

That voice. Colin whispered to Bea, "Who's that cop there?"

"Lieutenant Hoyle. He's running this now."

"He spotted me when I first got to the hospital, and he let me go. And we need someone to get how serious this is."

" 'Get' what?" Bea's voice dropped lower, and fiercer. "Invisibility, bulletproofing, and now using that 'protection spell' to make more skein by feeding people to it? —Oh yes, Zara told me what Eric tried doing to her," she added. "You know once you tell them about the skein, this'll never be about protecting you, or stopping Eric."

It can't mean you have to shoot someone when they're helpless, or risk your badge over it. Even Eric.

Colin stepped past her, toward the door.

"Wait!" Zara snapped. "You heard how the police spoke about you. It's not safe."

"It's not getting any safer." Not for Terri, trapped by her injuries and waiting for Eric to come after her again, with Colin afraid to step away or sleep at all. They needed that police protection.

Colin reached up to the crown of his head. His fingers dragged the skein back, and a *thought* magnified the motion to make the stuff split and peel away, down his head and on down his body.

Zara's breath caught when his face appeared. He'd only had a glimpse himself, of the raw scars on his face and arms, from trying to control what the spell did to the skein. Now just pulling the stuff away from the gashes stung worse than any bandage—

He kept his eyes looking past her, and kept his features steady as he flattened the skein to slide in under his shirt. At least she didn't have to see his pain too.

It's either keeping a full police watch here, or Eric wins.

He opened the door.

"Hey!" "That's him, what the hell—"

The two nearest uniforms closed in on him. One scruffy beard, the stocky build on the other—of *course* those were still the two that had broken up his fight with Eric in the church, the two he'd lashed out at. He looked around for Hoyle, but the lean older man he remembered was nowhere in sight.

The bigger cop grabbed him and wrenched him around in an arm lock. "Don't you move!"

"If he was going to fight," Bea said, "why would he be here? Think."

"Sure you'd say that," the other said. "We know about you and your boyfriend."

They just go right to that, when Bea and I never let it happen.

Colin gritted his teeth. "Where's Lieutenant Hoyle?"

The cop's grip tightened. "What's it matter? You hit my partner, da Costa."

"So hit me!" Colin flung back. "You want us even, fine. But I'm telling you, it's the same man who's been attacking all of us."

"Hit you? You think I'm stupid?" The cop shoved Colin a step, toward Zara watching it all. Her lips were clenched white to keep silent.

The two cops pushed him down the corridor. Colin tried to move with them, to keep pace and walk with some dignity. Sure, enough concentration could spread out the skein under his shirt sleeves and give his arms the strength to fling the cops off, but he needed them to *listen.*

"That's enough."

Hoyle stepped into view. Colin knew him by his calm voice—and the way the officer's grip went slack—more than the lean build and the wisps of red hair that he'd glimpsed in his first minutes here.

"Lieutenant." Bea's voice came from behind them. "Colin has come forward to explain his side of the last few hours—"

Hoyle held up a hand to cut her off. "Thank you, Simms. We'll discuss your suspension later." He turned to Colin. "Now, let's talk, the two of us."

"Just tell him the truth," Bea said. "That Eric Rowe actually is that stealthy—"

"Coaching a witness?" Hoyle warned. "Now, this way."

"Sir?" That was the cop who had Colin's arm.

Hoyle waved them to back off. The cop let go, and Colin stepped clear and followed the lieutenant away.

For a moment they could have stepped into normalcy, no officers watching them or need to hide from anyone, only the quick stride of the man in front, and the doctors and nurses they passed. Except for the glances Colin caught from some of them, at the marks on his face.

Hoyle stopped them at a simple junction, where stepping around the corner gave them a hint of privacy. He gazed over their surroundings, and turned to Colin. "All right now…"

"Can you help Bea?" Colin found the words gushing out. "She's a cop who chased down a murderer—"

"And tried to shoot that murderer when he was captured."

Shooting to wound *him!* Colin wanted to say. But Hoyle probably knew that too.

And the lieutenant went on "It's only the fact that Eric Rowe is still such an obvious threat that's kept charges from being filed so far." He let out a sigh. "Her sergeant and I are doing what we can. But, did you really come here to defend your friend?"

"No." Colin squared his shoulders. "I came to defend my *family*. You've got witnesses now that prove Eric held my sister prisoner, and he grabbed my mother trying to get her back. He's still trying."

Two doctors in white walked by in the corridor. Hoyle let their footsteps pass, then said "Is that why you're here? Go on."

"Alright. Look… I know Detective Simms was bending the rules when she let me near the case at all. But I know a bit about Eric. I was the first one to recognize it was him, and I was right."

Hoyle's eyebrows rose, slow and thoughtful. "How'd you manage that?"

"His voice." Colin drew himself up taller, sloughing off the weight of the last day's fighting, anything to make the truth credible. "Eric Rowe used to be our friend; he was *engaged* to Terri. Not that we had a clue he'd been all twisted up by finding she'd survived the earthquake. But he'd been holding her prisoner for all three years, and when we found where he kept her…"

He looked at the floor a moment, until he forced out the next words.

"Then I rushed in ahead of the cops, and pulled her out myself. I know, it would have been cleaner if I'd let all of you do that."

"Awkward, but understandable after so long," Hoyle nodded.

"Thanks. But the next minute was when it went south: Eric caught us in the street and attacked. I'm sorry I left Bea and the others there, but I did get Terri away from Eric for a while. Then tonight he set a trap—"

"Never mind that now." Hoyle's eyes locked onto Colin's. "Several of our officers tried to bring you back, but you got away from them all in broad daylight, carrying your sister. You want to tell me just how you pulled that off?"

"Well, the Hillside's my home turf, I guess more than for the officers there." Colin frowned; one mention of *how* from Hoyle and he turned evasive? But he went on "And I only had to make it to the top of the hill, above the streets—"

"You make it sound easy." Hoyle waved that aside. "I know a bit about you, Colin da Costa. Some martial arts, but mostly you've been a workhorse for your mother's community efforts since you left school."

"Because we lost Terri." It sounded defensive, even to Colin's own ears. "I guess that's me. What are you saying?"

"That being able to throw a punch doesn't tell me how you left Rayo Hill's Finest in the dust. Not that morning or when Rowe escaped tonight, and then a third time with me here." He leaned forward, gaze boring into Colin. "We have a four-time cop-killer out there. But you, you bring your sister and then your mother out of danger, and you come back with those scars…"

He waved at Colin's face.

"I need to know how that's possible."

"You need to know it *is* possible, or Eric will just keep killing," Colin flung back. *I'm stalling again*—but he felt his fists clenching, ready to push back the more Hoyle leaned on him. "You can't stop him with ordinary guards."

"I asked you how *you* got past us."

"Too easily. I mean, can your cops be ready for the smallest little sign that someone's creeping up on them? Can you keep them in pairs as if any moment could be the one someone gets hit?" At least that kind of protection might make Eric back off. He waved around the corridor; any corner of that space could be Eric creeping in if they turned their backs on it.

"You're explaining security to me?" Hoyle scowled. "How is that different from how I'd protect any victim?"

"It has to be better! Eric's already lured Zara out and grabbed her once, to get Terri back. He'll try again if you can't stop him." He leaned in to meet Hoyle's gaze. "That is the real goal, right? Bringing him down?"

"Four. Dead. Cops. Of *course* bringing him down is the goal."

"Glad to hear it." Colin stopped to let his breathing ease. "I just don't think your protection here will do it."

"The security is fine." Hoyle took a step into the main corridor, and waved. Two uniformed cops marched into view.

Colin stared—they couldn't be *arresting* him now, could they? But the two men held back, still a few paces away.

Holding his voice even, he told Hoyle "I hope you're right. One other thing: when Bea shot Eric, he was reaching for a weapon. And even then he was strong enough to break away from your cops, and me. And take Zara."

"That's still hard to believe," Hoyle said. "Even the way this case has gone, the more you claim, the harder it is to swallow."

Does that mean... "If you believed it, would you let Bea off the hook?"

"This isn't a negotiation," and Hoyle glanced at the two cops. Like they might have overheard that, like he couldn't make promises in front of them, but...

But, what would Bea want? Colin felt the extra glimmer of hope in his mind turn harsh and ugly. Bea was the one still fighting to keep the skein's secret to themselves; trading it for her badge would be a betrayal.

And... did he need to give the whole story right now, if he could just make them open their eyes?

"I asked you a question," Hoyle said. "Tell me how you keep dodging us, and I *might* look the other way for tripping over our investigation."

A bluff. It had to be.

But Colin's teeth clenched. Threatening to take him away, with Eric still out there?

Through his teeth he said "But, you *are* hunting Eric, and watching for when he makes his next move here, right? Like he was more dangerous and more tricky than anyone you've chased, ever?"

"What are you saying?" Hoyle said. "We've tracked cop-killers be-fore."

"You think you're ready for him?"

Colin stole one more glance past Hoyle and the two cops, down in-to the corridor. Then he said,

"Prove it."

and dove past them down the wide hallway.

His first running steps flung him almost into a nurse with a tray, but he twisted aside. Another long moment later he heard the shout that tore open his head start: *"Grab him!"*

They took the bait. *Good. I think.*

Colin charged down the corridor, flinging and wringing all the strength his worn-out muscles had into clawing for another inch of speed. It was still his own strength, with no chance to shift the skein to around his legs yet. Voices rang out ahead of him, closing him behind him. He threaded past another pair of nurses, twisted up one side that looked more empty, then one more…

Far enough.

Out of sight for a moment he flattened himself against the wall, and willed the skein to come flooding out. The silver-green substance surged out from under his clothes and encased him again, and another thought *twisted* light around him. He gasped for breath, clenched his lungs still against their ragged sound…

The two cops barreled by him, too fast to glance at some discolora-tion against the wall. An intern charged after them, shouting warnings.

Before they got too far, Colin dashed the other way, still blurred against sight. The skein casing his legs drove him forward in long—loud—steps, and he heard the cops behind him react to the noise. For five long steps he darted by, too quick for anyone to focus on the pass-ing blur.

Then he ducked around another corner and slowed, and slipped be-hind a counter. He could hear them searching, shouting their confusion—and determination. The determination they'd need, to slow Eric down.

I could have told them. Showing them the whole thing would be so much easier... but Lieutenant Hoyle's prodding had just been too much. Bea knew them better, and she might be right.

Right now, putting the police on guard had to be enough.

ABOUT THE AUTHOR

"Whispered spells for breathless suspense."

Ken Hughes dreams of dark alleys and the twenty-seven ways people with different psychic gifts might maneuver around each corner. He grew up on comics and adventures before discovering Stephen King and Joss Whedon, and he's written for Mars mission proposals and medical devices, making him an honorary rocket scientist and brain surgeon. Ken is a Global Ebook Award-nominated urban fantasy novelist, creator of the Shadowed Steps series, the Spellkeeper Flight, the Mirrorman, and many more series of supernatural thrills.

Don't get him started on puns.

Find more books and join the Overview newsletter at:

KenHughesAuthor.com.